Y0-EEF-268

OTHER BOOKS BY BRIAN JOHNSTON

The Gift Horse Murders
The Dutch Treat Murders
The Good Luck Murders

WITH MALLETS AFORETHOUGHT

A Winston Wyc Mystery

BRIAN JOHNSTON

OTTO PENZLER BOOKS
New York

**OTTO
PENZLER
BOOKS**

OTTO PENZLER BOOKS
129 West 56th Street
New York, NY 10019
(Editorial Offices only)

Simon & Schuster Inc.
Rockefeller Center
1230 Avenue of the Americas
New York, NY 10020

This book is a work of fiction. Names, characters, places, and incidents
are either products of the author's imagination or are used fictitiously.
Any resemblance to actual events or locales or persons, living or dead,
is entirely coincidental.

Copyright © 1995 by Brian Johnston

All rights reserved, including the right of reproduction in whole
or in part in any form.

Manufactured in the United States of America

1   3   5   7   9   10   8   6   4   2

Library of Congress Cataloging-in-Publication Data
Johnston, Brian, 1944–
With mallets aforethought: a Winston Wyc mystery/Brian Johnston.
        p. cm.
        I. Title.
PS3560.03873W58   1995
    813'.54—dc20
    94–36019
        CIP

ISBN 1-883402-44-1

ACKNOWLEDGMENTS

I would like to thank Marta and Thurston Greene, Esq. for their invaluable introduction to the world of professional croquet. Also, I must give credit to Thurston (a friend I can always count on for a delightfully bad pun) for the title. For their numerous favors, a nod of the head to Jan D'Luhosch, Fast Eddie Boyle and Aki Busch. Small things mean a lot. A bow at the waist to John Sayles for his uncommon support and patience. A thank you to Meg Ruley. And speaking of patience, the Flo Nightingale Award (and a special thanks) to Kate Stine.

For my mother,
Kathleen June Miller,
with love

WITH MALLETS AFORETHOUGHT

CHAPTER
1

Filofax in hand, Sackett Corbally rechecked the number he had written down against the one on the door. Could it be he'd entered the wrong building? The dust, the peeling paint, the exposed light bulbs, these were not the environs Sackett would have expected of a prosperous historian. Was that an oxymoron? Prominent didn't necessarily mean prosperous, but really, there was a homeless man asleep in the lobby. Of course it was still possible that beyond the frosted-glass door pane awaited a different world, a hushed, tasteful world of leather chairs and Palladium prints.

Stepping back, Sackett checked his reflection in the glass: black cashmere pullover, loose black Armani sport coat and pants, black cowboy boots (which brought him up to six feet three and a half) and the final article of intimidation, the sharp white square of his clerical collar. For gaining a stranger's trust, nothing worked better than this simple patch of white. Sackett understood the impact of a first impression. Unlike some, he thought, as he tapped lightly on the glass.

Sackett hesitated in closing the door behind him. His feelings of uneasiness were not lessened by what he saw. The unattended oak desk piled high with papers, the low shelves stuffed with documents and magazines, maps and photographs, the stalagmites of books that leaned in toward the door, all had the look of clutter not industry. The fingers of his right hand went to his chest as if seeking a cross.

A frosted-glass partition wall straight out of an old grade-B detective movie separated the front area from the back. Voices could be heard on the other side. Closing his eyes and uttering a short prayer of assistance, Sackett knocked loudly on the office door. The voices stopped. A shadow appeared against the glass and moved quickly toward a door on the far left. The cheerful, round face of an Asian woman peered out at him.

"Ohhh, I'm so sorry. I did not hear you enter." Coming into the room, the woman positioned herself behind the desk. "Have you been standing here long?" Her voice was crisp, almost British.

"No, no, but I'm not sure that I'm in the right office." Sackett stared. The woman was extraordinary looking. Flawless white skin, almond-shaped eyes, the ebony hair cut tight to a face which was perfectly round and so white that the bright red lipstick she wore shimmered and glowed as if the lips were about to burst into flame.

"Which office would you like to be in?"

Pulling the Filofax from his jacket pocket, Sackett read the name aloud. "Mr. Winston Wyc. Architectural historian."

"You are in the correct office."

"Oh, well eh . . . good." Sackett tried not to give the room a disapproving glance, but he couldn't help himself.

The woman followed his gaze. "It's a mess, I know," she nodded, "but, believe me, it was worse. You see, I've only been Mr. Wyc's assistant for a short time." Her smile seemed to imply that that was all the explanation needed.

Sackett's expression implied he wasn't convinced. "I called earlier. My name is Corbally." This woman was quite a jewel amid all this litter and Sackett appreciated the rare gem. He presented a broad smile of his own.

"Ahhh yes, Mr. Corbally." The woman glanced at a paper on the desk. "You're right on time. I'm sorry . . . we've been distracted."

"Please, you mustn't be sorry." Dropping his voice and eyelids a notch, Sackett found a more seductive register. "You must be very busy, Ms. . . .?"

"Hamaguchi. Kiko Hamaguchi."

"Yes, a lovely name. A lovely woman."

Kiko gave Sackett a strained smile. "Is it Mr. Corbally, or is it Father Corbally?"

"I'm an Episcopal priest and we, as a rule, tend to be casual concerning titles. Please call me . . ." He leaned in. ". . . Sackett."

Kiko leaned away. "What?"

"Sackett. My first name is Sackett."

"Like in potatoes?" Kiko gave him a charmingly bemused frown.

It was Sackett's turn for the strained smile. Hint taken, he backed off. "A family name. A bit WASP I admit, but then that's what I am. We're a dying breed."

"A dying wasp, Mr. Corbally?" Kiko's expression was all concern.

Sackett couldn't tell if he was being mocked or not. Most women found his name attractive, even a little sexy. He was saved by the entrance of Winston Wyc, who, being focused on a book in his hand, didn't see him.

"Kiko, I'm afraid you're wrong. It *was* the *Armenia*. Where you got the idea it was the *Betsy Ross* . . ." Winston looked up. "Oh, hi."

"This is Mr. Corbally, the man who called this morning."

"Hello, Mr. Corbally, I'm Winston Wyc." The two men shook hands. "Please call me Winston."

"You must call me Sackett, then." Sackett immediately regretted his quick glance back to Kiko, whose beautiful round face was all raised eyebrows and mischievous grin. The two men stared at each other. Sackett's uneasiness returned. In his mid-thirties, Winston Wyc was as tall as Sackett but not as thin. He wore neither coat nor tie and what he did wear had no character: a wrinkled, blue oxford-cloth shirt and jeans. With sneakers. Sackett was appalled. Winston's long hair was combed straight back, covering his collar with dark curls. His face was handsome but too wide, a working-class face. It could have been a tough face had it not been for the eyes, which were clear and thoughtful. Sackett felt uncomfortable and overdressed. He'd come here to meet a well-known historian and had been introduced to the handyman.

Winston turned back toward his office. "Well, come in, Sackett. Have a seat. Would you like some coffee, tea?"

"No thank you."

"Kiko and I were arguing about which boat was racing the *Henry Clay* when it caught fire. That's the boat on which A. J. Downing was riding when it caught fire and sank."

"My God," said Sackett, stopping at the door. "When did this happen?"

Winston couldn't tell if Sackett's concern was genuine or not. "In 1852."

"Oh. That was some time ago."

Winston was impressed. If Sackett was at all chagrined, he didn't let it show. "Downing was a well-known architect of the period. He was on the *Henry Clay* when it got into a race up the Hudson River with the *Armenia,* something steamboats did in those days. An older version of drag racing, I suppose. Anyway, Downing's boat overheated and . . . well . . ." Winston could see that Sackett didn't care. ". . . and we lost a good . . . eh, architect."

Sackett had followed Winston into a much larger room that was almost as cluttered as the reception area. Filing cabinets piled high with papers lined the walls. A tall, wide bookcase, the type found in libraries, ran down the middle of the room defining two separate spaces. Twenty feet long and ten feet high, the bookcase was crammed with books on either side. Each space had a desk, a computer and its own pile of confusion. Stacks of the *New York Social Register* and back issues of the *Real Estate Records* sat on the floor. Wall space not taken with cabinets was covered with maps. Pinned to the maps were photos, newspaper articles, drawings and blueprints of buildings. Winston motioned for Sackett to sit in a large wing chair that stood just inside the doorway. Sackett watched as Winston cleared a space on a desk to sit.

"Sorry for the mess," said Winston. "It seems no matter how often Kiko and I sort it out, it quickly creeps back."

"I would take that as a measure of success." Smiling, Sackett couldn't help wondering if his seat was as dusty as the arm of the chair. If so, his black outfit was going to need some attention before he went back on the street.

"Yes, I suppose so. I should move to bigger quarters but I really like this office, this building. The architect was Comstock before he really got into his Beaux-Arts period. The influence is evident, though, in the high arched entranceway and the pediment above it." Turning slightly, Winston picked up a piece of paper that lay behind him on the desk. He handed the paper to Sackett. "You may or may not have noticed, but the stairway you came up has some wonderful wrought-iron scrollwork. That's a sketch I did yesterday of the newel post in the entranceway. The management company for this building is going to replace it and I'd like for them to have it reproduced exactly. It's typical for the 1870s, but hard to find today. This building hasn't changed much since it was built and I like that. Not that I'm a nostalgia freak, but I enjoy that sense of historical connection, of constancy."

Historically accurate and complete with original dirt, thought Sackett. He handed back the drawing. "Walking down your hallway I felt . . . almost as if I were traveling back in time."

"You did? Well . . . what can we do for you?"

Even though he'd gone over it more than once, Sackett took a moment to gather his thoughts. The less Winston Wyc knew, probably the better. He cleared his throat.

"My father, Clement Corbally Sr., has, over the last ten years, bought and stored on the family estate a number of old buildings which he would like to now erect into a . . . a what?

A little world of sorts, a reconstructed village from the past."

"Like Sturbridge Village?" offered Kiko as she entered. Taking a seat at the other desk, she took out a notepad and began writing.

"Yes, a miniversion, I suppose."

Winston spoke. "You don't mind if Kiko takes notes, do you? I find it sometimes clarifies things later."

"Not at all, as long as what is said here is kept confidential." Casually, Sackett ran a finger over his clerical collar.

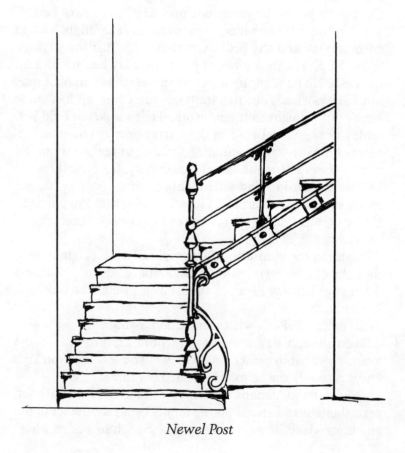

Newel Post

"But of course, of course. Please continue."

"Well, the family has some concerns about Father's project: the work involved, the time it would take and, eh, the cost of such an endeavor. We have expressed these concerns to Father and he has agreed to our seeking an expert in the field so that we can all have a clearer understanding of the situation. I inquired at the Historical Society and you were highly recommended."

"Uh-huh. Anything interesting?" asked Winston.

"Pardon?"

"The old buildings. Are any of them of architectural interest?"

"I . . ." Sackett shook his head. "I couldn't tell you. They're all bits and pieces covered with numbers. I suppose that's where you come in. Or you." Sackett smiled at Kiko.

"Are there plans of any kind? Blueprints? Written histories of the buildings?" asked Winston.

Sackett thought of Sam Harris and the reams of paper he and his father pored over. "It's possible my father has some. I've seen what look like blueprints in his study."

"I see." Winston wondered if Sackett understood the considerable work involved in what he wanted done. "Has your father been planning this for some time or is he in the beginning stages?"

"He's been at it for a while, I guess. But nothing's been started in terms of actual buildings going up."

"Doesn't he have consultants assisting him? I mean, a 'reconstructed village from the past' would involve the advice of architects, engineers and contractors who specialize in that sort of thing. Historic restoration on that level, if done properly, needs a lot of planning." Winston waited for Sackett to answer.

"Well, yes, there are others," he finally replied.

"And can't they give the family the advice you're seeking?"

Sackett took a moment to recross his legs and appear thoughtful.

Winston continued. "And there're the local planning board, the zoning laws, the neighbors. Is this village for personal enjoyment only or will the public be invited?"

"Good heavens, no. I mean I don't think so." It was a thought Sackett hadn't considered: Was his father going to invite the public to Longmeadow? "Look, to get back to your question concerning Father's assistants, the answer is yes, of course he has help. Lots of it. But that's the problem, isn't it? I mean, what kind of advice is a man . . ." Sackett smiled over at Kiko, ". . . or woman going to give the family if there's the chance they might talk themselves out of a job?"

Standing, Winston walked around behind his desk. "You say your father has agreed to a third opinion?"

"A third opinion?"

"There's your father's, there're the family's concerns and then there's my opinion should I take the job. I'd be the third opinion." Winston could see from Sackett's look of surprise that a third opinion hadn't been considered.

"Of course, I understand. I wasn't thinking. It's possible, I suppose, that you could suggest an alternative approach to, eh, everything."

"Or not suggest anything," added Winston. "I'm certainly not against, let's say, taking sides, as long as I agree with my client, Sackett. Developers versus neighborhood organizations, building owners versus the Landmarks Commission, whatever. I've worked for both sides of the fence. My experience, though, is that these groups are nothing compared with the family versus family. You can appreciate my concern, certainly."

Sackett's chest rose and dropped with a deep sigh. "Yes, I most certainly can appreciate the problems of being caught in the middle." Making a tent of his long fingers, Sackett pretended to give the problem some consideration. Actually, for him, the conversation was becoming a bore. Maybe it was time to sprinkle a little truth around. Either that or take out the checkbook.

"Look, I admit I'm less than enthusiastic about the project

WITH MALLETS AFORETHOUGHT

but believe me, I'm not the only one. I don't need an expert to tell me that there's a lot of money involved and I'd be lying if I said that aspect of the project didn't bother me, and not only me, but my brother and sister as well." Sackett paused. "But there are other concerns beyond the money issue. My father is an old man and not a particularly healthy old man. A project this size could possibly prove too much for him." Sackett stifled another sigh. "I really think it might shorten his life."

Sackett was so obviously full of bull that Winston and Kiko exchanged a quick is-this-guy-for-real look.

"Well," said Winston, "have you talked to his physician?"

"Dr. Somerset is older than Father," snorted Sackett. Suddenly, Sackett leaned forward, his voice earnest, his expression sincere. "Look, I need someone to give me some advice here. I'm looking for someone outside the tight little circle of gung-ho assistants that have made my father's project their lifework. I need to know that this historic village is sane and sensible, that the money being spent is not crazy. I want you to come up to Longmeadow and talk to my father, to go over the plans, to sweep the dust from those piles of lumber and see if there's anything under there that could possibly warrant reconstruction. I'm a religious person, Winston, obviously, but sometimes peace of mind can only be achieved through secular intervention. I need that third opinion so I can sleep at night." A checkbook materialized in Sackett's hand. "How much are we talking for a day of consultation? Eighteen hundred? Two thousand? Twenty-five hundred?"

"It's not a question of payment, Sackett, it's eh . . . it's . . ." Winston couldn't think of one good argument for not accepting twenty-five hundred dollars. He noticed Kiko staring at him, her eyebrows working themselves into a frenzy. "It's knowing that I'm being hired for the right reasons. The family, including your father, has to know that I'm there merely to review the available material and offer my professional opinion. That I'm not there taking sides. That I'm not a prejudiced witness championing *your* concerns for the project.

19

Under those conditions I'd be willing to come up for an afternoon. The fee would be four fifty." Winston ignored Kiko's little gasp. For a second he thought that Sackett was going to say forget it. His expression was that of a small child whose team had just lost. Slowly Sackett rose. Leaning on Winston's desk, he wrote out a check and slid it across to Winston.

"I want you to know that I agree with you." Sackett's voice had gone flat. "I'd have it no other way and you can be sure the family, and my father, will know the situation. I certainly don't plan on embarrassing anyone."

"You can appreciate my position," said Winston.

"Completely."

The next ten minutes were spent signing a contract, setting a date, getting directions and cleaning off Sackett's Armani suit.

"Sorry about the dust," said Winston.

"Patina," smiled Sackett. "I'll call before next Friday. I certainly hope you plan on bringing your nice assistant. The countryside is beautiful this time of year."

As the door closed behind Sackett, Winston picked up the check.

"I liked his first offer," said Kiko with a frown.

"It's not the way I do things," said Winston. "You accept big checks like that and before you know it the office starts to lose its comfy feeling." Grinning, Winston handed the check to Kiko. "Not to worry. We'll be okay. I guess that's for two days."

Kiko smiled. "Nine hundred dollars. Maybe this man's father needs a full-time historian with a nice assistant to help arrange a little village."

"Sounds to me like all the positions are filled. Should be an interesting afternoon. Maybe I should have asked who the project manager was. I might know them."

"It would be nice to spend an afternoon in the country."

"Have you ever been to this part of the country?"

"I'm not sure."

"It's a very strange place and I'm not talking about people

with their hats on sideways, either. I'm talking wealthy people with their *horses* on sideways."

"You mean sidesaddle?"

"Whatever. I'm talking people who *sleep* with their horses and dogs, their neighbors' dogs. People who think anywhere west of the Hudson River is unexplored territory. People who *still* think Richard Nixon got a raw deal. Take my word for it, it's a strange world. I say beware."

"Warning received and noted."

Winston paused. His last two exploits involving this part of the world had resulted in his finding dead people. Murdered dead people. It had made for tense working conditions. But this wasn't a real job, it was a consultation. Quick in, quick out. Take the money and run.

"Let's go to lunch," said Winston. "Courtesy of one Sackett Corbally. I'll explain a few things about the country."

"Nature," smiled Kiko. "What a thought."

"You know I've never had a butler. All these damn years and not one." Clement Corbally Sr. allowed his two sons a quick smile. They were beginning to irritate him.

"Is that what you'd like, a butler?" Sackett gave his brother a look of annoyance. The old man was being evasive.

"I didn't say that." Leaning back in his club chair, Clement Sr. stared up at the ceiling. They were ganging up on him and he didn't like it. Some silly notion about calling in an impartial third party. The moment called for anger but he didn't have the energy. It was either too early or too late, he couldn't decide. Until he could escape, Clement Sr. had to keep his sons off the restoration issue and the butler thing was all he could come up with at the moment. "Haven't I kept the damn place full of cooks, maids, cleaning women . . . Christ, can't pass wind in this house without someone buffing something."

"Father, please."

Sackett was getting exasperated, noted Clement Sr., wondering if he could get the young fool to stomp out of the room. Gripping the chair arms, Clement Sr. grudgingly unfolded himself from his chair. A stiff string of horsehair rose with him. In an otherwise fastidiously kept home, Clement Sr.'s club chair was, as Mrs. Corbally often stated, "a problem piece." Clement Sr. stumbled slightly. Rising was becoming difficult. Lately, when he sat too long, his legs went to sleep.

"Like some help?" Clement Corbally Jr. asked his father

but he didn't move to assist him; he knew better. His father gave him a wry smile.

"Not yet, mister. Not quite yet." Moving slowly, Clement Sr. leaned for the French doors that led out to the breakfast patio. The late afternoon sun through the glass would feel good on his face. Like an old reptile on a rock, Clement Sr. grinned at some inner amusement and waited for the heat to revive him, get his circulation moving again. "Clement, fix me a drink."

"Father, it's barely four."

"So what?"

"It's too early. You might . . . I mean . . ." Clement Jr. looked over at his brother for support.

"I might what?"

"You might fall asleep in your soup again," answered Sackett.

Clement Sr. tried giving Sackett a withering look but he couldn't sustain it. Age *was* taking its toll. There had been a time when a look from "Old Wicket" could clear a room.

"That wasn't the fault of my Scotch, it was my family's dinner conversation."

"I'm sorry we bore you so much. I was unaware you paid that much attention to what we said," growled Sackett.

"I hang on your every word," Clement Sr. growled back.

"I'm delighted to hear that, Father." Sackett punctuated his sentence with an insincere smile. "And if that's true, how about hanging on these . . ." Sackett spoke quickly. "Myself, and I might add the rest of the family, have decided to—"

"Enough! We've been through this."

"Not really. It would seem that every time it's brought—"

"I have worked hard all my life to provide my family with a comfortable and happy home." Old Wicket pulled himself up to his full six feet three. "I deserve at this stage, this new and exciting stage of my life, a little understanding. A little sympathy would be nice, too. And what about a little . . . a little . . ."

"Empathy?" asked Sackett.

"You're damn right. That, too." Turning back to the French

doors, Clement Sr. gazed out at the bluestone patio, the low barberry hedge and beyond, the long expanse of lawn and woods.
From this window all the world belonged to Longmeadow, the
Corbally estate. It was one of Clement Sr.'s favorite views. A butler, tray in hand, would look very handsome with that as a back-
drop. The old man noticed that the *Philadelphus coronarius*
shrubs needed a haircut. And the roses hadn't been dusted
lately. Maybe he could use gardening as an excuse to escape the
concerns of his family. Or maybe . . . Clement Sr. turned to his
namesake. "How're the plans for the croquet match going?"

The question took Clement Jr. by surprise. "Oh, I . . . fine,
fine."

"Good." Clement Sr. almost shouted the word. "Listen,
this is your first hosting, as it were, and I've been thinking I
should do something special for you."

"That's really unnecessary, Father, I . . ."

"And I think I've come up with just the ticket."

"Wait a minute," said Sackett. "First it's talk of butlers and
then we get the indignant speech and now it's something special for Clem. I would like to get back to—"

"Just a second, Sack." Clement Jr.'s curiosity had been
piqued. It was rare for the Old Wicket to bestow gifts.

"In the corner, Clement, you'll find a case. Fetch it, please."

Clement Jr. returned with a wooden box three feet long,
four inches high and six inches wide. Placing it on the low
refectory table, he ran his hands over the highly polished
cherry wood, the brass hinges. He gave his father a smile.
"It's so beautiful."

"Looks like a small coffin," noted Sackett.

"Does it?" Clement Sr. decided to ignore the remark.
"Richie made it. Go ahead, open it."

Resting the lid gently on the table, Clement Jr. stared into
the box. His brow furrowed slightly.

Clement Sr. leaned forward, his hands supported by the
table. "What's the matter?"

"It's yours."

"It *was* mine."

"You're giving it to me?"

"I'm passing it on. It's what fathers do. Let's say it's a legacy."

"I . . ."

"You what?"

"I don't know what to say."

Although addressing Clement Jr., the old man grinned over at Sackett. "Say nothing."

Not entirely moved, Clement Jr. nonetheless made a ceremony out of lifting the croquet mallet from its baize resting place. An attempt had been made to clean the old club, but it still bore the dents and scrapes of a lifetime of striking. Although bound by rings of brass, the lignum vitae head had begun to split in several places. The soft suede handgrip covering the Malacca cane shaft had gone black and threadbare where the palms had sweated.

"The Nationals were won with that mallet, boy. Beat the English too, by God. No one else has ever held it."

"I don't know what to say," repeated Clement Jr.

"So you said. How about 'thank you'?"

"Yes, but of course, thank you, Father. I appreciate the gift. I really do. . . . It's, well . . . I hope you won't be offended, but it's a bit on the disfigured side."

"You don't have to use the damn thing, you twit. As I said, think of it as a . . . a warm-up legacy."

"A legacy?"

"If you like, a memento. Or better yet, a reminder." Cackling, Clement Sr. shuffled over to his humidor.

"A good legacy can often take the edge off a loved one's departure. Or so I've heard," noted Sackett.

Clement Sr. took a moment to give Sackett a hard stare.

Sackett spoke. "Father, if we're all done here, I'd like to get back to . . ."

"The only one with a departure in their immediate future's going to be you, Brother Sackett. You wouldn't happen to know about some notes I've received lately? Would you?"

"Notes?" Sackett's pause was a beat too long. "I'm afraid not."

"Uh-huh." Having taken his time in selecting a cigar, Clement Sr. snipped off the end. "This is where the butler would come in handy. He'd do all the cutting and the lighting of matches. All I'd have to do is inhale."

"Perhaps he could squeeze your chest, too," said Sackett. "Then all you'd have to do is enjoy the moment."

"Well, that'd be a sight better than this moment, Mr. Smart-ass, and another thing . . ."

"The balance of this mallet is extraordinary, Father." Clement Jr. had found a croquet ball and was lining it up with a table leg. "It feels like it has a mind of its own."

Sackett shook his head. That mallet probably had a bigger brain than the man flourishing it. "Could we get back to the question at hand? Please? I feel the moment slipping away." With his right index finger, Sackett flipped the lid to the cherry box shut. The sharp crack was a little too loud, a little too aggressive. The two men stared at each other a little too long. Turning his back to his son, Clement Sr. went to the French doors. After a pause he opened them and went out onto the patio. Sackett turned to his brother.

"You're a big help. Together we might have convinced him that this project of his could be ruinous. You shouldn't be so intimidated by him, and if all the legacy you need is that damn mallet then so be it, dear brother, but I would like something more. A comfortable future for one thing."

"I'm beginning to wonder if you're not blowing this whole thing way out of proportion. Why shouldn't Father have a little fun in his old age?"

"He's had nothing but fun his whole life, for Christ's sake."

"This whole tantrum just seems a little grasping, Sack." Clement Jr. knocked the croquet ball across the room. Sackett winced as it dented the mahogany baseboard.

"Great. Nero fiddled and you play at croquet. I hope you wake up before it's too late."

"You keep mentioning the whole family, Sack, but it's really only you that's so upset, isn't it? Hiring someone to come up and appraise Father's project after he's worked so hard. How do you think he's going to take it? Why don't you just back off? Go stack Eucharist cookies or something."

After a cold glare and a loud, weary sigh, Sackett huffed from the room and joined his father standing at the barberry hedge.

"Father, would you please let me . . ."

"I can hear it now: the sound of hammers, the shouts of workingmen. It's exactly what this tomb needs."

"If you don't mind, I—"

"It will do you no good, boy. This project that you keep resisting is more than just some harebrained idea the Old Wicket's thought up to waste the Corbally fortune."

"We're all genuinely happy that you've found something to occupy these long hours of retirement, but don't you think the same thing could be accomplished on a smaller scale?"

"Listen to me. I've spent a life wasting more than money. There's been time and energy and potential and . . . God knows what else. I should have thought of it sooner but . . ." Clement Sr. stopped. It was not a good idea to expose so much, to be so forthcoming. "How old are you?"

Sackett could see where the old man was heading and he wasn't interested in listening to the "wasted life" lecture. Just because his father was feeling guilty in his old age didn't mean the rest of them should suffer. Sackett and his siblings understood their privileged positions in the world and had no problems with being advantaged. Their days were full and their hearts held no regret.

"My age is irrelevant to this conversation. As for squandered lives . . ."

"Late thirties, right? And what do you do? Really? Pretend to be a priest? Go on retreats? Reading and traveling is not considered a vocation in the real world."

Sackett was wounded. The fact that he hadn't managed to finish seminary didn't make him less the priest. It was a heart and soul thing. Straightening, Sackett took a step backward.

"Let's stop all this blather about the real world, shall we, Father? Corballys don't live in the real world. And since when did digging a hole in the ground and throwing all your money into it equal a communion with *mundus verite*?"

"Cut the Latin crap, I'm talking focus. I'm talking useful exertion."

"You're talking great deals of money, Father, with no idea or consideration as to how much is needed or will be needed. I called Phillip yesterday and he said you had set up some kind of foundation or something to finance this nonsense. That you were trying to transfer large amounts of the Corbally trust—"

"Phillip Waltham is an accountant with the soul of a ledger book. He knows nothing about . . . about art."

"Art?"

"But of course." Grinning broadly, Clement Sr. waited as Sackett brought himself under control. "Think of my project as a work of art, a thing of beauty. Not like those damn things your brother makes and hides all over the place."

Taking a moment to pull on his cigar, Clement Sr. gave his son a quick, mental once-over. Such a good-looking lad, and intelligent, in an academic, parochial way, but what a dud. His brother might be a misguided pervert, but at least he got off his duff occasionally what with his so-called art projects and his croquet obsession. Sackett did nothing but contemplate the possibility of doing something. The philosopher-priest talking of mission and liberation theology. Horse dung is what it was, not a life.

Taking a second to wet down a minor unraveling of his cigar, Clement Sr. gave his son an appraising glance. The boy *was* bright. When motivated, he did well. It was just that his interests were so screwy, at least to Clement's way of thinking. Was it possible his son could be motivated to take an interest in history? Maybe the boy felt left out in some odd way. Suddenly, Clement Sr. had an image of them working side by side on the project. Why hadn't he thought of that before? And what if something should happen to the Old Wicket? Why, the boy could continue the work, a sort of Corbally and Son, Inc. As crazy as the idea sounded, Clement thought he might give it a whirl. Stranger things had happened.

"What are you grinning at?" asked Sackett.

"I have an idea."

"Now what?"

"You won't like this idea initially, but give it some thought." Clement Sr. took a moment before answering. His tone needed an adjustment. A sincere and genuine delivery was called for here.

"I'm waiting."

"Why don't you come aboard the village project? Be my assistant. Then you could see that it's not the burden you envision."

"You're kidding?"

"Not at all." Clement Sr. warmed to the idea. Why he hadn't thought of it before was a mystery. "How do you know you wouldn't like it? Why not work with me for a few days? See if it grabs you in any way."

"Muck about with you among the rotting timbers? Not likely."

"Not even a few days?"

Sackett looked horrified. Clement Sr. could see that it wasn't going to happen, that it was too late. He should have gotten the boy interested when he was much younger. The realization made him sad.

"I'm sorry you feel that way," said Clement Sr. Quickly, his sadness turned to resentment. "I had thought maybe you could learn something useful. Something that might carry you beyond the end of the driveway. What a ridiculous idea: that we might work together on something."

Sackett could only stare at his father. The man had finally

gone off the end of the pier. "Good try, Father, but I'm not interested. Listen," Sackett spoke quickly and with intensity. "I've learned of someone who could come up and chat with you about your project. He knows about these things; he's someone who could review the project and make an intelligent assessment as to what it's going to cost, not just in money, but in time."

"Miles and Sam can do all that."

"Sam possibly, but Miles Northingham is a television personality and, if you don't mind my humble opinion, a bit of an opportunistic ass. I don't think he'd be all that impartial."

"Maybe I'm missing something here, but I don't think the family has—"

Clement Jr. appeared at the door. "Father, this mallet is extraordinary."

"I'm glad you like it," said Clement Sr. His vision of a Corbally and Son, Inc. resurfaced in his mind. If he couldn't get Sackett interested in his project, then Clem Jr. was a possibility. "Forget about croquet for a minute, son. Come join me and your brother."

Taking his son by the arm, Clement Sr. led him out onto the patio. His elder son gave him a wary look.

"What is it, Father?"

"You know, son, I might not be around that much longer . . ."

"Nonsense."

"Well, I am seventy-two. We old people can have terrible accidents. Bones go, no support, and there you are, a disastrous crash. One never knows."

"Yes . . .?" Clement Jr. didn't like the idea of bones going.

"This project of mine, you know, it's a great responsibility, not to mention the money. I could use a partner. Someone to help me . . . run things. Now what do you think yourself about my little project? Don't think about what Sack says, what do *you* think?"

Clement Jr. peered over at his brother. "Help you run things. I don't know."

"You do believe the idea has merit, don't you?"

Hesitantly, the younger man nodded in the affirmative. "I'd have to study it more, but yes, it seems to be a good idea. If kept small, that is." Clement Jr. gave his brother another quick glance.

"Good. I'd like for you to take a look at the project and then decide if it interests you in any way."

"I'd be your assistant?" asked Clement Jr.

Clement Sr. nodded. "In the event that something should happen to me, not that it's going to, but just in case, then I'd like to have someone within the family be part of the project. Do you see what I mean?"

"I do." Clement Jr. nodded slowly. He had to be careful. His father's sudden camaraderie could mean trouble.

Sackett could restrain himself no longer. "Really, this is absurd. Clem isn't interested in this project. No one is but you, Father."

"Beat it," snapped the old man.

"I will not 'beat it.' " Sackett turned his full attention to Clement Jr. "What are you thinking? He doesn't need a partner. He's just looking for support from within the family. He's conning you." Sackett wheeled on his father. He punched out his words one at a time. "You are a raging menace."

"A menace, am I?" The old man went to snatch his mallet back from Clement Jr. but the younger man held on tight. "Ohhhhhh, a menace, am I? Well, let me say this, Brother Sack, my know-it-all son, I'm still in command. It's me, Clement Peel Corbally, who pays the bills around here, who controls the wills and guides the legacies to their proper resting places." His voice rising, Clement Sr. began to pace, his cigar poking the air. "And you can bet your brother and sister would love a little extra on their plates when the Old Wicket finally pegs out for good."

"Are you threatening me, Father?" Pretending not to care, Sackett kept his voice low and nonchalant.

"You're damn right I am. I'm being a raging menace. How do you like the real thing?"

"Not particularly. If you'll excuse me I have things to do."

"Good idea. Run off and conspire against your old dad."

Taking a few deep breaths, Sackett calmed himself. "I think you're making a mistake, that's all. If we can't discuss it then we can't. But I'm not done yet. I have someone coming up to review the project and if—"

"You what?"

"I decided to go ahead and—"

"You have someone coming here?" Clement Sr.'s face was scarlet.

"I do."

"Forget it. You have no business doing that—"

"His name is Winston Wyc and he's very—"

"Winston Wyc?"

"That's right. You've heard of him?"

"Of course I've heard of him." Stepping away, Clement Sr. took a second to calm himself. Seeing that his cigar had gone out, he tossed it into the hedge. "You have Winston Wyc coming up here? When?"

Sackett's nerve was slipping, his voice lost its edge. "For lunch. Friday."

Old Wicket stared hard at his son for several seconds, but then his expression relaxed with a chuckle. "You might have a little priest in you after all, boy. Somebody up there likes you."

Sackett couldn't believe the change in his father. "Then . . . you mean, you'll see him?"

"Don't look so gleeful or I might change my mind."

Clement Jr. spoke. "Who is this Winston Wyc?"

"He's an architectural historian," answered Clement Sr. "A good one. I have his book on eighteenth-century New York City. Very readable."

"Well, you certainly pushed the right buttons," said Clement Jr. to his brother.

"I thought it time that Father and Mr. Wyc met. He's a sensible man, this Mr. Wyc."

Snorting, Clement Sr. gave Sackett a look of tempered animosity. "And I'm not a sensible man. Don't push it."

"I didn't mean it quite like that. I only meant . . ."

"I'll meet this Mr. Wyc under one condition," interrupted Clement Sr.

Sackett's guard went up. "What condition?" Father had capitulated too easily.

"That I see him alone. Just the two of us."

Sackett realized he'd better not push it. "Sounds fine to me."

"Then it's done. Go read your Bible or something."

Hesitantly, and with a long last look at his brother, Sackett went back into the house.

For a long moment, Clement Sr. stared at the open French doors.

"Everything okay, Father?" asked a bemused Clement Jr.

The Old Wicket came out of his reverie, a big smile on his face. "Okay? Hell yes, everything's okay. Look, how about that Scotch? There's much to discuss. I must initiate the new recruit into the mysteries of old buildings."

"Could we begin initiations tomorrow, Father? It *is* late and I see George waiting for me down by the wisteria."

Stopping at the door, the Old Wicket looked back to where the sun was settling behind the locust grove. The end of the great lawn was bordered by a wisteria arbor, and standing in its shadow Clement Sr. could see his son's friend George. The smile left his face.

"Why does he lurk so? Why can't he just come up to the house?"

"He's not lurking, he's waiting. There *is* a difference."

"I say he's lurking. Any normal person would come up and wait in the kitchen or someplace." Clement Sr. directed his comments toward the arbor.

"That's not fair," protested Clement Jr. "If you were nice to George, he might feel comfortable about coming up here. No one enjoys being snarled at all the time."

"George is—" Clement Sr. stopped. What was he going to say? Why did he feel so weak? All at once the fight went out of him. The emptying began at his shoulders and swirled down his body like water from a tub. The sensation left him exhausted, his legs wobbly. Shaking his head, he sat in a wicker chair. "Fine, fine, we can start . . . tomorrow."

"Are you okay?" asked Clement Jr.

"Would you stop asking me that?" The statement had very little force. Clement Jr. gave his father a curious look.

"If you say so. See you in the morning?"

"In the morning."

Falling back into the chair, Clement Sr. watched his son amble down the lawn toward his friend, who had left the safety of the arbor and was walking out to meet him. A slight breeze made him shiver. Was it possible he didn't have the strength to continue this project? And was it something he really wanted? Maybe Sackett was right. Maybe it was too late to be erecting monuments. And these notes he'd been finding lately. These threats. As he started to doze, Clement Sr. wondered who was leaving them and whether he should take the notes seriously. Friday he would meet Winston Wyc, the historian. He was looking forward to that. And then he was asleep.

CHAPTER
3

"John Corbally was brought over to the colonies by Caleb Heathcote in 1690 to be his master carpenter. Family histories say he was 'intelligent, tall and of comely countenance.' "

Winston smiled. Clement Corbally Sr. might have been describing himself. And probably was if the glint in his eye meant anything. On the ride up to Longmeadow, it had suddenly occurred to Winston that Sackett might have arranged this meeting without the senior Corbally's assent. Even with the little Winston knew of Sackett, that was certainly a possibility. "Oh, yes, Father, how silly of me to have forgotten. Oh well, since you're here." It had been with some trepidation that Winston rang the entrance bell. Oddly enough, Sackett hadn't been there to greet him but Clement Sr. had been aware of his coming and had received Winston with polite, if reserved, good cheer. A ruddy-cheeked man with flyaway white hair, dressed in overalls over a white shirt and tie. Winston had liked him immediately.

"Did well, too. Married a rich widow, took her money and ran with it. By the time he died, at the ripe old age of eighty, he'd amassed an estate of thirty thousand acres. Not bad for a man who was self-educated."

"He never could have accomplished that had he stayed in England," added Winston.

"Hell no." Clement Sr. grinned at the middle distance. "America must have been one heck of a place in those early years."

Good looks and charm can still take you far, even today,
thought Winston. A rich wife doesn't stand in the way, either.
"And this house we're in now. Is it standing on that tract of
land?"

"No, no. That was down in Putnam and Westchester
Counties. Want another splash there?"

Winston shook his head no as Clement Sr. raised the
Scotch bottle. "If only I could, but I have to drive back to the
city this afternoon. It's very good." Even though he was quite
fond of his Scotch, especially a single malt, Winston was not
in the habit of drinking it so early in the day. A lunch of
Stilton cheese, pâté and water crackers had been brought into
the study by an elderly Mexican woman.

"Aberlour. Excellent for the price." Clement Sr. poured
Winston a shot anyway.

Nodding in agreement, Winston slid his glass closer to
himself and out of Clement's reach. He hadn't been in the
man's study five minutes and the Scotch and cigars had
materialized. At first Winston had been hesitant to participate, but he had quickly realized that for the senior Corbally
it was a ritual of approval, for had Clement Sr. not liked him,
these items of male bonding would not have appeared. With
his cigar, Winston pointed at the large document stretched
out on the table between them.

"But this land grant, it's for Longmeadow?"

"It is." Clement explained. "Old John had quite a few children survive, five sons and three daughters. Except for one,
the girls married well and moved off to other parts. As you
know, in those days the land was still ruled by the laws of
England and that meant the land was passed on to the eldest
son. In his later years John was elected to Assembly and
wielded some influence with the governor. He was able to
acquire individual land grants here in Dutchess County for
those younger sons and in so doing guarantee them a good
life. By that time there was a limit on grants of two thousand
acres. This grant is written for that amount of land."

Winston studied the document. "Let's see here . . . at two thousand acres this grant must have been issued before 1753 . . . ahhh, there it is: 1743."

A slow smile spread over Clement's face. Here was a man he could talk to. "Seventeen forty-three. Before Osborne came to be governor with his instructions from the Crown to give grants of only one thousand acres."

"And to make sure the quitrents were paid."

"Not that anyone paid him any attention," chuckled Clement. "Probably why he committed suicide."

"So which ancestor was granted Longmeadow?" asked Winston.

"That was Roger Corbally, John's youngest." Having risen, Clement moved over to a group of pictures hanging on the wall behind his desk. "This is him."

Following, Winston studied the man's profile. There was no doubting he was a Corbally. Clement and Roger could have been twins. "You bear a strong resemblance to him," noted Winston.

"We all seem to inherit the same features. These gray eyes, the long nose. Sackett, whom you've met . . ." At the thought of his son, Clement frowned. ". . . has the same Corbally profile, although I'm afraid he's . . . he's . . . Let's just say the boy could use some guidance." Clement moved on to another picture. "This was my father, Peel Corbally. He's the man who built this house."

"I noticed when I drove up that this house was relatively new. Colonial Revival, and since it's built of brick, I'd say middle twenties."

"Nineteen twenty-seven." Clement smiled.

"But there must be an older house around. The original manor."

"Torn down, I'm afraid. In fact, this house was built on top of the original foundations. I was brought up in that older house. Marvelous edifice. One of those rambling old things with a hundred and fifty years of one addition after another

37

tacked on here and there." With a wistful grin, Clement remembered those days. "My God, it went on forever. The old kitchen led off to a large pantry and then the dairy room, with a huge sink." Screwing up his face, Clement walked his mind through the maze of rooms. "Let's see, there was a storage room for firewood and after that . . . a tack room of some kind, had a small fireplace and then, oh my goodness . . . then there was the four holer." Clement chuckled. "Can you imagine? The entire family out there on a Sunday morning. Now we pretend nobody has bodily functions. Ridiculous."

Winston watched as Clement tried to remember the sequence of add-ons that made sure a person wouldn't have to deal with bad weather, back in a time when there was no central heating. In the 1600s these continuous structures were banned by many towns as being firetraps. A fine was imposed on any farmer who didn't obey the law, but there was no record of a single person ever paying that fine and by the 1700s the ban was nonexistent.

". . . and finally you wound up in the carriage shed. That's where the old man parked his Bearcat. Right next to an old landau. You weren't supposed to go near that damn Bearcat, although I'd sneak out there sometimes and just sit in it, pretending to travel the dusty back roads that were everywhere in those days. What a car."

"Did you ever get to drive it?" Winston asked with genuine curiosity. He loved listening to older people talk of their early years, remembering the exotic-sounding names of things long gone.

"Hell, no. By the time I could drive, we owned a Packard. Two Packards. The kind Cagney and Raft drove in the movies."

"You should write a personal history of those times," said Winston. "I've often thought more people should do that, even now. Put on paper those remembrances so that their children, their grandchildren, would have some idea of what the day-to-day living was like. Particularly now when things seem to change so quickly."

"It's a damn good idea and one I keep telling myself to do. *Go* through all the histories, I keep saying to myself, *and* the photo albums *and* the letters and put together a written and visual profile of the Corbally clan, all under one cover. It's still in the 'telling' phase."

"This idea you have for an historic village seems to follow in that vein."

Sucking at his front teeth, Clement studied Winston's face for any clue as to his possible thoughts on the subject. Winston's expression remained neutral. "I can imagine Sackett gave you an earful on that topic."

"Not much, really. I got the feeling he was worried about cost and . . . well, your health."

"Hah!" guffawed Clement. "My health. The boy's worried about his inheritance. Thinks the Old Wicket's going to leave him penniless. Well, I just might. Wouldn't be a bad idea, to my way of thinking. As you might or might not know, I've hired a man to take care of the logistical end of things just to keep the expenses to a mild roar. Although, I must admit, having spent the last hour with you, I might have been hasty in that hiring."

"I take that as a compliment," said Winston.

"Uh-huh."

"If you don't mind my knowing, who did you hire?"

"It's two people, actually. Came as a package. Maybe you've heard of one of them, TV fellow, name of Northingham. Miles Northingham. Has some history show on NBC. Very popular. He's okay, bit of a blowhard, but doable. I really hired his partner. An historian name of Sam Harris. Good man."

"I know Sam Harris," said Winston. "He is a good man. Used to work for the New-York Historical Society. I haven't seen him in a few years, though. What's he up to?"

"Works for this TV guy. Does the background for the shows, I believe. Gump and Whistler did the engineering and Pat Bell helped me with the fieldwork. Now there's one hell of a good woman."

Winston nodded his approval. Clement Sr. had gone out and hired the best in the business.

"I had known Sam Harris at the society and went looking for him when the engineering was done. I needed someone good to pull it all together. By the way, Sam thinks the plans are just fine." Clement Sr. gave Winston a sly look over his half-glasses.

Winston shrugged. "I think Sackett just needs someone outside the project to look at the plans and tell him it's feasible."

"I've been telling him that." Clement's voice was on the edge of anger.

Deciding to change the subject, Winston lightly ran his hand over the old grant. "Not many people still live on the land their great-great-grandparents owned."

Clement smiled, realizing that he'd been a little sharp. "Sorry, but the boy upsets me sometimes." Turning, Clement sat at his desk and pulled open a drawer. "Let's see if I can find something here . . ."

While the man rummaged, Winston admired the slant-top desk. He placed it between 1750 and 1780. American made, in the rococo style popular at that time. The decorative shells were finely carved and the slight bombé front would indicate it was made around the Boston area.

"You're right. Not many people have that privilege. Although, sad to say, it's no longer two thousand acres. Somewhere here I have a survey of the original grant. I had this fellow in town superimpose it onto a modern map just for the fun of it. See what might have been mine." Cackling to himself, Clement thumbed through some papers. "It's here somewhere."

"Roger lose any land after the Revolution?"

"Nope. Actually, Roger didn't live to see the Revolution, died in 1765, but his son Jefferson did and he was of the new breed. Didn't think of himself as part of the British gentry. Got himself in trouble, too. You see, in 1772 the Crown was hot on collecting taxes, needed to replenish the war chest, and it began seriously investigating who owned what. If a man couldn't prove ownership to their satisfaction, then the land was reclaimed and opened to yeoman farmers who developed the land and were therefore easier to keep track of . . . and tax."

"So Jefferson had trouble with the Crown?" asked Winston.

"When his grant was investigated he couldn't come up with a letter of exemplification."

Winston thought a moment. "That was an attested document issued by the government. Am I right?"

"Correct. Basically it was a piece of paper with an official seal that stated the land grant was genuine. Well, Jefferson couldn't produce one and God knows what his father, Roger, had done with it. The Crown tried to take back his land."

"Obviously they didn't succeed."

"Damn right they didn't, and I'll tell you why. In 1763 the government of New York began evicting farmers who had bought their land directly from Indians because they hadn't been issued the proper warrants. The real reason, of course, was that other men, influential men, wanted that land. Where is that damn map?" Pulling open another drawer, Clement rummaged as he talked. "In 1765 there was a farmer's revolt up and down the Hudson valley."

"William Prendergast," said Winston.

"That's right. He was one of the leaders. Wonderful story about his wife, a Quaker woman. Supposedly, when she found out they were going to hang him, she put on her best dress and hat and rode her horse for five straight hours right down into New York City and to the Council House, where she pleaded his case. It was never recorded what she said but it must have been something, for the Council rescinded the sentence and gave Prendergast a year in jail." Clement shook his head. "Must've been one hell of a woman. Ahh, here it is."

Getting up, Clement carried the map over to the refectory table, where the land grant document lay.

"This darker line shows where the grant lands were. Goes up to Connecticut there. Two thousand acres wasn't considered much in those days, but a man could make a decent living. Better than being shuffled off to a life in the military or something. As a joke, I showed this map to my neighbor, that come-up-on-the-weekends malcontent Eliot Barker. Told him I wanted my land back. God, did he get huffy." Clement had a good cackle at the remembrance of it. In the process he lost his train of thought. "Where was I?"

"Tenant's revolt."

"That's right. Turns out Jefferson wasn't much interested in farming and instead became a land surveyor and schoolteacher. When the tenant's revolt happened, Jefferson sided with the tenants and for very little money sold his tenants the land they were renting. Almost twelve hundred acres. Of course, the men in power didn't like that, thought it treason to their class, so when the investigations started in '72 he was singled out. Probably wouldn't have been investigated at all had he behaved more like a man of the gentry. All the other wealthy landowners booted the farmers off their land, calling them squatters, and rented the land to others, houses and all. When the Revolution came there were many grudges settled and quite a few landowners were run back to England. Because of his political stance and his goodwill, Jefferson was given back Longmeadow and spent the rest of his years in comfort teaching school, doing a little farming, a lot of fishing. With inherited monies he made some intelligent investments and enjoyed his later years. He died in 1801."

"What a story. Make a good book."

"I've always thought so. Now, let's get down to the reason you're really here: Corbally Village." Reaching past the map, Clement retrieved his glass and drained the remaining Scotch. "Ahhh." Catching Winston's worried expression, he shot back a look of bliss. "Fuel, Mr. Wyc. It's what keeps these old bones churning."

From an old umbrella stand that held, in place of umbrellas or canes, cardboard tubes, Clement selected the biggest and brought it back to the table. Popping off the end, he took out six rolled sheets of architectural blueprints and renderings. As he unrolled them, a smaller piece of paper fluttered to the table.

"What's this?" asked Clement, picking up the paper. "I'll be damned."

"What is it?"

"Oh, nothing. Someone around here's been leaving me these damn notes. Quotes from the Bible."

But Clement had gone rigid for a second and turned quite pale.

"Notes concerning the project?" asked Winston, whose interest was piqued.

"I suppose so. Here, what do you make of that? Found one down in the barn, one on my desk and now this one."

The note had been typewritten on a kind of heavy paper which was made to look like parchment, all dappled brown and wrinkled. Winston read the note to himself.

> For which of you desiring to build
> a tower doth not first sit down and
> counteth the cost, whether he have
> wherewith to complete it?
> LUKE 14:28

"Could be advice or a threat," said Winston.

"Could be."

"Is it possible someone doesn't want you to pursue this project?" Once he said it, Winston realized that that was exactly why he was here at Longmeadow. He'd been hired by Sackett to review the plans and, if possible, talk Clement Sr. out of the idea. "I mean, besides Sackett?"

"Hard to tell, but there's not many in the family spend much time with the Bible other than him."

Clement Sr. obviously thought it was his son.

43

"Why not confront him with them?" asked Winston.

"I should, I guess, but . . . hell, for some reason it's not that easy. The thought that he'd do such a thing . . . I don't know. Look, I shouldn't have brought it up. Damn thing caught me by surprise. Let's get back to the business at hand."

"Sure." Winston slipped the offending piece of paper under the larger renderings. Clement was once again his garrulous self.

"Now this is the first phase. Only five buildings. Blacksmith's forge and living quarters, that's here. General store and storage shed, here. The family that owned this lived on the second floor. This small building belongs to a hatter. This is a one-room church and this structure here is a mill owner's house. I have five more buildings including a grain mill. It took me ten years to find these buildings and bring them here. Four I actually got through Sturbridge Village. Being who they are, they get offered old buildings all the time by communities that have some old place they think has some historical significance. They're very good there about passing on information. If they didn't need the thing, they'd give me a crack at it. The first building to go up will be the church. It's a real beauty. Comes from up near Utica. Strong Dutch influence."

"All these buildings look to be mid-nineteenth century."

"Eighteen forty to just before the Civil War. That's the time period I have in mind. A small backwoods community, that's all. I'm not trying to compete with Sturbridge Village. What I see happening is a teaching situation. Each year during the summer months, twenty or twenty-five people pay a certain amount to help restore an old structure. I have Sam Harris to help with the historical details and a young fellow named Richie Baire to oversee the hands-on construction. Excellent woodworker. And through Miles I've got the television people interested in doing three or four shows a summer right from the construction sight. That alone would bring in enough to cover building costs. Tuitions would help defray salaries and whatnot. I admit it's still not enough to cover all the costs, but I've put together a trust that hopefully will make up any deficit. The start-up costs will be considerable. Have been considerable. But there you are."

"Obviously, I'm not familiar with your resources, but this project has to cost in the millions. Have you pursued government funds at all?"

"The last thing I want is the government involved. Maybe later." Clement stared down at the blueprints. "I realize why you're here, Winston. Sackett must have gone on at some length about his threatened resources."

With a shrug Winston indicated that that was a possibility.

"The reason I agreed to see you and to tell you what I have is because, one, I'm familiar with your work and have admired it, and two, I knew that once you saw what I was doing, you'd approve. Not that I need it, of course."

Winston smiled back. "Of course."

"If I could get that damn boy to spend ten minutes with these plans, as you have, then he might understand what's going on. He might take an interest."

"Could it be there's a third reason you had me up?" asked Winston, who just realized that what the old man really wanted was for his son to share his interest.

Chuckling, Clement began to roll up the prints. "It might have crossed my mind."

Helping with the prints, Winston smiled and said, "I'll suggest it as a possibility."

Clement reached for the Scotch bottle. "I'd appreciate it. Something for the road?"

"No thanks." Watching Mr. Corbally put the bottle down, Winston thought the man looked suddenly tired.

"Well then, you must come back. I've got a whole barn full of history sitting on this property and I know you'd enjoy seeing it. I'd walk you down there now but . . . well, the old legs say no."

"I'd love to come back."

The two men left the study and walked down the hall to the entrance foyer.

"Quite impressive this double stairway," noted Winston.

"It's a copy of the stairway in Drayton Hall down in South Carolina. Not exact, of course, but close. My father had visited there and remembered liking it. He thought it quite grand. Next time you're up we'll do a tour of the house. There's a McIntyre fireplace in the living room." Clement steadied himself against one of the newel posts. "I'd better go sit down."

The Scotch? wondered Winston. "It was nice to meet you, Mr. Corbally. I hope to see you again, soon."

The two men shook hands.

"I'll call," said Clement. "Have you up again. Take care."

"I have my sketchbook with me here. Would you mind if I did a quick rendering of the staircase?"

Clement Sr. turned and headed hesitantly back down the hall. He spoke over his shoulder. "Sketch away. Don't mind me. Let yourself out the front, there. Damn legs."

Winston watched him until he was back in his study. Sackett might have been using the health question as a ploy but Winston wasn't so sure. Clement Sr. didn't appear very well. And those notes. What was that all about?

The large foyer that Winston stood in was divided by columns into two distinct areas. The paneled entrance area had a small coatroom off to the right. On the left was a six-foot-long bench on which to sit and remove soiled boots. In the late 1600s, when it had been made, it would have been called a stool. Next to the door was a sweet little Hepplewhite gaming table with its flat side pushed to the wall. On this sat the mail. Curious, Winston separated it with an index finger. Was it possible that Sackett or his siblings lived here? Other than for Mr. Corbally, Winston found a few letters for a Mrs. Corbally but that was all. Taking out his sketchpad, Winston sat on the bench and eyed the staircase. At one time he had lugged a small Minolta around to take photos of architectural details that he found interesting, but had eventually abandoned the camera. Putting it on paper forced him to look at the detail and become familiar with it in a way that never happened with a photograph.

On the other side of the columns was the double stairway that led to the second floor. Of dark mahogany, it was heavily carved and quite beautiful. In the wealthy colonialists' home, these stairways were the first items visitors would see as they entered the house and so were treated as showpieces. The newel posts, the handrails and the balustrade turnings were always done by the best wood turners money could buy. This reproduction was no different.

Completing the drawing, Winston let himself out. He stood for a moment in the gravel drive, looking up at the immense structure. Kiko should really see this house. When he came back, and he would, he'd bring her with him. And speaking of Kiko, Winston checked his watch. If he hurried, he could beat the evening rush hour.

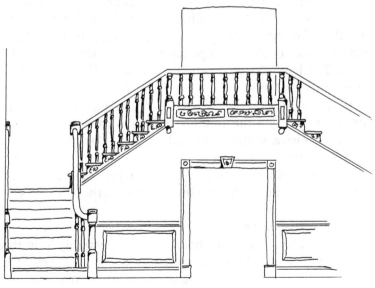

Main Staircase

CHAPTER 4

Miles Northingham stifled a yawn as he tried to concentrate on the TelePrompTer. He knew he was supposed to stare just to the right of the damn thing, his gaze and words meant only for that special viewer, but today he didn't care. If his eyes appeared dead from his straight reading of the material, that was just too bad. Who in the hell cared about door latches?

". . . and these original doors in old houses can often still have the original wrought-iron thumb-latches. Made of malleable iron by local blacksmiths, these thumb-latches consisted of five hammered pieces." Leaning forward, Miles picked up one of the metal pieces that lay on the table before him. "The hand grasp, this half circle here. The . . . eh, lift. That's this, eh . . ."

Miles could see Sammy Harris, his assistant, waving at him from between the TelePrompTer and camera 2. What's that little nitwit jumping around for now? thought Miles as he picked up another piece.

"The lift had the thumb press on one end and went through a hole in the door to lift . . . this . . . the bar. And you have the staple which held . . ."

Miles realized that he'd been holding the wrong piece initially. What he'd called the hand grasp had actually been the staple. This would have accounted for Sammy's damn arm waving. Without picking up any of the remaining objects, Miles continued quickly.

". . . the bar against the door to keep it from flopping around
. . ." Miles grinned at the camera. ". . . and the catch, a notched
piece spiked into the doorjamb into which the bar rested."

Making a hammering motion with his hands, Miles
moved down the table.

"Sometimes the lifts were secured by swivels, the swivel-
lift latch, as it was called . . ."

Miles droned on. He had no idea what any of the metal
objects were and he didn't care. The home-viewing audience,
for the most part, knew less than he did, and if he got the
dates wrong or held up the wrong latch, who'd know? The
important thing was they thought he knew, and if Dr. Miles
Northingham said this piece of iron was a Norfolk latch or a
Blake's latch they'd buy it and two minutes later forget he'd
ever mentioned it. The fact that his show was so popular had
always baffled him. At one point on a promotional tour, he
had realized that ninety percent of the people who watched
him on TV didn't even live in an old house. They were looking for something that Formica, Sheetrock walls and plastic
moldings weren't giving them. They'd buy reproductions of
these latches and install them in their split-level ranch, or
worse, their apartments. Sammy said people needed these
things to give them some sense of tradition, a connection
with the past. Miles felt it was like putting one of those fake
wells in your front yard and about as affected. What in the
hell was that all about? Miles realized the TelePrompTer was
blank and everyone was staring at him. Sammy looked as if
he'd just been fired. Miles hurried.

". . . and so that's it for this week. If you should want a
transcript of today's show just send five dollars to the address
on the screen and . . ."

"It's over, Miles. You're off the air." Joesy, the production
manager, stepped into the light.

"It is?"

"Didn't you hear the exit music? What were you doing out
here? Having a damn religious conversion?"

"The hell with you. Maybe latches bore me to tears. Come on, Sammy, we have to talk."

"Next taping in one hour. We can redo this mess then." Joesy shook her head. Miles had already bullied his way out of hearing range.

Miles waited for Sammy to enter his dressing room before slamming the door. "What's with the damn latches? Two shows we do latches? I'm up to here."

"The mail's running that way. We did doors and windows and suddenly the people want hardware. It's the natural order of things . . ."

"The hell with people. It's like those five shows we did on Native American dwellings. *Five shows*, for Christ's sake!! Longhouses! The ratings went down."

"You're right. That was a mistake. We should have stopped at four . . ."

"Three."

"Okay, perhaps three, but those were good shows. We got a plaque from the Esopus Indian Historical Society honoring us for those shows."

"Well, whoop de fucking do." Falling into his chair, Miles leaned back to stare at the ceiling.

Sammy waited a minute before speaking. "You held up the wrong . . ."

"I know that." Miles smacked the chair arm, his voice rising as he spoke. "I held up the damn staple instead of the thingamajig. Who cares? I do that to amuse myself. To give your skinny little arms some exercise." Standing, Miles moved over to the refrigerator he kept in his dressing room and took out a beer.

"We have another taping. In about an hour," advised Sammy.

"Great. I have time to drink the whole six-pack." Miles drained an entire can and opened another.

Shaking his head, Sammy reached into the briefcase leaning against his chair and removed a large folder. Carefully he took out some papers and spread them on the dressing room counter. "Shall we review the next show?" Sammy took Miles's silence as an affirmative. "The show is on porches. It's the beginning of a three-part series."

"What?"

"You should already know this. Didn't you read the material?"

"I glanced at it. I don't remember the three-part-series stuff. Porches are small, for Christ's sake. What's to talk about for an hour and a half? And stop with the sighs. You're driving me nuts." Miles sat down. "Okay, okay. Read the stuff to me. Slowly."

As Sammy began to review the material, Miles shut his eyes and thought about how bored he was getting. He was tired of the show. He was tired of old buildings, old hardware and old everything. He was particularly tired of Sammy Harris. Twice he'd asked the producers to find someone else, preferably a nice-looking woman historian. They had said forget it. Sam was the best. Over the six years of the show, Miles had gone through three historians, but the last, Dr. Samuel Harris, had been around for three. Having been on the staff of the New-York Historical Society, Doctor Sam, as the crew called him, lent the show some credibility. He was responsible for the show's topics, the scripts and overseeing the three people hired to answer the mail. The "mailbag" portion of *From Mortises to Mullions* was important because it provided ideas for topics and filled up ten minutes of a half-hour show. The mail hounds, as Miles called them, would cull out what they thought might be interesting and give this over to Sammy, who would make the final decision. He would then script answers to the picked questions and the day before taping have Miles memorize them. The effect was such that Miles actually came across as sounding authoritative. But the reality of the situation was that Sammy Harris was the show. Without him nothing would happen. In some vague way Miles knew all this and was careful not to alienate Sammy too much, but at the same time he never let Sammy forget who was boss, who made the big money. Miles could hear Sammy's voice off in the distance.

"What?" Miles opened his eyes.

"Were you asleep?" asked Sammy.

"No, I wasn't asleep. Just thinking. I don't like it. Not even a little bit," said Miles.

"So what don't you like?" Sammy was hurt.

"The whole damn porch thing. Didn't we do porches last year?"

"It's that time of year, Miles. Summertime people want to know about their old porches. They sit on them and they notice the porch isn't doing so well: rotten decking, rotten fascia, rotten rafters, something's missing, maybe. Sixty percent of the mail is running porches."

"I thought the mail was running hardware."

"That was a month ago. Now it's porches."

"And I know why. You had me mention porches a few shows back. We should never have done it."

"It's how we stimulate interest, Miles. You know that. Mention cornice moldings and suddenly all the mail is cornice moldings. I had you mention porches because porches are a smaller version of the house itself. They need much of the same materials and building expertise of the main structure but are smaller and easier to expose so one can illustrate and fix the problem without tearing apart an entire building. Anyway, this porch is different from the last one, Miles. It's a terne metal roof. We've never done a terne metal roof."

"I don't like roofs. I don't like ternes. They give me the willies."

Sammy gave out a sigh. Most people would ask what a terne metal roof *was* but not Miles. His lack of curiosity was staggering.

"Don't start with the sigh stuff, Sammy." Closing his eyes, Miles leaned back. "I want to do lighthouses again. Go to the beach. It's summer, Sammy. Time to take off the clothes. Check out the girls."

"Look, Miles, you don't have to get on the roof. We can do the whole thing from the studio. John can go out with the video if necessary for demo, but I don't think we'll need it. We bring in a guy to solder the pans, that's the hard part, and you just explain what he's doing."

"Solder the pans? What is this, a kitchen roof?" Miles snorted a laugh.

"That's what they call the metal sections. Terne is a tinplate alloyed with a large percentage of lead. You have to solder them together. It's a good show, believe me. We've already torn off the old roof, see. Now we show how to copy the existing hip structure and the ornamental rafter ends and put on the sheathing. Then we solder the terne metal. Good for two weeks. You could read the script while taping since the camera's going to be on the pans." Sammy knew Miles liked reading.

"Who in New York cares about porches? Tell me that."

"New York isn't just Manhattan. You know that. People out in Bensonhurst, City Island, they have porches that were built in the twenties, thirties. That's the time we're talking about. Besides, you're being seen by all America now, Miles. You have to remember that." As if Miles could remember anything, thought Sammy.

Standing, Miles leaned close to the mirror. "My mother had a porch on the front of the house. Had that green Astro-stuff on it. Was nice. You think this beard's too red? Maybe a nice white streak. Make me a little distinctive looking."

"You mean distinguished looking?" Sammy couldn't imagine the man being any more distinctive looking. At six feet four, two hundred sixty pounds and with a flaming red beard, Miles was hard to miss.

"Whatever."

The phone rang and Sammy picked it up. "Hello. Yes. Yes. Sure, put him through." He covered the mouthpiece. "It's Mr. Corbally."

"Which one?" asked Miles.

"I don't know. The receptionist only said . . . oh, hi. How

are you, Clement? . . . That's nice to hear. I'm looking forward to this weekend. . . . Sounds wonderful. . . . Sure, he's right here." Sammy mouthed the word "senior."

"Clement, how are you?" Miles's voice became all smiles. "That's wonderful. Are we still on for this weekend? . . . Uh-huh. . . . Uh-huh. . . . Well, of course I know it sounds like a lot, but I feel it's what's needed. These men are willing to put big bucks into the project, but the project has to be big, too. You can understand how investments work. . . . I know you are, but it's not as out of control as you're saying. . . . No, no.. . . Of course I understand. How about we talk this Saturday? . . . It's possible we can slim it down some. . . . I don't think that's necessary, Clement. Let's don't be thinking that way. . . . Certainly. . . . Could we wait until this weekend? . . . Yes, of course, I understand completely. . . . I sure will. My best to Lucille. . . . You, too." Miles waited for the click before speaking into the mouthpiece again. "Old fart." Miles was upset. Standing, he slammed the phone down.

"What was that all about?" asked Sammy.

"Oh, nothing." Miles's voice was choked with sarcasm. He headed for another beer. "Clement's not happy with the new idea. Might be a 'bit much.' Damn guy's got more money than God and . . . damn." Miles popped the tab on his beer. "These men I've lined up aren't going to be interested in two shows a summer. What's in it for them, for Christ's sake? We're talking money here."

"It's possible the expansion idea *is* too much. We could always get money elsewhere, Miles. The government's a possibility."

"Get real."

Sammy had liked the original microvillage concept. When Clement Corbally Sr. had come to him with the idea, Sammy had been excited. The village could be a place to explain old structures from the ground up. It would be an excellent way to demonstrate old building techniques, to teach and educate on the various methods used by the old-timers. Corbally

54

Village, as it would be called, would be a permanent teaching facility, someplace real that would expand the role of *From Mortises to Mullions*. There were historical organizations that taught a limited few specific aspects of the restoration arts, but this would encompass all aspects and reach millions. Dr. Miles Northingham would become the patron saint of architectural preservation. The show would do more to demonstrate American history than even Ken Burns could imagine. The problem was Miles. He kept wanting to expand on the project. Neither Sammy nor Mr. Corbally thought expansion necessary.

"You know how I feel about this," said Sammy. "I think small is better, and I also think that if we push for expansion we'll lose Corbally. I've worked too hard to have this whole . . ."

"Can it, Sammy pal. We've been through this. You see this whole thing as part of a TV show. Well, the hell with that. You have to quit thinking small, Sammy. Where would we be if our forefathers had done that? I'll tell you where, living in one of those damn longhouses we spent so much time on, that's where. I'm not thinking one dinky TV show twice a summer, Sammy my man. I'm thinking a whole damn television studio. A studio dedicated to the history of this great country. A cable network that shows nothing but U.S.-of-fucking-A. history. And what better place to broadcast from than somewhere right in the middle of that history? And Longmeadow is the place. Besides, it would keep start-up costs wayyyy down. You hear what I'm saying? Don't you want to be a part of that?"

"The village?" whispered Sammy.

"Sure, we can have the village. It's a must. It would be like one of those movie lots the old film studios used to have. But, you see, it wouldn't be just a boring old village, hell no. It would be a hot place with cameras rolling and history going out over the airways."

Sammy Harris could only stare. Even Miles could see that Sammy was in pain. He switched gears.

"I'll tell you what. I'll do another porch show if you can find another lighthouse or something. What else do they have at the beach that's old?"

Sammy didn't respond.

"Okay, Sam, okay. Come back to life, for Christ's sake. You're probably right, it doesn't have to be a whole network. But even you have to see that we could do more with this project. Aren't you bored with this *Mortises to Mullions* thing? Aren't you ready to move on to bigger and better? We're being given that opportunity." Sitting opposite Sammy, Miles lowered his voice to a brotherly tone. For a second he considered taking Sammy's hand. "Look, your job is history, Sammy. My job is presentation. You don't know these men, Sammy. I do. They move in different circles. They have influence and money. They don't care about history, they care about bucks. *They* like my idea. *They* see the possibilities. These are men who got where they are by *not* thinking small. Let me ride with it for just a little longer, okay? Let me have a crack at old Clement. If I can't convince him, I'll drop the whole thing. That's fair, isn't it?" Miles gave Sammy his special smile, an eerie expression that fell somewhere between a sneer and a dog grin.

"We can talk about it later," said Sammy, who looked as if he might burst into tears at any moment. "I'll see if the control room is ready. Please read the script again." Without looking back at Miles, Sammy made a quick exit.

Miles studied his beard in the mirror. He was going to have to watch himself with Sammy. Sammy was needed to keep Clement Sr. in line. The two had the hots for each other. But once the project was off the ground, Sammy Harris was going to *be* history. Miles Northingham was just starting and nobody, no weasel-faced history prof or any ancient, gray-eyed, croquet-playing WASP, was about to stop him.

CHAPTER
5

"Interesting," said Winston as he replaced the phone. At that moment Kiko entered the office.

"What's interesting?"

"Remember my friend Henry Thayer over at the *Times*? Does the television reviews. I called him to ask about this Dr. Miles Northingham I was telling you about. He had some charming things to say about the doctor."

Kiko gave Winston a questioning look. "And . . .?"

"Well, I'd heard rumors concerning this guy and thought I'd check up on him. Turns out his real name is Charles Miles and he's not a doctor of anything. Bull maybe."

"Oh? Miles Northingham isn't an historian? His show is really big."

"So I've heard, but he used to push used cars on late night television. Called himself The Mountain Man. Seems he had a small following. Appealed to the insomniac crowd."

"How'd he get from that to what he does now?" asked Kiko.

"Henry's not sure. Charles Miles must have had what the network was looking for. Apply some veneer, add a history degree or two, and voilà: TV historian. Seems the guy's always in trouble with the network. He has a bad habit of talking up products other than the show's sponsors. A tool with its name showing placed conveniently for the camera, that sort of thing. There's a question of payola, but the man's so popular the network growls and looks the other way."

57

"Hmmmm. Do you think Mr. Corbally knows about this?"

"I couldn't tell you. It's really not my business to interfere. It's just that I liked the old guy, and when he mentioned this Miles character I thought I'd follow up on some rumors I'd heard. Did you try Dr. Harris again?"

"I did. The television person said he was out of town."

"I wonder if he's up at Longmeadow. Well, thanks for trying."

Kiko set a piece of paper on Winston's desk. "Here's a reply from that group fighting the convent demolition. Seems they weren't very happy with your findings."

"That's to be expected. It's a nice building but I'm afraid it's not that nice. Now what's that look?"

Kiko's beautiful face had grown cloudy. "I don't know . . ."

"You'd like to save the convent?" asked Winston.

Kiko nodded in the affirmative. "It's so wonderful. It just seems a shame to pull it down."

Only six months out of graduate school, Kiko still confused age with merit. Winston could remember feeling the same way, but with experience his attitude had changed. It was an old battle in the preservation ranks: to preserve or not to preserve. Or more to the point, to designate or not to designate. The process for saving old structures was long and complicated and involved getting on someone's historic preservation list. That could mean the local level or the National Register of Historic Places. Determining what was eligible for designation and what was not was often a matter of opinion.

"The problem here," continued Winston, "is that this neighborhood's lawyers based their entire case on the fact that the convent was the only good example of Beaux Arts architecture in the surrounding area. That's like saying the American League is a good example of a baseball team. The term 'Beaux Arts' encompasses a broad range of styles and, as I mentioned in my letter, the lawyers need to be more specific. Just around the corner is a much more interesting example by the architect John Carrère. And I'd have to say that the convent, with its lack of facade ornamentation and its flat roof, waffles in an area somewhere between Italian Renaissance and not-very-interesting."

With a frown, Kiko went and sat at her own desk. "If they take it down the developer will put up some horrible building made of black glass. He'll stick a marble portico on the front and call it postmodern Colonial or something."

"He might, and I agree with you that that would be too bad. The neighborhood association wanted me to verify their opinion concerning the convent. I couldn't do that. My credibility was on the line, and had I thought the building was a good example of Beaux Arts, I would have stated as much. That was not the case. This building wasn't designed by Cass Gilbert. It was the work of a lesser architect for some robber baron who owned only one railroad and who wound up selling his house to the church during the Depression."

"You don't think it's worth saving?"

Leaning back, Winston let out a sigh and thought about saving the convent. "If the building's in good structural shape, why not? And you're right, it's certainly more attractive than what will probably go up in its place, but that's something else altogether. The neighborhood should fight for adaptive reuse, concentrate on the 'character' of the neighborhood. There are no other tall buildings in that area, and that could be in their favor. Also, the economy's not so great at the moment. Maybe a long, expensive legal battle wouldn't interest the developer. You know, developers can be nice guys, too."

Kiko expressed her opinion of that by screwing up her nose.

"No, it's true. I've worked with developers who were good people. I know there are many architectural historians who feel that that should be a crime punishable by having to sit for a full year staring at the Time-Life building on Sixth Avenue. But those people are usually ensconced in some academic wonderland and don't have to worry about paying the rent. History for me is a business. If it was the other way around, my business would be history."

"You should put that on your business card."

"Now, now, it's the real world talking here. Look, you'll have many chances to save buildings, but they'll deserve to be saved."

"King Tut's tomb would have been in trouble had . . ."

The phone rang.

"Saved by the bell," chuckled Winston.

Frowning at Winston, Kiko picked up the phone. "Hello . . . Yes, it is. . . . Yes, Mr. Wyc is in. Could you hold a moment, please?" Blocking the receiver, Kiko mouthed the word, "Sackett."

Rolling his eyes, Winston took the phone. "Hi, Sackett, how are you? I was going to call you later. Did you get my letter?" Periodically shaking his head at Kiko, Winston listened for a full minute before answering. "But those were not the conditions under which I took the job. I think the project has merit. It has been carefully planned and, if developed in the way your father said, could conceivably cost much less than you believe. . . . Yes, you're right, it's still going to cost a lot of money." Winston listened some more. "What about my suggestion of you working with your father? You wouldn't have to go into the history business but it would give you a better idea of what was going on. You might even be able to help keep the costs down. . . . I see. Impossible, huh? I'm sorry to hear that. . . . One more session? Wellll . . . why not. That's fair. . . . Okay." Winston smiled over at Kiko. "Certainly, we'd love to. July the second. . . . Sure. Two o'clock. . . . Thanks. . . . You too. Bye."

Winston let out a long sigh.

"Didn't go for it?" Kiko asked.

"Didn't go for it, is right. Thinks I've been hoodwinked. Feels he paid for more than one try. And he did actually."

"And that means another visit. Did I hear the word 'we' used?"

Winston smiled. "You did. We've been invited up to attend

a lawn party on the second of July. Sackett feels that that would be a good time to have another talk. All together this time."

"A weekend in the country. What a nice idea."

"How about an afternoon in the country?" corrected Winston.

"Oh, come on. We could do a tour of historical houses or something. Write the trip off as research."

Winston laughed as he wrote in his appointment book. "For less than a month on the job, you're learning fast. Next you'll be condemning buildings for profit."

"That will never happen." Rubbing her palms together, Kiko shivered with delight. "I see a chance to get out of the city. Let's enjoy it."

"Believe me, the country is overrated."

"Just one night? We could have dinner in one of those cute little inns. Drinks in front of the fireplace."

"It's July. A bit warm for fires."

"We'll have them crank up the air-conditioning."

Laughing, Winston considered a weekend with Kiko. At first, when he had hired her, he had thought about asking her out but decided against it, realizing that restraint would be better for office harmony. A whole weekend could be dangerous.

"It's a thought." Winston stayed noncommittal.

"Don't wait too long. That's next week and we'd have to make reservations." Kiko gave Winston an expectant look.

"Okay, okay, I give up. I know of a good place to stay, too. It's called the Ruddy Rooster and it's run by ex–New Yorkers who have a firm grasp on the irony of the whole thing. At least the wife does. You'll love it."

"I can't wait. I don't know why I'm so excited, but I am."

"Maybe it's your work environment?" mused Winston aloud.

Kiko smiled. "It is pretty oppressive."

"Speaking of work . . ."

"Goodness." A worried expression crossed Kiko's face.

"What is it?"

Kiko stood. "What am I going to wear? And don't give me that look. Everything I own is black. Not very country."

"Well then, why don't we have Georgio come up and outfit you in something . . . safari. After all, it is a write-off."

"No dumb jokes, please. This is serious."

"For someone who's constantly beating me over the head with the feminist viewpoint, you sure do care an awful lot about appearances."

"What's that have to do with anything?" Placing her knuckles on Winston's desk, Kiko leaned in to talk. "What? Feminists can't look nice? I can see we're going to have to sit down and have a talk, Mr. Wyc, on what's important and what's not."

"I'll tell you what's important right now. That's lunch."

"A not very sophisticated defensive ploy, Mr. Wyc, but I think you're on to something. Come on, let's go out. You can buy me lunch and I'll explain a few things concerning appearances. You might have me on Beaux Arts, for now, but when it comes to style . . ." Kiko shook her head. "This could be a long lunch."

CHAPTER
6

Kiko had thought they should rent a Mercedes. She said you couldn't arrive for a lawn party at the Corballys driving a fifteen-year-old Volvo; besides, it was only for two days. Winston had said it was too much money and there was nothing wrong with his car. Other than the missing side window in the back it was a classic. Kiko had complained of the whooshing noise coming from the rear of the car but had fallen asleep five miles outside the city limits and had remained asleep all the way to Longmeadow. Winston had concentrated on the music of Natalie Cole and the passing countryside, lush with the greens of summer. As he approached Longmeadow, Winston realized that the prospect of seeing Sackett no longer bothered him and that a pas de deux between father and son might provide high entertainment.

The long driveway up to the estate house was lined with tall oaks and white fencing. The trees formed an irregular tunnel of sorts with the front portico of the house, the light at the end. Unlike on his first visit, when the house had seemed void of all human presence, the grounds were now alive with people. Blocking the drive near the house were seven or eight cars waiting to be parked in a field to his right. Young men dressed in orange baseball caps could be seen running back and forth from the field to the cars. Pulling in behind the last car, Winston leaned over and gave Kiko a gentle prod.

"Go away," she said.

"We're here," answered Winston.

Raising her head, Kiko suddenly came to attention. "What's going on? Is this the right place? There're so many people."

"Looks like what the gentry around here call a 'telephone party.' Everyone's invited."

"Do I look okay?" Instantly, the visor mirror dropped and there was an inspection. "I look terrible. Why didn't you wake me sooner?"

"You look wonderful," replied Winston. And she did. Kiko's idea of country wear was an ankle-length, red polka-dot silk dress that clung to her as if it were in danger of falling off a cliff. She appeared very chic to Winston, although he couldn't help thinking that in some vague way she looked like a war bride. Maybe the light-colored straw hat with blocked crown she had brought would erase that impression.

A kid in an orange baseball cap pulled open the door and handed Winston a slip of paper with a number on it.

"Party's round that way," the kid intoned.

No sooner had they stepped from the car than it shot away.

"Good thing my dress didn't catch in the door," said Kiko, "or I'd be parked over there right now. Now, how does the hat look?"

"Quite chic."

"It's not too manly?"

Giving Kiko an exaggerated once-over, Winston shook his head no. "I don't think anyone's going to notice the hat."

"What's that mean?" Twisting herself, Kiko tried to see what she looked like from behind.

"It means you look beautiful."

Kiko gave Winston her own once-over. "What does it say in the company bylaws about holding the arm of the boss?"

"The bylaws don't apply twenty-five miles past the city limits."

With Kiko on his arm, Winston followed the other couples past the front of the house and the east wing to where a sculptured privet hedge gave privacy to a garden beyond.

Stopping short of entering the garden, Kiko turned to admire the house.

"This is quite the place. What do you think? Thirty rooms?"

"Twenty big ones," answered Winston. "It's one of the largest Colonial Revival houses I've ever seen. You'll like the inside. The architect reproduced an original interior, not like a lot of these places where the interior would have been much more contemporary. Can you tell me when it was built? Within five years?"

"Aren't we on vacation?"

"Not yet. This is the research part of the trip."

"Okay." Kiko studied the house. "Colonial Revival . . . so it has to date from around the 1880s to . . . well, the twenties. Until the late teens, very early twenties, the exteriors were almost always wooden . . . so the brick facade would indicate it was built in the twenties and I doubt if it was built just before or during the Depression . . . so I'd have to say, mid-twenties. Nineteen twenty-six. How's that?"

Winston smiled. "I knew I'd hired you for a reason."

"Bingo, heh?"

"Don't look so smug. You were off by almost six months."

"Take it out of my pay. On second thought, maybe you'd better not. This dress cost me a fortune."

Laughing, Winston led Kiko through an archway in the hedge. Suddenly the world was all rose beds and topiary and bubbling humanity. An almost exact copy of Clement Corbally Sr. was standing just inside the hedge greeting people as they entered. He wore a white polo shirt and bright red pants that didn't quite reach his ankles. "Hi, I'm Uncle Carl Corbally," said the man. "Official greeter for the Wistfield Corballys." Chuckling to himself, Uncle Carl Corbally leered at Kiko.

Winston introduced himself and Kiko.

"Friends of Sackett?" asked the man, his huge, bushy eyebrows raised in query.

"Sort of." Winston smiled. "We share an interest in architectural history."

"My nephew?" Uncle Carl's expression was one of mild shock. "Are we sure we have the right Sackett? Well, make yourselves at home. Have a drink, talk nonsense and leave the silver alone." Uncle Carl wheezed a laugh to show that he was kidding. Winston wasn't so sure. Brushing past Winston, Uncle Carl greeted the couple behind him. Kiko and Winston moved into the garden.

"Do I look like I might touch the silver?" asked Winston.

"Well, now that you mention it . . ."

"Gosh, thanks."

"Check out these bushes," said Kiko. "They've been shaped to look like animals. What do you think this one is?"

"Obvious," answered Winston. "It's a coati."

Kiko laughed. "A coati? I think I need a cocktail."

Drinks in hand, the two wandered about the garden, nodding at others and commenting on the roses. Soon they were standing in the back of the house looking out over a great lawn. In the center of the lawn was a large, perfectly flat, raised area that resembled a rectangular putting green approximately one hundred by eighty feet. Arranged on the blemish-free surface of short-cropped grass were six symmetrically arranged, thick metal archways, their whiteness sharp against the intense green veneer. In the center of the court was an Indian's small totem of bright stripes to echo the color of the balls scattered about. Leaning against one of these archways, or wickets, were two mallets. At one end of the court area several guests sat quietly talking within the shade of a gazebo. Two hundred feet past this, at the far end of the lawn, stood a long arbor wrapped in the thick vines of an ancient wisteria, its flowers hanging like huge clusters of grapes.

"Look at the size of those mallets," observed Winston. "They look a lot bigger than the backyard variety."

Kiko shook her head in disapproval. "Everything here seems a bit too much, if you ask me. It would make a nice public park."

"Do I detect a note of hostility, Ms. Hamaguchi?"

"Not from me. I find all of this perfectly normal."

"I bet. Let's see if we can locate Mr. Corbally. I think you'll find him more to your liking. He's a rough in the diamond, as it were."

Rolling her eyes, Kiko fell in behind Winston.

"If I'm correct about this, Mr. Corbally's study should be just down here. I remember it looked out on a patio in the rear of the house. More than likely that's where he'll be hiding."

The brick wall of the east wing extended out from the main house by twenty feet, providing a sheltered area for the patio. This wall was covered with a well-developed espalier of peaches. Thirty feet opposite this wall was a one-story clapboard extension in which were set French doors and a large picture window looking out over the lawn. Its flat roof was contained with a railing and appeared to be a second-floor porch. A low, thick barberry hedge ran along the open side. Across from the hedge was another set of French doors that led into the main house.

"This is it," said Winston. "Those doors lead into the study. Look at these peaches."

As Winston inspected the fruit, Kiko crossed the patio and peered through the French doors.

"There's someone sitting at the desk," she mumbled into the glass.

"Are they . . ."

"Winston? Winston Wyc?"

At that moment the other set of French doors flew open and a short, round man stepped from the house. Dressed in religious black, a dash of white at the neck, with a black cape that flapped behind him at each purposeful step, the man looked like Zorro gone to seed. With arm extended, he strode across the patio toward Winston. The two shook hands.

"My goodness, what brings the famous Mr. Wyc to these parts? Has someone been murdered?"

Smiling, Winston turned to Kiko. "Kiko, I'd like for you to meet the Reverend Simon Tart, the Vicar of Wistfield, and an old friend."

Simon bowed at the waist. "My pleasure. And please, young lady, promise me you will not go into the garden, for the roses will surely wilt with jealousy before your beauty. And I do love those roses."

Even though the vicar said this with the utmost sincerity, Kiko couldn't help noticing the impish twinkle in his eyes. "Thank you for the compliment, Mr. Tart, but I've already been in the garden and the roses all seem perfectly happy."

"Then they are finer roses than I thought and better for your having walked among them."

"Oh, please." Kiko giggled.

"And you, Winston. I didn't know you were friends with the Corballys."

"I'm not, really. I . . . eh, did some work for the son Sackett and because of that I met the father. We share an interest in history."

"Oh, he loves his history. I'm always having to remind him to beware the false idol. But he's a good man."

"And a wealthy man," teased Winston.

"Please, Mr. Wyc, you know I prefer the healthy soul to the wealthy soul, and although the Church does harbor those pastors whose hearts can be reached through the collection plate, I pray each morning that I'm not one of them." Simon gave the heavens a quick mock-concerned glance. "But isn't this a party? You may find this hard to believe, Kiko, but occasionally even an ascetic like myself has to get his head out of the clouds and concentrate on more mundane persuasions." With a wink, Simon patted his substantial girth.

"Odd you should mention that, Simon," answered Kiko, "but I was just saying the same thing to Winston here. The man spends too much time thinking about work."

"It is odd," nodded Simon, "for I was of the impression that the man had some Irish in him."

"That's enough," said Winston. "I can see I should never have introduced you two." Winston held up his empty plastic cup. "I need more broth."

"Ah, there's the Irish," said Simon with a grin. "I wondered where it . . ."

"Simon?"

A tall, handsome woman appeared in the doorway.

"Lucille, I'm sorry but I was waylaid. I want you to meet some friends of mine. Or perhaps you've already met?"

"No, we haven't," said Winston.

Simon introduced Lucille Corbally, the wife of Clement Corbally Sr. The woman wore a soft, dark green leather dress hung with a leather fringe from the sleeves and the hem. The dress was gathered at the waist with a delicate silver belt, and at her neck a pendant of silver and jade glowed against the dark green of the cloth. Her long white hair was plaited and held in place with a pale yellow headband. Lucille's patrician face seemed oddly out of sync with her ensemble.

"I'm so glad you could both come. Clement did carry on so about Winston the other night, a parallel soul or somesuch."

"We were just looking for him," said Winston. "I'd like to say hello."

"If he's not here, then he's probably down at the barns. I see his little cart isn't parked in its normal place. Perhaps Cybil knows."

"Knows what, Mother?"

At that moment another woman appeared at the French doors. For Winston, these doors were beginning to take on the aspect of C. S. Lewis's magic closet. How many more wonderful creatures would emerge from within? This one was a younger version of Lucille, tall and willowy and pretty. Her dark hair was cut short at the chin line and bounced when she moved her head. Her pale blue eyes were bright and bold. She wore Birkenstock sandals and a sleeveless blue dress with a buttoned front. Once again Simon did the introductions.

"An historian?" Cybil's blue eyes gazed intently into Winston's. "I'm sorry but you seem far too young."

"We come in all shapes and sizes."

"Winston was looking for your father," said Lucille.

"As soon as the guests started to arrive, he hopped on his cart and drove away toward the barn. No more than half an hour ago." Cybil smiled at Winston. "It's a short walk. I could show you the way, if you like."

"Why not?" interrupted Kiko, who had not been included in Cybil's suggestion.

"Kiko and I are a team," explained Winston. "That is, we work together."

Cybil smiled at the thought.

"I'm afraid I'm going to have to ask you to stay here," said Lucille to her daughter. "Sackett was supposed to assist me but he seems to have disappeared." Lucille turned to Winston. "Clement should return soon. Why not wait with something to drink and eat. It's all on the piazza. Cybil, you come with me. This caterer hasn't a clue."

Leading Winston and Kiko back toward the rose garden, Simon bubbled with praise for his hostess.

"Marvelous woman. Rare for one of her station. Has some odd thoughts concerning one's spirituality, but I forgive her. Lucille feels comfortable with anyone, from the impoverished to the fortunate. Should all of this vanish tomorrow, I truly believe Lucille would hardly notice."

"Oh?" Winston raised an eyebrow at Kiko. Simon's point of view of the world tended to the parochial. The vicar had been coddled and subsidized by the wealthy of Wistfield for so long and with such earnestness that the real world had in many ways become a mystery hinted at in the Sunday *New York Times* or on the six o'clock news. If the less enamored of his flock might have wished him to be more alert to outreach, the conservative majority were quite happy with his humorous and agreeable sermons. American society might be riddled with serial killers, the homeless, savage gangs or what-have-you, but in Simon's little sphere, civilization had stopped expanding with the death of Thomas Hardy. If there were no Tess or Eustacia to comfort him as he briefly pondered these societal ills, then he could certainly imagine them entering his life at some point and making him whole. As befits a man of his calling, Simon was infinitely patient.

"You haven't seen Sackett, have you?" asked Winston.

"Not since I arrived. I think the presence of a real priest embarrasses the man. As you may or may not know, Sackett has his . . . eh, shall we say dreams. One mustn't be too harsh."

"You mean, Sackett isn't a priest?" asked Kiko.

"He went to seminary but never completed the work. One or the other didn't meet expectations. Which one I couldn't say."

"I'll be darned." Kiko raised her eyebrows at Winston.

The population of the garden had doubled in size. The piazza, as Lucille called the porch off the east wing, was dense with people getting drinks and helping themselves to canapés. Caterers' helpers, in white shirts and black pants, passed through the crowd with their trays, appropriately solemn and discreet.

"Can I get you two something?" asked Winston.

"No thanks." Raising his hand to a passing caterer's assistant, Simon plucked a napkin from the offered tray. "I'll just take one of these and one of these and one of these." From another tray he snared a glass of white wine for himself and one for Kiko. "The Wistfield version of the moveable feast, dear. You run along and get your favorite poteen, Winston. I'll entertain Kiko with malicious gossip about those around us."

Standing in line, Winston watched Kiko laughing at Simon's remarks. The man looked rounder and shorter each time he saw him.

"Scotch, please. One ice cube, no water," said Winston to the bartender.

"My goodness," said the woman beside him.

"I should drink it neat?" asked Winston, turning to her.

"That's up to you, darling. I was wondering about the agitation over by the pool. What could be going on?"

As if summoned by a silent whistle, the guests, first in twos and then as a group, collected at the other side of the garden. Drink in hand, Winston caught up with Simon and Kiko.

"What's going on?" he asked.

"It would seem to be Uncle Carl," said Simon. "If it's what I think, then we should get over there."

Simon directed Winston and Kiko around the hedge and onto a walkway that led past the garden to a large swimming pool. The three came out at one end of the pool while the remaining guests were crowded at the other. On the opposite side, two elderly men looked prepared to enact a duel. At the moment they were standing back to back, their pistols raised to their chests, their eyes staring straight before them. Winston noticed that one of the performers seemed much more eager than the other. The eager one was addressing the crowd.

"The year is eighteen aught four and the scurrilous Aaron Burr is still smarting from his defeat in the United States Congress, a slap in the face that will dog him all his days. In cowardly style he has coerced the fine gentleman Alex Hamilton into a shooting match."

Uncle Carl was bombastic in his presentation. The guests smiled and listened attentively.

"Today we will reenact that black moment in history. Ready, Rodney old man!"

Rodney did not look ready. Uncle Carl began shouting numbers.

"One!"

He took one pace forward. The other man didn't move.

"Two!"

Another step. Rodney was beginning to visibly quake. The pistol banged against his shrunken chest. Winston could see Lucille and Clement Jr. trying to work their way through the crowd. Lucille had one arm raised and was shouting something. Uncle Carl must have heard her for he picked up the pace.

"Three, four, five . . ."

"Carl! Put that gun down now!" Lucille's voice was coming in clearly.

"Six, seven, eight . . ." Rodney had finally found his legs

and was hesitantly moving away. Winston was surprised by a short, stocky man who suddenly went by him in the direction of Uncle Carl.

"Nine, ten . . ."

Turning, Uncle Carl shouted something about cowardly traitors and pulled off a shot. At that exact moment the short man reached Uncle Carl and grabbed him by the waist. Both men flew head over heels into the pool. Across from where Winston was standing, the cowardly traitor stopped, wavered and went down. For a second the world stalled. Then, as if on cue, all the guests began to move. Some attended to Rodney while others reached out to rescue the bathers.

"Should we do something?" Winston tried not to sound too enthusiastic.

"Is that man hurt?" cried Kiko.

"I'm a priest," sighed Simon. "I suppose I should go look at him."

Winston, who wouldn't want Simon near *him* in an emergency, watched from the opposite side of the pool as Simon stood pontificating beside the fallen duelist. While Lucille scolded from the edge, guests assisted Uncle Carl and his tackler from the pool. A caterer offered the dripping men something from her tray. Lucille joined Rodney and the others, and there was a great amount of concerned inspection and slapping of clothes. Kiko, who had followed Simon over, came back shaking her head.

"No visible wounds," she said. "I think poor Rodney's going to need a strong martini when he gets home. Uncle Carl might need a strong lawyer. When do they close the gates to this asylum?"

"They give plenty of warning. I think a loud horn goes off."

"And you were a big help, Winston." Kiko's expression was one of feigned disapproval.

"I was always taught to give the victim lots of breathing room. Look, before they do shut the gates, let's go find Mr. Corbally."

"Show the way, brave leader." Kiko and Winston left the excited crowd behind. "Speaking of shootings, what was that Simon said when he greeted you? Were you here because someone had been murdered? What did he mean?"

Winston laughed. "It's a long story. Let's just say I've had some unfortunate adventures in these parts and Simon was involved."

"Come on. How about a hint?"

Winston explained as they walked back through the rose garden. "A few years ago I took a job in Wistfield in which, quite by accident, I discovered someone who'd been murdered. Simon has always kidded me about it."

"Murdered? That's horrible."

"It was an adventure I wouldn't want to repeat."

Kiko glanced back at the pool area. "Well, it almost happened again. You were right about the country. It's a strange place."

"Amen to that," said Winston.

CHAPTER

7

Winston and Kiko stopped at the piazza for a traveling cocktail. Cybil was there arranging platters of hors d'oeuvres.

"What's all the commotion?" she asked.

Winston plucked some salmon from the table. "Uncle Carl was giving a history lesson."

"Not Burr and Hamilton?"

"That's right," answered Kiko. "This has happened before?"

Cybil offered Kiko a plate of stuffed mushrooms and a look of displeasure. "I'm afraid so and more than a couple of times. Was anyone hurt?"

"I don't think so," said Kiko. "When we left, Rodney, that was the poor victim's name, was walking away under his own steam."

"Rodney? Oh no, that's Mother's favorite neighbor. I do hope he's all right."

"What seems to be Uncle Carl's problem?" Winston took the presented mushroom.

"For some reason, no one knows why, Uncle Carl, when he's drunk, thinks he's related to Alexander Hamilton, which he isn't. Or maybe that he *is* Alexander Hamilton. That part's fuzzy."

Winston remembered that a descendant of Hamilton's, Robert Hamilton, had been married to a woman who had turned out to be a bigamist and who had tried to palm off another woman's child as her own. There had even been a shooting or a stabbing involved. Winston couldn't recall the details. It was possible that Uncle Carl might possess some of this woman's genes.

"Anyway," continued Cybil, "after a few drinks, sometimes he discovers Aaron Burr is present and finagles a rematch."

"He actually challenges them to a duel? And they accept?" Winston tempered his incredulity with a sip of Scotch.

"Well, you see it's not initially proposed as such. Uncle Carl's too cunning to actually slap someone with his glove or whatever it is you're supposed to do. He casually brings up the Hamilton-Burr thing in conversation, talks about duels in general and before you know it he's staging one. The other person rarely understands that Uncle Carl is serious. Luckily, there have been no injuries. Yet."

"I'll stay clear of Uncle Carl," stated Kiko.

"Like my father, Uncle Carl is a history nut. The three of you would probably have a lot to talk about," Cybil said to Winston with a mischievous grin.

"Is he the older or younger brother?" asked Winston.

"Neither. Actually, he's my father's first cousin. They sort of grew up together and they share the same birthday, and for that reason many in the family think of them as brothers."

"Speaking of your father," said Winston, "Kiko and I would like to visit with him. If you could head us in the right direction . . ."

Glancing up, Cybil took in the action at the end of the garden. "Oh boy, here they come. I don't think I'm up for the excited crowd scene at the moment. Come on, I'll take you to Father."

Grabbing one more slice of salmon, Winston fell in beside Cybil and Kiko.

At the end of the lawn and past the wisteria, the ground fell away in a gentle slope to a view of a rolling meadow. A dirt road, bounded on one side by a stone wall and on the other by a post and rail fence, wound its way down to several old barns. In the dry dust of the roadside grew wild chicory and out in the fields the whites of Queen Anne's lace, fever-few and ox-eye daisies. For Winston it seemed as if he had stepped into one of the many photographs his mother kept of her native Ireland. The meadow, with its gentle roll and jutting gray rock, needed only a thatched-roof cottage to complete the fantasy.

"I'm not usually taken by country scenes," said Winston, "but this little landscape is beautiful."

"This is my favorite part of Longmeadow," said Cybil. "When I was younger, Father and I would walk down to the barn there and he'd tell me stories or recite poems. He'd stand at the barn, his chest forward, his hand waving in the breeze, booming Robert Service at the top of his lungs." Cybil mimed his movements. "I'd laugh like a little nut. He hasn't done that in a while. I'll have to insist on a performance when we find him."

"Someone's coming," observed Kiko.

From the direction of the barn, Winston could see Sackett approaching. Because of a hollow in the road, his head was visible first and then, as if rising from a hole in the earth, the rest of his advancing figure. Even from a distance he appeared to be agitated, moving quickly and with determined stride. Sackett had his sport coat slung over his shoulder. He hesitated when he noticed them and put the coat back on. The three waited.

"Hello, brother dear."

"Cybil. And Winston and Kiko. How nice to see you." Sackett was curt.

"Is something wrong?" asked Cybil.

"Oh, nothing at all. Father insisted on my meeting him at the barn and then he doesn't show. I come all the way down here and he's not there."

"Well, it's not that far, is it?" Cybil's tone was mildly scolding. "Maybe he's with Richie."

"Richie's not there, either. I looked."

"We could wait for him together," said Winston.

"I've done my waiting. Twenty-five minutes I had to stand around in that dirty, dreadful barn."

"He must be around somewhere," said Cybil. "I saw him get in his cart and head down this way over an hour ago."

"His cart's there all right."

"Then he's down here."

"Oh, I don't doubt that. Probably off with Richie talking wooden gutters or some such nonsense. Just like him. Mother said he wanted to tell me something important. Just had to meet with me when I've got cars full of guests arriving up at the house." Pausing, Sackett took a moment to calm himself. "I apologize, Winston. I've allowed my father to upset me. But I think this might give you some idea of what I'm up against. As you can see, your proposal of getting together on this silly project is just too far-fetched."

"I'm sorry to hear that," said Winston, although he did think Sackett was overreacting. "I wonder what was so important."

"Nothing, absolutely nothing. He . . . he was going to have another go at me, I'm sure." Turning, Sackett glanced back toward the barns, started to say something and then changed his mind. "Again I apologize, but I must get back to my guests. If you still plan on going farther, tell Father I waited long enough."

With that said, Sackett, first checking to make sure none of the dirty, dreadful barn had settled on his dark blue sport coat, started up toward the house. Standing in silence for several seconds, the three watched him walk away.

"Is that like your father?" Kiko asked Cybil. "To forget Sackett was coming?"

"My father probably waited twenty-five minutes himself and, thinking Sackett wasn't coming, gave up and went on to do something else."

"Let's go see if we can find him," said Winston.

The first barn they approached was a huge structure. The foundation wall was constructed of fieldstone, rose six feet above ground level and formed a large lower space for livestock beneath the actual first floor. The first floor was lit with small mullioned windows spaced every ten feet. Winston counted fourteen windows. Above the stone foundation, vertical boards rose two stories, terminating in a gable roof that added another eight feet to the impressive building. A hundred feet past this barn was another smaller barn that looked to have been recently renovated. Partially hidden by this building was what appeared to be an old Airstream trailer, its beautifully rounded silver corners glaring in the sunlight. Winston moved over to the side of the large barn to inspect a door that was set into the stone.

"This side door here is exquisite," he said.

"It looks like something out of a fairy tale," added Kiko.

Cybil laughed. "I used to be scared of this door," she said. "I thought a troll lived here."

"Would you mind if I drew a quick sketch of it?" asked Winston. "I find it quite fanciful."

"Of course not," answered Cybil.

From the inside pocket of his sport coat, Winston took out his small sketchpad. "I like the hinges. Some local blacksmith had quite the imagination."

"There. What do you think?" asked Winston, showing Cybil his artwork.

"I like it. I think you've captured its trollness very nicely."

Winston laughed. "I'll take that as a compliment."

The three moved around to the front of the barn, where two large sliding doors had been pulled open to reveal the interior. Piles of stacked lumber and architectural details could be seen resting in the shadows. To the left of the entrance, leaning against the wall, was a fully realized Federal-style doorway with slender side windows and a gracefully curved fanlight. Winston stared back into the barn, letting his eyes adjust to the darkness. Mr. Corbally's golf cart was parked just inside the doors.

"That's a smart way to get around," said Kiko.

"Father's legs haven't been so great lately. He bought this so he could come down here. Billy, that's my son, thinks it's the best thing since Batman."

"You have a son?" asked Winston.

"I have two sons. Billy who's ten and Gordon who is four."

"Two sons?" mumbled Kiko under her breath.

"Look at all these interesting pieces," said Winston, moving slowly through the architectural elements that lay stacked on the barn floor. "This Federal doorway is wonderful. Kiko, check out this banding that runs around the casing. It looks Egyptian. I've never seen that before." Having moved farther into the barn, Winston suddenly came to a stop. Before him, and just below the hayloft opening, stood a carefully stacked and numbered pile of roof rafters. In the shadow of the dim

Barn Door

light that shone down through the opening, Winston found the man they were seeking.

Clement Corbally Sr. lay stretched out on the pile, his body limp, his eyes staring blankly up at the dust motes that swirled in the light above his head. The old man had dressed for the party. Instead of overalls he wore red plaid pants, a white polo shirt and a string tie, its silver clasp as dull and gray as his vacant eyes. Winston hadn't seen that many dead people but he recognized one when he did. He turned around and moved quickly back to the women.

"Is there a phone in that trailer behind the barn?" asked Winston.

"No," answered Cybil, "but there's one in Richie's shop. That's in the other barn."

"Maybe I could use it?" Winston wasn't quite sure of what to do. An emergency call seemed appropriate, but what of Cybil? Her father lay dead just behind him. Winston's legs felt wiggly, incapable of movement. He could feel himself starting to panic. Mr. Cool, that was him. Kiko resolved the dilemma for him.

"What in the world is that?" she asked.

"What?" mumbled Winston. Before he could stop her, she was past him.

"It's . . ." Kiko hesitated, her hand went to her mouth. "Oh, my God!"

"What is it?" asked Cybil.

Winston stopped Cybil as she tried to go past him. "It's your father. He's had an accident."

"Father?" Cybil shook her arm loose from Winston's hold and went by him. "What are you talking about?"

For thirty seconds Cybil didn't move. She stood rigid, her arms pressed tightly against her sides, staring at her father. And then slowly her arms lifted and her hands began patting the air as if swatting at invisible small fires. Suddenly, she stumbled forward, catching herself at the last second from falling against the stacked rafters. Winston moved to assist her but Cybil's voice stopped him.

"I'm okay. But could someone please go up to the house and get Dr. Chapman? He's wearing a pink shirt."

"Cybil . . .?" Kiko's voice was barely audible.

"Really . . . I'm all right. Please hurry."

Kiko touched Winston on the arm and then she was gone. While watching Cybil, Winston was aware of Kiko's short, rapid steps moving away from the barn. Many minutes passed. Slowly, deliberately, Cybil moved closer to her father. Placing her hand on his head, she carefully stroked his hair. If she was conscious of Winston, he couldn't tell.

He looked up at the opening above him. Had Mr. Corbally fallen from that hole? At the moment, it certainly looked that way. His body had an unnatural twist to it, as if he were some Raggedy Andy tossed by a child onto a pile of wood.

A sharp inhale from Cybil brought Winston's attention back to her. In the dim light it appeared as if Mr. Corbally had been carelessly laid out on a funeral pyre and was only waiting for Cybil to light the flame that would lift his soul to heaven.

CHAPTER
8

It was one hour later and Winston stood at the garden entrance watching the ambulance leaving. A few guests still milled around looking solemn and confused. Kiko was seated near him, her eyes glazed, her body slack. Sackett came toward them from the direction of the driveway. He appeared surprised to see they were still at Longmeadow.

"How's Cybil doing?" asked Winston.

"Simon's with her and Mother up in the house," answered Sackett. Winston thought he seemed strangely calm for a man whose father had just been found dead. But then, people reacted very differently to stressful situations.

"Sackett, I didn't know your father very well, obviously. But in that one visit I had with him, I connected with a kindred spirit. I liked him very much. Please accept my . . ." Winston looked over at Kiko, ". . . our sympathy."

For a long moment Sackett stared at his hands. "Thank you. You might be right concerning the kindred spirit thing. Father enthused rather energetically about you the other night. Not something he did often, I can assure you."

Particularly toward his own son? thought Winston. "That's nice to hear," answered Winston.

"Look . . ." Sackett paused. He appeared to change his mind about what he wanted to say. "Look, I must get down to my brother's cottage. In all this . . . this disaster, I suddenly realized that Inclement hasn't heard of Father's accident."

"Inclement?" asked Winston.

"My brother's named after father. He's Clement Jr. My sister and I have always called him Inclement. He hates it, of course."

"Of course."

"Inclement wasn't 'up' for a party today. Had to stay at the cottage and paint instead." Sackett shook his head as if nothing was more important than a party. "I'm sorry about the weekend. I know that . . ."

"Please, you don't have to apologize." What an odd man, thought Winston. He appears more worried about offending his guests than the fact that his father just died. "Look, we're keeping you . . ." Winston nodded over at Kiko.

Standing, Kiko offered her hand to Sackett. "I'm sorry."

"Thank you." Sackett held Kiko's hand. "You know . . . I'll have to speak to Mother, but something has to be done with Father's buildings. An inventory, maybe. They won't be needed now, I wouldn't think, and I see no reason for . . ." Something in Kiko's expression made Sackett stop. He dropped her hand.

"We'll call," said Winston.

"Yes, of course. Well . . . *dies infaustus,* as they say. If you'll excuse me." Sackett strolled away in the direction of the pool.

"That guy's a twerp." Kiko spoke in a whisper.

"Maybe he's in shock," answered Winston. "You know, I'm a bit in shock myself. I could use some moving scenery."

"And some fresh air," added Kiko.

"I think we should head home," said Winston. "I'll call Simon from New York." Kiko nodded in agreement.

As they made their way across the gravel turnaround, the front door of the house opened and two men emerged. One looked like a grizzly bear in a sport coat and the other his addled keeper. The four nodded at one another. Winston and Kiko had continued on five paces when the keeper, a tall, thin man with sharp features, called out to them.

"Winston Wyc?"

Stopping, Winston turned to face the man. "Yes?"

"Winston Wyc the historian?"

"My goodness," said Winston. "It's Sam Harris." The man coming his way was thinner, gaunter than Winston remembered, but it was Sam Harris. "I apologize, I didn't recognize you. I'm not thinking clearly at the moment."

"It's no wonder. This whole thing is . . . is dreadful, isn't it? Clement and I were friends. I . . ." Sam Harris shook his head in disbelief.

The bearlike man stuck out his hand. "I'm Dr. Miles Northingham."

Sam started. "Oh, sorry, I should have introduced you."

Winston introduced Kiko.

"Aren't you the person on television?" asked Kiko.

The large man was obviously flattered at being recognized. "Yes, I am. Saturdays at ten."

"*From Mortises to Mullions*," said Winston, who suddenly realized whom he was talking to.

"*From Mortises to Mullions*," echoed Miles. "As an historian, do you watch it?"

"I don't own a television."

"You're kidding." Miles obviously couldn't imagine anyone not having a television set. "You should get hold of one. I'd think, as one interested in history, you'd find the show very rewarding." Miles stopped himself. "At least, I hope you would."

"I'll make an effort," said Winston.

"I'm Miles's assistant on the show," added Sam, a touch of pride in his voice. "I've been there for three years now."

"Has it been that long since I've seen you?" asked Winston. "The last time we spoke, you were still working at the society."

"I . . . I decided to branch out. I find the TV work very stimulating. Something new all the time, the . . ."

Miles interrupted. "Are you in the same field of study as Sammy?"

"Architectural history, yes," answered Winston. "So is Kiko."

85

A shadow passed over Miles's face. "You're friends of the family?"

"Not really. I only met Mr. Corbally once and that was at the invitation of his son Sackett. I liked the man quite a bit. We shared a common interest but then, it would seem, we all do."

"Yesss . . ." Narrowing his eyes, Miles gave Winston a suspicious look. "Did you talk to Clement before . . . before his accident?"

"No, I didn't get the chance. Why?" asked Winston.

Sam cleared his throat. "We . . . eh, we have been working with Clement over the last six months on a project of his."

"The dismantled buildings in the barn?" asked Winston.

"That's right. You've seen them?"

"Just today. I was down at the barn looking for Mr. Corbally . . ." Winston directed this comment to Miles, ". . . when he was found."

"You were? It was you who found the body?" asked Sam.

"I'm afraid it was."

"My goodness," mumbled Sam.

A short silence followed.

"Well . . . maybe he's gone off to a better place," intoned Miles.

An even longer silence ensued.

"Of course, what could be better than Longmeadow, eh?"

Miles's attempt to lighten the mood brought a look of distress to Sam, who spoke quickly as if to keep Miles from continuing.

"Clement came to me with his village idea wondering if we could use it on the show. Not all the time and certainly not in the winter, but during the summer months. He thought that for the viewers it might be a real education in restoration. You know, to see an old structure being restored from the ground up. I thought it was a great idea and that's how we connected."

"The real thing, as it were." Miles took a deep, meaningful inhale. "The viewer would see me on location, explaining, educating as it happened. I thought the idea very exciting. Of course Clement was no fool. He understood there was money to be made on TV."

"A smart man," said Winston.

"Yesss . . ." Miles eyed Winston closely. "Very smart. I don't mean to pry, Mr. Wyc, but what exactly was your business here today? You say you've only met Clement once before?"

Winston took a moment to answer. Was the grizzly becoming territorial? Were there too many historians in the area? Had it been another time, under different circumstances, Winston might have considered discussing his reasons for being at Longmeadow, but with Mr. Corbally's death it no longer seemed necessary or appropriate.

"Purely social. As I said, we shared a common interest."

"You can understand my asking," said Miles, suddenly looking more social himself. "It was a big project and . . ."

"Is," said Sam.

"What?" Miles gave Sam a look of irritation.

"*Is* a big project," repeated Sam.

"Yes . . . is, certainly." Miles gave Sam a quick nod of understanding before turning back to Winston. "It's been a long day."

"I agree," said Winston. "I think Kiko and I have to get back to the city. It was good to see you again, Sam. And to meet you, Dr. Northingham. It's not often I get to shake hands with a television star."

"Please call me Miles. It was a pleasure to meet you and . . . Kiko, is it?" Miles leaned toward Kiko as if to pass along some important information. "You should see that that fellow gets himself a TV. He's missing out on some good things." With a guffaw, Miles suddenly turned and headed away from everyone. He called to Sam over his shoulder. "I have to get back, Sammy."

"Call me," said Sam to Winston. "Nice to meet you, Kiko."

Winston and Kiko watched as the two men disappeared into the rose garden.

"Was? Is? What was that all about?" Kiko gave Winston an exaggerated look of bafflement.

"There seemed to be some confusion as to the status of the enterprise," said Winston.

"I wonder how much Mr. Corbally's death actually affects the project."

"I would have no idea, but Sam certainly wasn't ready to quit. For him the project was obviously still on."

"That would be news to Sackett," said Kiko. "I got the impression he was ready to have a barn sale."

"You're right. Of course, Sackett doesn't know much about the project. That could be wishful thinking on his part."

"Maybe you'll get another call." Kiko raised her eyebrows at Winston.

"Perish the thought."

"You know, that Dr. Harris was the person I saw sitting in the study when I looked through the glass," said Kiko.

"Really?" said Winston. "Was Miles in the study, too?"

"I didn't see him, although he could have been."

"He was probably waiting for Mr. Corbally." Winston's statement was more to himself than to Kiko.

"Well, I'm ready to go home," said Kiko.

"Sure." Winston stared up at the house. "It's odd, I mean, I didn't really know Mr. Corbally, but I think I'm going to miss him. He was an interesting old man." Winston began walking toward his Volvo. "Come on. Let's leave these people to their grief. How about a drink at Brennan's?"

"How about two?" answered Kiko.

CHAPTER
9

Winston was ten miles down the Taconic Parkway when the thought hit him.

"Wait a minute," he said out loud.

"What is it?" asked Kiko. The two hadn't spoken since they'd turned onto the highway.

"It wasn't an accident."

"What wasn't?" Kiko peered out at the road.

"Mr. Corbally's death was not an accident. How dumb can I be?" Slowing quickly, Winston turned off the Taconic and onto a side road.

"Mr. Corbally's death? What are you talking about? Where are we going?" Kiko was confused.

Having found a driveway to turn around in, Winston was headed back to the parkway.

"We're going back to Wistfield. I have to call Simon."

"Going back . . ." Kiko shook her head as if to clear her thoughts. "You've lost me. I thought we were getting sloshed at Brennan's."

"That will have to wait." Winston struck the dashboard with the flat of his hand. "It's so obvious."

"What?" shouted Kiko. "Come on, you're being unfair."

"It must have been the excitement of the moment or something. The ambulance, people running around, it didn't dawn on me." Kiko went to protest but Winston raised his hand to stop her. "Where did we find Mr. Corbally?" he asked.

"In the barn."

89

"That's right, but where in the barn?"

Kiko thought about it for a second. "On that pile of wood."

"How did he get there?"

"He fell through that hole in the second floor?"

"But how did he get to the second floor? He sure didn't climb a ladder."

Kiko ran through her mind what she remembered of the interior of the barn. "I don't know. Were there stairs in back?"

"I didn't see any," answered Winston.

The two sat in silence for a full minute. Kiko finally spoke. "He didn't get around too well, did he?"

Winston shook his head in agreement. "Nope."

"He probably didn't crawl up on that pile of wood by himself, either," said Kiko in a soft voice.

"I doubt it. This might be nuts but I have to see if Mr. Corbally could have gotten up on that second floor by himself. There's something about all this that I haven't told you."

"What's that?" asked Kiko.

Winston explained about the notes that Mr. Corbally had been receiving.

"My God," said Kiko. "Threats?"

"It would seem so. Here's a gas station. I'm going to try and reach Simon."

Five minutes later Winston was back in the car.

"I was lucky," said Winston. "Simon had just gotten home when I called his house."

"What's the plan?"

"He's going to meet us on some road that runs behind the Longmeadow estate. He says we can walk in and look at the barn without disturbing anyone."

"How are the Corballys?" asked Kiko.

"Not good. I got the feeling Simon wasn't doing all that well himself, but he said he'd be willing to meet us."

"You know, I was thinking while you were in the gas station. We saw Sackett coming from the barn, remember? I mean . . .

he must have been there, or shortly after the . . . eh . . ." Kiko spoke with her head bowed.

"It had occurred to me," answered Winston, "but I don't want to think about that at the moment. We're going back to see if we can find some stairs. There might have been some in the back of the barn. I certainly hope so."

"Let there be stairs," said Kiko to herself. "Please let there be stairs."

CHAPTER
10

Simon had pulled his Chevrolet station wagon off the road and was waiting when they arrived. He had removed his cape and collar and was wearing a short-sleeved white shirt instead of the black one he'd had on earlier. Gone, too, were the jovial expression and the twinkling eyes.

"Thanks for coming," said Winston. "I know it's been a long day for you."

"Longer for others," replied Simon.

"You think it's okay to park here?" asked Winston.

"Heavens yes," answered Simon. "The one car that might pass will simply think we're bird-watching or hiking. This isn't the city, Winston, where one has to avoid the dreaded parking ticket. Wistfield raises funds in less contentious ways. And how are you, Kiko?"

"I'm not sure at the moment. It's turning into a very odd day for me."

"For everyone," agreed Simon. "Dealing with others' grief is part of the job and I've been doing it for years, but it never seems to get any easier. Shall we proceed? We only have about an hour and a half of light left. This path winds through those woods and eventually becomes the dirt road with the barns on it. That road used to come all the way to this road, but after the hurricane of '38 the town abandoned it."

No one spoke as Winston and Kiko fell in behind Simon and followed him up the path. They reached the barns within ten minutes. Simon looked over at the Airstream.

"Let me see if Richie Baire is in," he said. "He lives in the trailer and I don't want him to think we're prowlers."

"We'll be in the barn," answered Winston.

Winston hesitated before entering the barn. The sun had passed beyond the trees at this point and the cavernous interior looked darker, less inviting than before. The events of just four hours ago were still very real in Winston's mind. It would be a long time before he'd forget Cybil discovering her father.

"I'll see if there's a light." Winston inspected the wall next to the sliding door.

"Here it is." Having entered the barn, Kiko found a switch over by one of the horse stalls. A single light bulb, high up by the haymow opening, came on.

"It's not much but it's better than nothing," said Winston. He took a moment to survey the scene. The ambulance crew had done a good job of rearranging the area. If there had been footprints they were gone now.

"Are there any stairs behind those doors?" asked Winston. Kiko was inspecting the barn on the far left.

"Not over here."

"I was afraid of that." Winston made a slow circle around the stacked wood where Mr. Corbally had been found.

"What are you looking for?" asked Kiko.

"I have no idea," answered Winston. At the rear of the barn, he pointed to a ladder that was attached to the back wall. It ran straight up for eighteen feet and through a small opening onto the second floor. "I think that is the only way up, though."

"Mr. Corbally didn't go up those," observed Kiko.

"He certainly didn't," said Winston. "But I'm going to. Join me?"

"Forget it." Kiko tugged at her tight red dress. "I'm not really dressed for mountain climbing."

"Goodness gracious," said Simon, who entered the barn when Winston was halfway up the ladder. "You be careful."

"Kiko said she'd catch me if I fell," yelled Winston.

"In your dreams," answered Kiko.

The haymow was dark but a small door to the rear was open and let in enough light so Winston could see. An unused grain bin ran along the west wall of the haymow and some forgotten lawn furniture was piled near the opening. Hanging on nails along the east wall were a large assortment of antique reflectors, the type that held candles and were used to light house interiors before the discovery of electricity. Had Mr. Corbally come up to inspect these? Somebody had certainly been up there recently. The dust had been kicked up from where the ladder came through the floor all the way over to the opening through which Mr. Corbally supposedly fell. Winston peered out the small door to the outside. Another ladder was attached to the exterior barn boards and stopped about six feet from the ground. A path led off into the underbrush. From this height, Winston could see over the trees to the chimney pots of the main house. In the fading light, they reminded Winston of those old Celtic towers the monks hid in to escape the Vikings. Avoiding the disturbed areas, Winston circled over to gaze down through the opening in the floor. Simon and Kiko stood below staring up.

"Anything there?" called up Simon.

"Somebody was up here," shouted back Winston. "Whether it was today or not I couldn't tell you. I'm coming down."

Carefully, Winston walked around the opening and then studied the floor for any clues that might have been left behind. He couldn't be sure, but it appeared as if the footprints had been erased by someone moving his shoe back and forth.

It had gotten darker and more difficult to see. With one last glance out the open rear door, Winston descended the ladder.

"Someone was up there?" Kiko shivered with the thought.

"It appears so," said Winston, slapping dust from his pants.

"Mr. Corbally?" asked Simon.

"Mr. Corbally didn't climb that ladder," noted Winston. "At least, I can't imagine him doing it. Was Richie Baire in?"

"No one there," answered Simon.

"That's too bad," said Winston. "I would like to have asked him some questions."

"Could we go outside?" asked Kiko. "This place is giving me the creeps."

Once outside, Simon turned to address Winston.

"Now, Mr. Wyc, I've been a patient priest. You explained things briefly over the phone and there seemed such an urgency to your voice that I couldn't deny you your request." Simon paused. "You suggested foul play."

Winston repeated what he had told Kiko about the threatening notes and Mr. Corbally's bad legs.

"Who has these notes now?" asked Simon.

"I would imagine they're still in Mr. Corbally's study," answered Winston.

Simon was silent for a moment. "Murder," he finally whispered. He looked up at Winston. "That's hard to think about and even more difficult to imagine. Who would gain from such a heinous act?"

Winston hesitated before speaking. "I don't really know except that certain members of the family were upset about the amount of money being spent to underwrite Mr. Corbally's historic village project. That's a possibility."

Simon was incredulous. "Members of the family? That's ridiculous. I've known this family for twenty years and there's not one of them capable of hurting a flea, much less another family member. I can say positively that that possibility is out of the question."

"I hope you're right," said Winston. "I don't know the situation well enough to suspect anyone, really. Mr. Corbally was planning a large project involving a lot of money. There were other people involved, too. Whether any of them had a motive I couldn't say, but I really don't think Mr. Corbally fell from the haymow or climbed up on that pile of wood by himself. As I said, I had a meeting with Mr. Corbally in which one of those notes was discovered. The man was obviously upset by it."

The three stared at the ground for several seconds. Finally, Kiko spoke. "What do we do now? Do we call the police?"

"The police?" Simon was surprised. "I'm sorry but I don't think you have enough to go on here, Winston. Lucille Corbally would be horrified at that suggestion. Particularly in her present state."

"I disagree, Simon. I think we have reasonable doubts and the longer we ignore them, the harder it will be to prove anything later."

"Maybe, maybe." Unsure of what to do, Simon talked to himself as he walked in a tight circle. "I *could* talk to Lucille and ask her if anything odd has happened lately. Try not to arouse her suspicions. Or cause her undue grief."

"You could find those notes," said Winston.

Simon stopped. "I could do that too, perhaps." Simon noticed Winston's look of dismay. "I'm sorry, Winston, but the Corballys are not going to want the police barging around. It's difficult to explain but that's just not done. Particularly with so little evidence."

Winston and Kiko exchanged a look of disbelief.

"Call it a class thing, Winston. And what if, God forbid, it *was* a family member." Simon shuddered at the thought.

"Simon," said Winston, "there's the possibility that someone's been murdered. Don't we have a *moral* obligation to inform the authorities?"

"I think the Church's position on murder is fairly well documented, Winston," said Simon defensively. "Please, let's not argue. What's wrong with letting me talk to Lucille in the morning?"

"I don't think it's up to her." Winston was becoming upset, his voice tight.

"Did Mr. Corbally sleep on the second floor of the house or did he have a bedroom downstairs?" asked Kiko.

"What?" Winston and Simon spoke in unison. They both peered down at Kiko.

"If he went up and down the stairs in the house, there is the *possibility* that he went up the ladder. From what Winston said, he sounds like a pretty stubborn old guy. I don't know why he would want to go up there." Kiko looked up at the haymow of the barn. "But maybe he did and hurt himself and . . . and fell." Kiko shrugged. "That's a possibility too, isn't it?"

Pursing his lips, Simon gave Kiko a little smile. "It certainly is." He turned to Winston. "I see you're not the only detective in the firm, Mr. Wyc."

Winston wasn't convinced. He gave Kiko a look of disapproval. "Mr. Corbally didn't climb that ladder."

"At the moment, we do not know that," said Simon.

The three stood in silence listening to the birds sing good night to one another. Simon pointed up at the shimmering slates of the barn roof. "I believe that to be the last of the sun's rays. We should head back."

Once again, no one spoke until they had reached the parked cars. Simon took a moment to catch his breath, for the walk back had been done at a rapid pace.

"Listen, Winston." Simon took one last deep inhale. "I will talk to Lucille in the morning and then I will call you. One day isn't going to make any difference and it might save us all a lot of trouble."

Winston thought about it. "One day," he said finally. "But I don't like it. Mr. Corbally deserves better."

"Believe me," replied Simon, "Clement Corbally would have been the last person to want the police stomping around Longmeadow."

"What a thought," said Winston, "the justice system disrupting the Corballys. Wouldn't want a nasty scandal now, would we?" Winston's voice took on a mock, upper-class nasal tone.

"That's unfair," stated Simon. "We wait one day, ask the

right questions and *then* we decide. I believe Kiko agrees with me on this."

Hesitantly, Kiko nodded in agreement. Winston capitulated. "Okay, one day," he said.

Simon's face took on a sly expression. "Almost like old times, hey Winston?"

Winston forced a smile. "Let's hope not. I seem to remember that the last time we got involved in something like this we both nearly got ourselves killed."

"This is not the same and you know it. Well . . ." Simon looked at his watch. "Oh my, I have to go. I have a sermon to write. And don't look at me like that, Winston Wyc, even in death the world keeps going around. I hope to see you soon, Kiko, under different circumstances, of course. Good-bye, Winston, I'll call tomorrow."

With that said, Simon bustled into his car and drove off. Winston and Kiko stood in the dusk listening to the night sounds develop. Far off a dog barked.

"I suppose he's right," said Winston halfheartedly. "And you, too. It's just that . . ." Winston paused. "Oh, never mind. And whose side are you on, Ms. Hamaguchi? I didn't know that we had another detective in the firm." Winston smiled to let Kiko know he was kidding.

Putting her hands together, Kiko bowed at the waist. "Only number one son doing what he can to help, honorable Chan father."

"Funny, in that dress you don't look like number one son," answered Winston with a smile.

"This dress . . ." Kiko screwed up her face. "Does it still look okay?"

"The *dress* looks fine."

"Gee, thanks."

"I bet I look pretty good myself. Come on, let's get back. It's been one helluva long day."

CHAPTER

11

It was noon Monday and Winston still hadn't heard from the Reverend Simon Tart. Three messages Sunday and one that morning had been left on the vicar's answering machine but they had gone unanswered. The whole affair had put Winston in a bad mood and the instant it was lunchtime Kiko had excused herself to seek sustenance elsewhere. The demolition ordinances for New York City that lay on his desk had no appeal whatsoever. Winston jumped when the phone rang.

"Hello. . . . Well, hi Simon, thanks for calling. . . . Oh fine, fine. I think I just dumped coffee all over section ninety-seven dash thirty-one of the New York . . . Where in the world have you been? I've left twenty messages on that machine of yours. . . . Okay, four. What's going on?"

Winston listened.

"Gosh, what a surprise. . . . Sorry. Sarcasm's about all I have left at the moment. . . . You did? . . . She does? . . . Oh, I don't know about that. . . . I thought we were going to call the police. . . . Lucille's afraid of what?"

Winston listened.

"I'll probably regret this but sure, I'll come up. . . . Tomorrow? . . . Well yes, I know I was, but this is such short notice and . . . You're right, you're right. I'll be there. . . . Tomorrow at one o'clock. 'Til then. . . . Bye."

The hall door to the office banged shut and Kiko came sweeping into the back room. All morning she'd been sweeping around the office. She couldn't walk across a room without a certain lilt to her step. Her performance had added to Winston's bad spirit. With muted flourish, Kiko placed a brown bag on Winston's desk.

"I decided to come back and eat here. I thought your favorite sandwich might cheer you up. Genoa salami with honey mustard on a hard roll. There's a side of potato salad." Kiko stood smiling down at him.

"What makes you think this is my favorite sandwich?" he asked.

"Because you eat it every day?"

"Doesn't mean I like it. Could mean I have no imagination." Winston peeked into the bag as if it might hold live things. "I don't mean to rain on anybody's parade but what's with the bounce this morning?"

"Gee, you're welcome."

"Sorry. Thanks."

"And what do you mean by bounce?"

"All morning you've been flouncing around the office, full of vim and vigor. I'm not sure it's appropriate. Some vigor maybe, but can the vim. Whatever that is."

Snapping the rubber band off her plastic container, Kiko surveyed her green salad.

"Have I? Maybe I'm just glad to be alive. That whole episode this weekend made me realize how lucky I am. To be young and beautiful and bright . . . and alive." Kiko gave Winston an exaggerated look of haughtiness so he'd know she wasn't serious. "I've noticed the opposite in you."

"Me?"

"Vimless. And grumpy I might add. Want my radish?"

"I don't eat radishes. Not many years ago, when *I* was young and beautiful and bright and alive, I swore off radishes. And what do you mean, grumpy?"

"Curt, brusque, surly, mean-spirited . . ."

"Wait a minute. I haven't been like that . . . have I?"

"How about: depressed?"

Winston thought about it. "Doesn't this say something

100

about us? As individuals?" He spoke to the sandwich in his hand. "Really, Mr. Salami, what seems more normal to you? When pondering thoughts of murder, do you become elated or depressed?"

"That's not fair. I'm upset about Mr. Corbally, too, but it's affected me in a different way. I never actually met the man and it's different for me. I spent all day yesterday outside, watching people, wondering about their lives, their futures. I've never done that before. Being alive became important. And not just for me but for everyone."

"It'll pass." Winston caught Kiko's look of irritation. "Hey, I'm kidding. And I apologize. Maybe I have been a *little* grumpy, but I can't help it. I feel frustrated by this whole thing. That should change soon, though."

"Why's that?" asked Kiko.

"Simon just called."

Kiko put her forkful of lettuce back in the container. "What? Simon called and you didn't tell me?"

"I was going to but you were bouncing so much . . ."

Kiko's high spirits went sour. "I waited last night for you to call and I've been waiting all morning, just like you, for Simon to call and you couldn't tell me? That makes me mad." Rising, Kiko took her salad out into the front office. Winston followed her.

"I'm sorry. The nice sandwich you brought threw me off. I should have mentioned it."

Kiko relented but only slightly. "What did he say?"

"He said it had been difficult to see Lucille. That she hadn't wanted to see anyone until this morning. He apologized for not calling."

"And?"

"It seems that Mr. Corbally *had* said something to Lucille. In fact, when Simon began to 'suggest things,' as he put it, she was relieved to know that someone else felt the same way she did. He couldn't convince her to call the police, but she did say she would speak to me."

"To you? Why?"

Winston hesitated. "It's odd, but as I mentioned, I've been involved in some misadventures up in Wistfield before. I got lucky and solved a few . . . mysteries. Simon explained all this to Lucille and now she wants to talk to me. I think, though, that unlike Simon, I can probably talk her into calling the police." Winston sat on the desk. "I'm to go back up to Longmeadow tomorrow."

Kiko thought about that for a second. "By yourself?"

"It would be easier. Sorry."

"Chief detective gets all the fun."

"Someone has to be here, Kiko. I'll be back tomorrow afternoon. If all goes well, my meeting with Lucille will be the end of it for me. The police can take it from there."

"I guess you're right." Kiko wasn't convinced.

"Now . . . back to that convent problem." Winston rose.

"Yes sir. Whatever you say." Kiko turned and peered straight ahead.

Oh boy, thought Winston. Looks like another long afternoon.

Winston, Simon and Lucille were meeting in a small room off the master bedroom, a room that in another day and time would have been a sanctuary for the lady of the house. A place to indulge a private smoke, pen a letter, put some gossip in a personal journal or simply get away from the man of the house. Lucille had turned it into a photo gallery. The walls were covered with snapshots of the Corbally children growing up and of her late husband both as a young man and later in his life. There were very few photographs of Lucille.

They were seated around a small table. Lucille had carefully placed four pieces of "evidence," as she termed it, on the table in front of her. She wore a simple black shift and no makeup. At the garden party Lucille's hair had been tied up in an intricate pattern of braids. Now it hung loose, almost to her waist, framing her pale patrician face with a whiter shade. Winston thought, with her solemn countenance and sad eyes, she looked uncommonly beautiful. Genevieve in mourning for her king.

"Could I see those?" asked Winston.

A long, thin finger ferried the paper across the table. Winston had seen the first scrap he picked up, the one that had fallen from the blueprints that day. The other two scraps of paper were obviously from the same source. They all had the look and feel of imitation parchment. He read each carefully. He set them to one side.

Lucille slid a fourth item, a calling card, across the table. It was not the modern business card with name, number and service, but an actual calling card with the name of the visitor printed neatly in the center. The card had been presented by a William Laird. Someone had written above the name the words "rigor mortis."

"Who's William Laird?" asked Winston.

"We don't know," said Lucille.

"What's 'rigor mortis' mean? Other than the obvious."

No one knew.

"That's Clement's handwriting," added Lucille, indicating the scrawled words across the top of the card.

Winston inspected the card for a moment, turning it over, again reading the face. "Where did you find this?"

"I found it attached to those notes in the top drawer of Clement's bureau. The walnut one in his dressing room." Lucille held up a paper clip as if it might speak. "Under some legal papers."

"What kind of legal papers?"

"I don't know. Clement took care of all the legal matters." Lucille sighed. "I gave them to Biff."

"Is this a son I don't know about?" asked Winston.

"The family lawyer, Benton Wiggins," offered Simon. "His friends call him Biff." Obviously, Simon included himself with that particular in-crowd.

Winston stared back at the two before him. "Was there anything else?"

"Well . . ." Lucille appeared reluctant to speak. She looked at Simon, who continued for her.

"When I spoke with Lucille Monday morning, I mentioned the existence of some notes, these notes . . ." Simon indicated the papers lying on the table. ". . . and that we should try and find them. I said that you had seen one and that it . . ." Simon paused, ". . . and that it was of an odd nature. I asked . . ." Simon turned to Lucille, ". . . and I do hope in a tactful fashion . . ." Lucille bowed her head. ". . . if Clement had mentioned these notes to her and if he'd said anything concerning possible threats. Well, it just so happens, Clement *had* jokingly said several times recently that he was being stalked and that if anything should happen to him Lucille was to call Ward Townsley and say all bets were off."

Lucille spoke. "Ward and Clement bet on professional golf matches. They would pick their favorite player and arrive at some wager that would be collected at the end of the golf season. If there is such a moment. Whoever's player made the most money, or had fewer strokes or something, won the bet. As you might expect, I didn't take his talk of stalking very seriously. It would be like Clement to be arranging some sly way of getting out of the wager. I . . ." Lucille's eyes became moist. She looked at her hands in her lap. Simon reached over and laid his hand on hers.

"You couldn't have known, Lucille, that he was serious. It wasn't like Clement to ask for help. He was always . . . joking like that." Catching Winston's eye, Simon continued. "When we went to look for the notes, Lucille realized that Clement's study had been disturbed. That someone had gone through all the drawers in his desk and poked through his files. She said that Clement was very particular about how his drawers and files were arranged and that they weren't at all like he would have left them. It was then that we really began to feel that something was amiss. After further searching, we found the notes in his bureau. From what you had told me about that one note, I admit I hadn't been too concerned, but after reading this one . . ." Simon placed a finger on one of the notes, "this one from Kings about 'Set thy house in order; for thou shalt die, and not live,' I changed my mind."

Lucille visibly stiffened.

Lowering his voice, Simon once again took Lucille's hand. "I'm sorry. I know how difficult this must be for you. Winston and I could discuss this alone . . . if you wish?"

"No, no," whispered Lucille. "It *is* difficult but in an odd way it helps." Lucille took a sharp breath of air and let it out slowly. Then, with a stronger voice, she continued. "I didn't sleep much last night, I . . . I kept thinking about what Simon

had said and what we had found and . . . the thought of . . .
Clement being killed. At some point, I realized that I had
become angry, that this . . . stupid, stupid act of violence that
has taken my husband's life . . ." Lucille hesitated. "If indeed
it did happen that way . . . needed to be punished or forgiven
or something. It's probably not very healthy but this anger
has given me a strength, a purpose, an emotional bridge over
which I might be able to link a previous life with the one to
come." Lucille turned to speak directly to Simon. "I'm not
abandoning my grief but this anger I feel comforts me, reas-
sures me that an answer will be found. It has to be." Lucille
turned to Winston, her eyes moist with emotion. She spoke
quickly, trying to get her thought out before her strength
faded. "Simon told me about you, Winston. Of how you've
been successful in solving these types of crimes. It was you,
after all, who realized something was wrong. I want you to
help me, help my family. Simon says you will want me to go
to the police, that it's the only way. I'm going to ask you not
to do that, at least not at first. I want a quiet investigation. I
want no one to suspect . . . I want you to . . . I want you to . . ."
Her energy spent, her voice barely a whisper, Lucille bowed
her head. A tear fell onto the back of her left hand. Rising,
Simon took Lucille by the shoulders and gently encouraged
her to stand. Winston watched as Simon guided her into the
master bedroom. Softly, he shut the door behind him.

Winston stared at the walls, at the photographic history of
the Corballys. Pictures taken of them standing beside cars,
boats, on vacation, enjoying a long line of holidays. Many
were of Mr. Corbally standing on various croquet courts, a
trophy in one hand, a mallet in the other. To Winston's right,
in a corded silver frame, stood a recent photo, one of Mr.
Corbally standing beside the dormer Winston had seen in the
barn, his arm carelessly draped over the curved roof, his face
radiant with . . . what? Was it triumph or achievement or was
it anticipation? Winston was staring at the picture when
Simon returned.

"How is she?" asked Winston.

"Resting," answered Simon. "She took something her doctor has prescribed for rest. I think she'll be okay." Simon gave the closed door to the bedroom a quick glance and then he sat.

"How are the others?" asked Winston. "How's Cybil?"

"Cybil's boy Billy adored his grandfather and has taken his death pretty hard. Cybil has had to put off her own mourning to take care of *his* emotional needs. I haven't spoken with Clement Jr. but I understand he was very upset. It's Sackett who worries me. He seems to have distanced himself from the reality of the situation. Emotionally, he acts as if nothing happened. He talks about it all the time, which is encouraging, but his emotions seem to be in neutral. I've seen others react the same way. Sublimating grief is not a good thing. It always comes back to haunt you."

"You mean he's in denial?" asked Winston.

"In the argot of the day, I suppose so. At some point he's going to have to respond to his father's death."

"Maybe he is. Maybe he goes home at night and grieves. Keeps it private."

"I don't think so," answered Simon. "No, he . . ." Simon paused. His expression darkened. "Something that Cybil mentioned to me has me worried. She says you saw Sackett just before you found the body. That he was coming from the barn?"

Winston nodded that it was true. "His father had asked him to meet him there. Said it was important. No one seems to know *what* was important but Sackett claims he never saw his father. That he waited and then left." Winston glanced up at the picture of Mr. Corbally with his arm wrapped around the dormer and then continued. "I have a theory. I think it's quite possible that someone else was there just before Sackett." Looking at the closed bedroom door, Winston lowered his voice. "I think the killer might even have been up in the haymow when Sackett arrived. That the killer had carried Mr. Corbally up that ladder and tossed the body through the opening to make it look like an accident. That Sackett had arrived just after the body was dropped and that he might have even surprised the killer, who left by a door that goes out the back."

The two men sat in silence for a few seconds. Simon spoke. "So you don't think it was Sackett?" He was obviously relieved by the thought.

"I . . . I don't know. Sackett was adamantly opposed to his father's project and, as you said, he's acted strangely since the body was found. I would like to know what was so important. It could be that it . . ." Stopping, Winston shrugged.

Simon finished the thought for him. "That it put Sackett over the edge?"

"I don't want to think that. Right now I'm thinking someone else was there before Sackett."

Once again the men sat silently. Winston noticed the curious smile that had crossed Simon's dark countenance.

"You smile?" asked Winston.

"Not a smile, really." Reaching over, Simon tapped Winston on the knee. "My friend, you sound like a man on the case."

"Do I?"

"I'd say so. You're not the type to see this as an amusement, an entertainment."

Standing, Winston stared out the narrow window at the rose garden below. His thoughts were of his meeting with Mr. Corbally. A full minute passed without a word spoken. When Winston finally did speak, he did not look at Simon.

"Lucille will hire me to do a history of Longmeadow, something Mr. Corbally had been planning to do. It will be a memorial to him. I will have access to all his files and to the family. They are not to know why I'm actually here."

Simon stood and clapped his hands once. "Good man, Winston. Lucille will be heartened."

Winston turned. "It would certainly be smarter if the police were called now, but I will honor Lucille's request. Up to a point. The second there is a reasonable cause to suspect someone, and/or the minute I finish my research, then the police must be notified."

Simon nodded his head to indicate that he understood.

"When is the funeral?" asked Winston.

"The day after tomorrow."

"I will come up next Tuesday. The family should have settled a little by then and the memorial idea would make sense if done relatively soon. I'll stay until the end of the week."

"That's only four days," exclaimed Simon. "You can't possibly conduct an investigation in that period."

"My research shouldn't take any longer than that. I may be wrong, but I believe Mr. Corbally kept an extensive family history in his study." When Simon didn't respond, Winston said, "That's my offer."

"How about until the following Tuesday?" replied Simon. "That seems fairer."

Winston moved closer to his friend. "Simon, at some point I'll have been here too long. I still don't know how we're going to approach the police about all this."

"I suppose."

"Particularly since Mr. Corbally will have been buried by then. If Lucille is upset by the idea of police running amok at Longmeadow, she's really going to be upset when they start talking about exhuming her husband."

"My God," mumbled Simon.

The two men stood silently for twenty seconds, deep in their own thoughts.

"There's only one thing for it." Simon took Winston by the arm. "*You* must find the killer."

13

The following Tuesday, Winston once again pulled into the Corbally driveway. Off to his right a workman hayed the field that bordered the long drive. The sun was bright in the cloudless sky, there was no wind and the air smelled of newly mown grass. Swallows dipped and strafed behind the tractor, feeding on the insects thrown up by its churning blades. It was a perfect morning at Longmeadow. Winston had been asked to arrive early so that he could accompany the family on a picnic. A little get-together down at the boathouse. Nothing fancy, said Lucille. Work would have to start the next day. She insisted. A boathouse would seem to imply the presence of a lake or pond. Winston hadn't noticed any large bodies of water on his first visits but then he'd only been shown the immediate forty acres.

Stopping in the gravel expanse by the front portico, Winston took a moment to study the house. Houses, like pets, tend to reflect their owners. The style, colors, outdoor furniture, items left strewn about and maintenance were all elements that offered insights into the inhabitants without ever having to go inside, or for that matter, meet them.

The house was quite large, being easily a hundred feet long and three stories high. The front windows were double casements that went to the floor and could be used as doors. On the wings, the center windows had fanlights which echoed the one above the main door. Four fluted pilasters, two on either side of the portico, ran from the ground level up to a wide entablature that crowned the entire front of the house. Above this an ornate balustrade defined the roofline. The main structure was of brick and, except on the wooden pilasters and trim, was covered entirely with ivy. As in many Colonial Revival houses, there was much that would not have been found on the originals. Pediments above the arched windows were without supporting pilasters; windows on the second story were paired; and the wings themselves would almost always have been additions on original Colonial homes. The facade was neat and well maintained and, except for its size, as reserved and subdued as would befit a true member of the landed gentry. Winston wondered if there were a few bats in the attic.

Taking his small suitcase with him, Winston went up to the portico door and rang the bell. The door was opened by Cybil Corbally.

"I saw you drive up," she said. "Come in."

"Thanks. I hope I'm not intruding."

"Not at all. Mother said just today that she was looking forward to the company. If you follow me, I'll show you to your room."

Winston followed Cybil up the center staircase and left down the wide hall.

"Everyone's in the kitchen preparing for the picnic. Mother says she'll go because of the kids, but everyone in the family knows she loves picnics. And everything has to be just right. The hampers packed properly with the right flatware and utensils. And the food of course. Always the same thing. The cheese, St. André. Water crackers. Cold chicken and cold asparagus spears. Baguette. A good Riesling and a peach tart. No deviation. And apples. The boys like apples."

Dressed for a picnic, Cybil wore jeans, a gray tank top and cowboy boots. The tank top showed off the long graceful arc of her neck and shoulders. A fine line of soft dark hair began at her neck and ran down between her shoulder blades. Winston gazed at this as he followed her down the hall.

"You'll be staying here. I hope you like it."

The room was large and filled with light. Being on the back side of the house it looked down on the swimming pool area and the great lawn. Winston could see a man knocking balls about on the croquet court.

"This is very nice."

Cybil joined him at the window. "That's my brother Clement Jr."

"Inclement?" asked Winston.

"That's right. Who told you that?"

"Sackett. At the garden party."

"The garden party." For a second, Cybil's eyes went dark, but then it was over. "Do you play croquet?"

"I don't." Winston smiled. "Baseball, basketball, that sort of thing. When I was younger."

Cybil smiled back. "Normal sort of games, you mean?"

"Did I mean that?" Picking up his suitcase, Winston moved over to a low table and set the case down. "How is your mother?"

"Remarkably well, considering. She seems a little distracted since Father died but that would be normal, I would think." Cybil looked back out the window. "Yesterday I found her crying in the rose garden." Shaking the image from her head, Cybil moved over to the door. She stopped just before exiting. "It's one of the reasons we've all decided to go on this picnic. It would cheer her up."

"And you. How have you been?"

"I don't complain. Look, take a minute to unpack. We'll meet you downstairs?" Cybil had almost closed the door when she stuck her head back into the room. She smiled. "It's nice to see you again."

The family was all gathered out by the garage, a converted low barn that stood beyond the hedge on the side of the garden away from the house. An old Ford pickup had been converted into a hay wagon by throwing hay bales in the back for seating. Inclement and a short, well-muscled man, whom Winston recognized as the one who had gone into the pool with Uncle Carl, were already seated in the back of the truck. Before them, on the bed, was a large picnic hamper. A boy of ten or so, dressed in the current "homeboy" fashion, stood off to one side pretending to be bored while Lucille asked another young boy sitting in the cab if he wouldn't rather sit in the back with his brother. The kid obviously didn't think it was a good idea. Upon seeing Winston, Lucille came forward to welcome him. She wore a man's white T-shirt and oversized corduroy pants cinched tight at the waist. Around her neck was a light blue bandanna that matched the color of her eyes. Even in her picnic clothes, she had the look of a gentlewoman.

"Winston, thank you for coming." Lucille presented her cheek for pecking. "I hope you had a good drive up."

"Very good, thank you."

"I know you haven't had a chance to settle in or catch your breath or anything, but we're not going to apologize. Instead, we're going to wine and dine you down by the lake. You're not offended, I hope?"

"Of course not," answered Winston. "I'm honored you'd have me."

Lucille laughed. "You say that now. Have you met my son Clement and his friend George?"

"No, I haven't," answered Winston. The men acknowledged one another with nods and smiles.

"And this is my grandson Billy." Billy looked at Winston's shoes and mumbled something. "Sackett's about somewhere," added Lucille. "Cybil, would you convince Gordon he must sit in the back. I don't think Winston should have to sit in the wind."

"Could we get going?" asked Clement Jr. "I'm starving."

"I don't—" Winston started to speak but was cut off by Lucille.

"And you know Sackett won't ride on the hay. Musses his hair or his pants or some darn thing. Promise Gordon a candy or something."

As Cybil bent to convince Gordon of the benefits of fresh air, Sackett, with a large thermos in hand, came trotting out from the direction of the house.

"Oh, there you are, Sackett. I thought you had disappeared," said Lucille.

"Little chance of that, Mother. I've brought some coffee. Winston, how are you?"

"Fine, thank you. Yourself?"

"I'm okay."

"Think we could get there today?" Clement Jr. asked the sky.

"*Vincit qui patitur,*" intoned Sackett at his brother.

"Oh, please." Clement rolled his eyes.

"Oh, brother," mumbled Billy.

"All aboard," shouted Lucille.

Sackett drove and Lucille sat shotgun, Gordon riding between them. After exiting right out of the drive, the truck traveled for several miles before turning right once again onto a dirt road. This road wound its way through a majestically quiet hemlock forest before stopping abruptly at the edge of a large lake. Once it was parked, Billy was out of the truck and down by the water's edge, wrestling with an overturned-rowboat. Everyone but Winston had a specific chore, and while he stood watching the rest either unloaded the truck or opened up the boathouse or gathered wood for the fireplace.

The boathouse was a two-story affair built out over the water with the ground floor opened to the lake and storage space for two small boats. An outside stair led up to a large room with a fireplace on one wall and storm shutters on the other three sides, which were propped open to reveal wide views of the lake and the hills on the opposite bank. The room was full of tattered old furniture that had made the journey from living room to guest room to maid's quarters to boathouse. Instead of chic rattan-style furniture there were big comfortable sofas and chairs that the boys could jump up and down on and nobody would care. A long picnic table was brushed clean of mice droppings and a white-and-blue checked tablecloth was spread on it. Winston's offers of help were rejected, so he leaned against the fieldstone of the fireplace and watched. Finally everything was in place and the whirlwind died down. Clement, taking a pair of binoculars out of the hamper and hanging them about his neck, informed everyone that he and George were going bird-watching. They disappeared. Sackett, who had done almost as much as Winston in lending a hand, had already settled in a chair and was reading. Down by the lake, Winston could see Billy hindering his brother's efforts to get into the boat. With a shout from one of the windows, Cybil went out to referee. Lucille stood gazing dreamily out across the water. Winston decided to join Cybil and the boys.

"Is the lake stocked?" asked Winston as he came alongside the boat.

"It used to be," said Cybil. "I think the fish stock it themselves at this point." She gave Winston a sly grin. "Want to take a boat ride?"

"Mother . . ." moaned Billy.

"If it's okay?" asked Winston.

"Don't mind Billy," answered Cybil. "Anyone who isn't into rap music, just isn't."

"I don't listen to rap music often," said Winston, "but I do like Dr. Didi, The Boyz and Sister Salt."

"You know about Dr. Didi?" asked Billy.

"Sure," said Winston.

"Come aboard, Mr. Wyc," said Cybil with a smile. "First timers, though, have to row."

Later, after the meal, the boys insisted on having a fire and roasting marshmallows. The boys then proceeded to give names to each marshmallow as they rotated them in the fire.

"This is Mr. Phillips my English teacher," said Billy.

"He won't be very tasty," winced Gordon. "He has a wart on his face."

The rest of us sat at the table finishing the peach tart, drinking coffee or wine and exchanging small talk. Clement hadn't spoken in several minutes when suddenly he blurted out in a loud voice, "I have an idea I'd like to run by everyone."

"What's that?" inquired Lucille.

"Well . . ." Clement appeared undecided. "Don't anyone say anything until I'm finished."

"What is it?" asked Cybil.

"This project of father's, the historic village or whatever it was, I have an idea of what to do with it." He grinned at everyone.

Sackett's back went straight. "I didn't know we had to do *anything* with it," he said.

"I know Father set up a trust or foundation. He told me about it but I wasn't listening. I saw Miles and Sam when they were here yesterday and they told me the project was to continue. I've been thinking about all that and I have an idea that could bring in a few bucks."

"An idea?" asked Sackett.

"That's right, brother mine. How does this sound? Corbally's Historic Village of Colonial Amusements. Or something like that. I'm not sure about the name yet." Clement peered around at the bemused faces.

"What?" said Sackett.

"Corbally's Historic Vill . . ."

"I heard that part. What are you talking about?"

"It goes like this: if Miles and Sam build this village, then we add a sort of entertainment section. I've already thought of one ride: the Paul Revere. Very colonial, don't you think? It would involve mechanical horses."

Cybil threw back her head and laughed, a high, wonderful sound that filled the boathouse. "Are you serious?"

"Let's say I'm researching the idea."

"What does that mean?" asked Sackett. "What's the research? A visit to Disneyland?" Sackett turned to his mother. "*If* Sam and Miles build this village? What in the hell is he talking about?"

Lucille hesitated before answering. "It's true. There's some question as to whether the project is to continue or not. Biff will let me know tonight."

"Impossible!" Sackett hit the table for emphasis. "It can't be true. I'm sure that the project died with Father. IT HAD TO!"

"Really, Sack," said Clement. "I've never seen you become unglued so quickly. What's bothering you? Is it your precious inheritance? This idea is meant to make money." Clement added as an afterthought, "For everyone."

With effort, Sackett brought his voice under control. "Yes, yes, my dear Inclement, it's my precious inheritance I'm worried about. All the precious inheritances. Have you become completely deranged? Don't you see, we, you and I, all of us, we live a certain way, enjoy a certain lifestyle. If the Corbally estate is kept intact, all of us might go on enjoying this way of life for a long time. My God, Cybil's the only one of us who brings in any money at all and I think—"

Clement interrupted. "That's not true. There's my art sales and my tournament winnings. Unlike you, I could be independent."

"Urrrgh." Sackett looked as if he might explode.

"That's enough!" Lucille's command was sharp and icy. Everyone looked at his plate. Lucille took a deep breath. "We do not need a 'few bucks,' Clement. I don't want to hear any more of that talk. *And* I would like to remind all of you that we have a guest." She turned to Winston. "I apologize."

What could Winston say? Sackett got to his feet.

"I'm going for a walk." They all listened to him stomp down the stairs.

"What's the matter with Uncle Sack?" asked Gordon.

"He's pissed," answered Billy.

"Let's talk about something else," encouraged Lucille. "Let's talk about Billy's new school."

Later, as Gordon and Billy stalked about the room looking for some unfortunate insect they could sacrifice in the dying

117

fire, everyone helped clean up except Sackett, who had returned from his stomp and sat brooding in the corner, ignoring everyone.

"I think the green and white checks go better with this Chinese print," stated Clement, holding up a plate. "More ecologically correct, too," he chuckled.

"Don't be an ass," sneered Sackett from his corner.

"Excuse me," said Clement. "Did I hear clouds parting? Cybil, answer me this. What's the difference between Sackett and God?"

"Got me," answered Cybil.

"God doesn't think he's Sackett."

Everyone tried not to laugh except George, who exploded with a tight-lipped spray of a guffaw.

"I don't get it," said Gordon.

"That's because you have a tiny little brain," offered Billy.

"Listen butt—"

"That's enough," admonished Lucille. "Really, Cybil, you must speak to these boys concerning their language."

"It's all the television they watch," said Clement. He turned to Winston. "Since you're going to be here for a few days, you must come down and see what George and I have done with our cottage. Architecturally it's very interesting."

"Winston's an historian," corrected George. "Cutesy little cottages are not his line."

"I thought he was an architect, too," said Clement.

"Many people make that mistake," said Winston.

"Some people make worse mistakes than others," said Sackett to no one in particular. Having risen, he went down the stairs to sit in the truck.

"I think we should get back," Cybil said, "before someone gets—" She stopped herself just in time. Everyone gave one another an embarrassed glance and busied himself for leaving. Lucille, who hadn't seemed to notice, took Winston by the arm and let him escort her down the stairs.

"We have another guest this evening, Winston. Benton

WITH MALLETS AFORETHOUGHT

Wiggins, our estate lawyer, is coming up from New York. I think you'll like him. He's a very interesting man."

"The moment of truth," cried Clement.

"For goodness sake," said Lucille. "Stop being so silly, Clemmy." She turned back to Winston. "I was wondering if we could have a little chat before he arrives."

"Certainly," answered Winston.

"I've had a few ideas concerning this . . ." Lucille paused, ". . . this history you're to write."

"I'd love to hear them," said Winston. Glancing up at the truck, he noticed Sackett staring back at him through the cab window. Sackett instantly turned his head away, but Winston was surprised at the hostility of the look. He was reminded of the expression "If looks could kill . . ." One of the boathouse shutters slammed shut. The noise startled Winston and he looked back. Inclement and George stood watching him from the stair landing, curious expressions on their faces. Hadn't Lucille explained to everyone that he was there to do a history and that only? Was he going to have to watch *his* back while at Longmeadow? It wasn't the first time and it wouldn't be the last that Winston wondered if he was doing the smart thing.

CHAPTER
14

Upon returning from the picnic, everyone had scattered quickly with promises to meet again for dinner with Biff Wiggins. Winston and Lucille were once again seated in the small room off the master bedroom. Lucille sat with her back to the window. With the light behind her, a shadow fell across her face, dividing it into two halves of light and dark. Her eyes were hidden in the dark half. The lively woman who had directed the picnic and scolded her children was gone. In her place sat a woman whose mouth cut a thin, hard line, whose shoulders hung heavy and whose voice was barely above a whisper. Listening to her talk, Winston realized that for Lucille to contend with family, and him, was an act of courage, of determination. He wondered if she had the strength to proceed with the investigation.

". . . and then Dr. Harris and that Northingham man showed up yesterday," said Lucille, "and had a meeting with Richie down at the barn. I walked down there myself to see and hear what was going on. After much hemming and hawing, they said that the project was to continue and that it was Clement's decision, not theirs. I didn't say much. I didn't have to. The information came tumbling out of them like the confessions of small boys. I asked how much the project was going to cost. They finally admitted it was a lot of money. How much they couldn't say."

Lucille stopped to catch her breath. The thin, tight mouth got thinner.

"I didn't believe Clement would have done such a thing. Even in his most enthusiastic ventures, he usually took care not to jeopardize the family trust. I came back to the house and called Biff. He said it was a real possibility and that we would discuss it tonight. He's coming up this evening to read the will."

"Has the money been placed in this foundation Clement Jr. mentioned this afternoon? Is there such a thing?"

"There is," answered Lucille, "but its extent and how much money is involved, I don't know. Everyone seems hesitant to say. That could only mean one thing, the money is considerable." In a gesture of self-consolation, Lucille drew her arms around herself. "Winston, I'm . . ." She didn't continue.

For a minute, the two sat in silence. It took Winston a few seconds to realize that the faint clicking he was hearing from the outside must be Inclement practicing his croquet again. He thought of Sackett and his warnings that his father was spending the family trust and that the Corbally world was about to change. Lucille appeared frightened. Simon had said earlier that Lucille was capable of living without all this wealth. That she could be just as happy with nothing. Winston had doubted it then and he doubted it now.

Forcing a smile, Lucille endeavored to rally. Placing her hands on her knees, she sat straighter. When she spoke, her voice was strong again.

"Listen to me. I . . . I get tired."

"That's understandable," said Winston. "It's hard when we don't know. Uncertainty and concern can wear us down. I . . ." With a self-mocking chuckle, Winston shook his head. "Listen to *me*. I offer the obvious. I can't possibly know what it's like."

"But you're right. This situation concerning Clement's death is such a terrible secret. That I am able to share it with you, a stranger, is a great help. Clement used to tell me that when he was in the army there were men that he'd know for only a few months but that he and these men would become very close. That they would tell each other intensely personal things, things that they would never tell friends at home. It's odd, but I feel more comfortable talking with you than I do with Simon."

Lucille bent forward and Winston could see her whole face. The eyes were clear and they peered intently into his as if searching for imperfections. She held his gaze for a moment before continuing.

"This situation is difficult for everyone. It changes people. I see pettiness where there is usually strength, resilience where there is often hesitation. The . . . 'the children,' I was going to say. I still think of them as children and I know I shouldn't. Someday you will have children and you will always think of them as being young, no matter how old they get. I'm sure it makes life harder for them . . . but there you are."

Lucille collected her thoughts.

"Anyway, please don't judge them by their performances today. Their father's death is one thing, but this historic village project is intensifying the situation. You are familiar with such projects . . ." Winston went to object but Lucille held up her hand to stop him. "Maybe not on this scale but you know much more about it than anyone in the family. When I talked to Biff this morning, I explained to him what was going on and your involvement." Lucille once again held her hand up. "Let me finish. Like you, he wanted the police contacted but I told him no. He was furious, but he settled down eventually and he agreed to talk with you privately this evening. I want him to brief you on the legal aspects of this project. I want someone here that understands what's going on, that can talk to Dr. Harris and that Northingham man on an equal footing. As I started to say earlier, I don't think the children are capable at the moment and I don't feel strong enough to do it. Talking to these men is like my talking to men in a hardware store. They patronize me. I'm not up for the sly exchange of smiles, the incomplete explanations, as though I wouldn't understand. I . . . I hate to say it but I don't entirely trust them. I think they're too involved."

Lucille paused. When she began talking again, the words came out rushed and precise, as if she had memorized them.

"I do not want this project to continue. As far as I'm concerned, it died with Clement. Biff will do what he can legally, and from what he said this morning it will not be easy. Until we know what's to happen, I would like for you to act as liaison for the Corballys in their dealings with the others. I would like for you to finish the history at the price quoted and on top of that you will be paid a consultant fee for any liaison work. I need you at the moment. I need your interest and your expertise and I will not take no for an answer. There."

Catching her breath, Lucille sat back, her eyes again in shadow. Winston sat stunned. Upon opening his mouth, nothing came forth. He closed it.

"My goodness," said Lucille, more to herself than to Winston. "I did it."

Benton "Biff" Wiggins arrived one hour before dinner in a chauffeur-driven limousine. He was a short man with a barrel chest and a red face. His white crew cut and white mustache emphasized his sanguine appearance. There was something of the bantam rooster about him, especially in the way he walked on the balls of his feet, not unlike how James Cagney danced in *Yankee Doodle Dandy*. Although his flushed face glowed and he had a warm smile for everyone, his eyes were garnet hard and not amused. Winston and the man exchanged a few words but there was no time to talk about the project.

Biff dominated the dinner conversation. He possessed the bullish goodwill of a garrulous insurance salesman or senior partner. He would introduce topics and then give the table his opinions. Being in charge was his due. He'd gone to the head of the table without once wondering if that seat belonged to him. With infinite wisdom and patience, he enlightened and entertained all who would listen. Contrary insights were met with an amused expression and a shake of the head. The Corballys had been with the man before. They nodded along and pretended to hang on his every word. Several times Winston had wanted to flick mint jelly at him but had thought better of it. An influential lawyer with no sense of humor could ruin a life. With the lamb finished and the arugula salad almost done, the lawyer turned the conversation to Winston's presence.

"Correct me if I'm wrong"—if you dare, he meant—"but I hear you're doing a history of Longmeadow. I think that a capital idea. Do you have a publisher?"

"It's a private history," answered Winston.

Biff's good nature dimmed a little as he searched the other faces for an explanation. "You must be kidding? The Corballys are one of the great American families. Their history is the history of this country."

"Please, Biff," said Lucille, "let's not get carried away." Lucille was dressed all in black tonight, her hair pulled up and back to reveal silver and jade earrings that brushed her shoulders. Around her neck hung a very large Amerind neckpiece made up of jade, animal bones and feathers. She looked like a shaman for the D.A.R.

"What do you think?" Biff caught Sackett by surprise.

"I . . . I don't know. It's probably a good idea."

"Mother says it's a memorial to Father," interjected Clement. "Father would have liked that, so I'm all for it. I'm working on something myself."

"You are?" asked George, himself surprised.

"I am," answered Clement.

"You didn't tell me that."

"I was going to tell you later. I—"

Lucille spoke. "I'm sorry to interrupt, Clemmy, but Biff has to be back in New York. Maybe we should have coffee and dessert in the study while the will is read."

"Excellent idea, Lucille." Biff stood. Reaching behind his chair, Biff picked up a large briefcase. "I would first like to have a word with Winston. Could we have the front room?"

"Of course," said Lucille.

"Do you mind?" Biff asked Winston.

"Not at all," answered Winston.

All eyes were trained on Winston and Biff as they left the dining room. Biff waited for Winston to pass into the front room and then he shut the door.

"I don't have much time, Winston, so I'll get right to it.

First of all, I'm not at all happy with this investigation. I'm a firm believer in the abilities of the police, not that I trust them, but some of them know what they're doing. Clement Corbally was a friend of mine, and if he's been murdered I want the killer brought to justice. I don't feel this is a time for amateur theatricals. If you—"

Winston cut him off. "Excuse me, Mr. Wiggins, but you're a little out of line here. I tried my best to convince Lucille to go to the police but she wouldn't have it. If you were such a good friend of Mr. Corbally's, then you would know that he would have been against the idea himself. I have given Lucille a timetable, a *short* timetable, in which I will investigate this affair. After that, I *plan* on calling in the police. Captain Andrews is the local detective in charge of homicide and he's a friend of mine. Although, I admit, if I have to go to him with this, that friendship will probably suffer, but that's beside the point. Tomorrow I will begin what's necessary." Winston paused. "I believe you have some legal information for me?"

If Biff was upset by Winston's reprimand, he disguised it well. A smile grudgingly made its way across his face. "Well, I guess I've been told."

"I thought your time was short, Mr. Wiggins?"

"Let's back up here, shall we? And please call me Biff. Maybe I was wrong. Maybe things will work out. We'll know soon enough, won't we?" Winston didn't respond. "You must understand, Winston, that I've been taking care of the Corballys for a very long time. They are a wealthy family. I see opportunists in every nook and cranny." He shot Winston a quick insincere smile. Biff spoke as he searched through his briefcase. "You wouldn't know a Dr. Harris or a Mr. Northingham, would you?"

"I know Dr. Sam Harris," answered Winston. "He has a reputation as a good historian."

"What about this Northingham fellow? What's his story?"

"Only that he's a television personality. I think beyond that there's not much to consider."

Biff smiled. "You're right there. Northingham's background doesn't indicate much interest in history. My office did a little investigating of its own. Before he turned to television the man was an actor supporting himself selling used cars. Clement was well aware of the fact but it didn't seem to bother him. Getting the television people involved was a way to defray costs. Mr. Northingham's producers had assured Mr. Corbally of a substantial retainer in return for which they could use the village for four shows in the summer months."

"Did this agreement with the television people include Mr. Northingham? Or was it strictly with the producers?"

Biff smiled at the question. "The agreement included Northingham." Biff pulled papers from his case. "Here they are. Okay . . . my concerns have to do with Mr. Corbally's trust, which was, and quite possibly *is*, to provide financial support for this historic village. Do you know much about trusts, Winston? I suppose you don't see. Well, a trust is set up by a settlor, or individual who creates the trust. The settlor, in this case Mr. Corbally, names those individuals or that organization who will administer the trust. These are the trustees. There is always a joint tenancy of two or more trustees. Clement designated himself as a trustee, which isn't a good idea, and two other people." Biff paused.

"Sam Harris and Miles Northingham," said Winston.

"That's correct," answered Biff.

"Now, trustees are selected according to the confidence the settlor has in them to discharge their duties in good faith. In law, a trustee cannot personally reap any advantage to the detriment of the trust. If there's the possibility of a conflict of interest, then the courts can remove a trustee."

"Like sharing in television revenues?" asked Winston.

"Exactly." Biff pursed his lips; his quick, silent reappraisal allowed that maybe he was rethinking Winston's abilities. He handed Winston some papers. "This is the trust agreement. Now, in joint tenancy, if one of the trustees dies, the others usually take equal control of that share."

"Usually?" asked Winston.

"When there're as few trustees as there are in this case, the court can, and should, appoint someone else to fill the vacated position. That's what I'm going to push for here. I strongly feel that one of the family should be a trustee. It makes sense since the person to vacate was a Corbally."

"Who did you have in mind?" Winston couldn't imagine.

Something in Winston's voice made Biff look up. Smiling, Biff went back to his notes. "That hasn't been decided."

"How much money is involved?" asked Winston.

Biff hesitated. "Fourteen million dollars."

Winston could only stare.

"You're right," said Biff in response to Winston's gape. "It's a lot of money."

"Is there any left?" asked Winston. "I mean, in the family coffers. If that's the right word."

"Good enough word," answered Biff. "Yes, there's money left but . . . the coffers have been depleted considerably."

"Why did Mr. Corbally do it?" asked Winston. "Why so much?"

"Seed money."

Biff took out another sheet of paper and handed it to Winston.

"Eventually, with revenues from television and from the educational programs, much of the money would have been replaced. At least, that was Clement's intention."

"Replace the fourteen million?" Winston was incredulous.

"The fourteen million is placed in trust, hence the designation, and it's the interest on the principal that's used to underwrite the project. That amount is considerably less and it is that that would be replaced. The idea is that at some point the project is self-sufficient and the fourteen million is not needed."

Biff checked to see if Winston was still with him. Winston nodded that he was.

"Now, a trust is finite," continued Biff. "There's always a

time limit. In this case, we're talking ten years, which is relatively short in the life of a trust. Clement felt that the village should be established at that point and able to support itself. If not, then the trustees could reconsider and reestablish the trust for five more years. That would be it, though."

"So," said Winston, "in essence we're talking fifteen years in which fourteen million dollars of the Corballys' money is out of circulation."

"Well, probably only ten. To go five more years is complicated and involves extensive auditing by an outside company. The guidelines are strict, but you're right, it *could* go fifteen years."

"That would be another good reason to have a Corbally as a trustee," noted Winston.

"Yes," said Biff, nodding. He began to put papers back in his briefcase. It was time to go.

"How does this affect the heirs?" asked Winston. When Biff appeared reluctant to say, Winston explained his asking. "Fourteen million dollars, to me anyway, is one hell of a lot of money. If I had been counting on its benefits, I might, let's say, go to certain extremes to make sure it didn't go away."

Biff assessed what Winston had said. "It's hard for me to believe that . . ." Pausing, Biff reconsidered. He'd been a lawyer too long. "The children receive a moderate income from their trust funds. It's just enough to live on, but that's it. Right now they have to watch their pennies. This fourteen million doesn't affect them directly at the moment. Lucille inherits most of the estate, although there is a small growth in the trust funds of about fifty thousand. A token gesture, really."

Throw a token my way, thought Winston. "What if Lucille should die before the ten years is up? Who would benefit when the trust is dissolved?" he asked.

"When a trust is set up, a beneficiary has to be named. In this case, Clement had most of the money going back to Lucille, but should she die, then the children would receive the bulk. There're some historical organizations who benefit and four million is divided equally among his grandchildren."

"The grandchildren? That's nice of him."

"I suppose," said Biff. Zipping his briefcase closed, he stood. "I better get into the study." Reaching inside his suit coat, Biff presented Winston with a business card. "If you have any questions or if you learn of anything, please let me know."

The card reminded Winston of something. "I have one quick question. You don't happen to know or have heard of a person named William Laird? Mr. Corbally didn't mention him, did he?"

"No. Why?"

Winston explained.

"I'm afraid I can't help you." Biff stood for a second in thought. Something had occurred to him. "There *is* something else concerning the trust funds for the children. I'd forgotten."

"What is it?" asked Winston.

"Clement Jr. He doesn't get much from the estate."

"Why's that?"

"When young Clement was in college he got involved with some guru or other. Wound up giving the man nearly all of his trust fund. He lived in some collective for a while but eventually came to his senses. Of course, by then it was too late to reclaim his money. Mr. Corbally had me look into it but there was nothing to be done at that point. I must say, I can't conceive of young Clement . . ." Pausing, Biff glanced at his case. "Well, there you are. It's probably information an investigation such as yours could use."

Biff was halfway to the door when he stopped and turned.

"I wish you luck, Mr. Wyc. I think the Corballys just might be in good hands." With that said, he was gone.

CHAPTER 16

Winston wasn't sure what to do. He could go upstairs and sit in his room but that didn't appeal to him. He could go for a ride or he could take a walk. Winston wandered back through the dining room and into the kitchen. Juanita, the Corballys' cook, was arranging little cakes on a tray. The room smelled of coffee.

"Hello, señor."

"Hi, Juanita. We haven't been formally introduced. My name's Winston. You'll see me hanging around for a few days."

Juanita nodded. "I understand. That is Jimmy. He works for Señor Biff."

A large man sat by the door eating cake. He wore the shiny black suit, shiny white shirt and shiny Irish face appropriate to the chauffeur.

"Nice guy, your boss," said Winston.

"He's all right."

"Work for him long?"

"Yup." Mr. Noncommittal.

"Would you like some cake, señor? Coffee?" asked Juanita.

"No thanks. I'll just explore."

Winston went into the breakfast room. His mother had been a maid for twenty years and Winston knew how much the help disliked guests who tried to be chummy. It drove them nuts.

Opening the French doors, he stepped out onto the patio.

The night was mild and full of stars. The din of a country evening always surprised Winston. There weren't taxis and garbage trucks, but crickets and frogs could make quite a racket. Moving a little to his left, he could see through the doors to the study. The Corballys sat listening to Biff. For a second Winston contemplated eavesdropping but then thought better of it. And then, caught by the light spilling from the house, he noticed someone over by the brick wall. The person had pushed himself against the trellis on the opposite side of the patio.

"Hello?" said Winston softly.

Realizing he had been seen, the person moved away from Winston and nearer the bayberry hedge. Winston moved toward the shadowy figure.

"Who *is* that?" asked Winston.

Suddenly the person took off. By the time Winston got to the corner of the house, the shadow had disappeared into the dark mass of bushes that shielded the rose garden from the pool. Cautiously Winston moved in among the bushes. No one was there. No one he could see, that is. Standing near the pool, Winston turned and watched the house. The snooper had been too quick for him but he could have sworn it was Billy, Cybil's older son. If true, what was Billy doing sneaking around the patio? Childish curiosity? A game of cloak-and-dagger? Winston wondered if Billy had discussed his inheritance with his grandfather. At that moment the study door flew open and a burst of light fell across the patio. Winston could see the top of Inclement's head as he stepped over the low bayberry hedge, came down the garden path and emerged opposite him along the pool. Not seeing Winston, he continued walking down the path that looped the great lawn and led eventually to the woods. Was this the way to the cozy cottage that George had mentioned? As no one else appeared to leave the house, Winston started back toward the kitchen. It was then he saw yet another figure leave the shadows of the porch, the one on which the canapés had been served that day of the party.

Winston froze. This person was too tall to be the other snooper. The figure moved over to the hedge from where he could watch the front of the house. Ten minutes passed and Jimmy the chauffeur came out of the breakfast room door and around the side to the waiting Cadillac. Another few minutes passed and suddenly there was noise from the gravel drive. Biff Wiggins could be heard on the portico saying his good-byes to Lucille. As the door shut behind him and before he could reach the Cadillac, the silhouette moved out onto the driveway and toward the lawyer. Winston didn't recognize the lurking man. Quickly, he moved over to hear what was said.

"Mr. Wiggins, do you remember me? I'm Richie Baire."

"Mr. Baire, you gave me a start. Yes, of course I remember. Mr. Corbally's restoration expert."

"Yes sir. Could I have a moment? I know it's late and you're tired but this is important."

Biff looked at his watch.

"It will only take a second, sir."

"Okay. What is it?"

"Would you mind if we sat in the limo? It'd be more private."

Biff thought about that for a second. "Sure. You have ten minutes. I must get back to New York by midnight."

Winston watched as all three men got into the limousine. He remembered that Richie Baire was the man who lived in the trailer down by the barns. Circling the house, Winston reentered by the kitchen and, using the entrance hall, went up the front stairs to the quiet refuge of his room. The day had been tiring, full of long drives, picnicking, boating, the Corballys and a big-shot lawyer. He would contemplate the whole in his dreams.

Winston woke early. It took him a moment to orient himself but the birds were a tip-off. Opening his eyes, he studied the clock and then the room. Longmeadow. After rising, Winston stood by the open window inhaling the freshness, watching the sun slide morning shadows across the croquet court. Not a cloud in sight. Winston thought of how nice it would be to look at this every morning instead of the blackened brick wall across from his bath. If the Corballys would put a Korean grocery and salad bar in the garage, he'd seriously consider leaving New York City and coming north permanently. Maybe.

Later, stopping on the stairs, Winston listened for movement in the house. All was silent. Coming down the hall toward the kitchen, Winston ran his hand along the chair rail of the paneled wainscotting. Early Colonial Revival houses, built before and just after the turn of the century, had simpler interiors than their prototypes and usually just grafted a few historical details inside and out to suggest a relationship with an earlier time. Heating and lighting considerations had kept rooms small, but by the teens architects were learning to incorporate the new domestic technologies of electrical wiring, concealed plumbing and central heating into their designs. This allowed them to open up and play with the space. By the twenties, American architecture was being influenced by Frank Lloyd Wright and by the geometric patterns of European modernism. For many architects, porticos and Palladian windows were a thing of the past. Most people, though, had a difficult time with the new designs. They *wanted* porticos and Palladian windows, and their homes reflected that feeling. But if the exterior of the home demonstrated a concern for past styles, the interior was kept simple by the dictates of expense and convention.

That had not been the case with Grandpa Corbally's home. Much time and expense had gone into shaping an interior that would have been the envy of any early well-to-do Colonial builder. The main rooms were heavy with decorative moldings and carvings, the fireplaces large and ornate. The living room was quite formal with raised paneled walls and fluted pilasters. The formal dining room was hung with hand-painted wallpaper depicting local landscapes. Heavy cornice work supported all the downstairs ceilings except for the kitchen area and the informal dining room, which would have originally been the old kitchen. Early architects were aware of and appreciated the way shadow and light played against each other in these heavy moldings. Originally, it had been a design consideration, but the relationship between candlelight and moldings was a lost art.

At the end of the entrance hall, Winston entered the study. The formality of the design elements in this room was softened by the personal effects of Clement Corbally Sr. The walls were hung with photographs of him hunting or in action on the croquet court. The early photos showed a Clement Corbally who was tall and lean, his attitude casual and confident, his smile relaxed and sure in its awareness of how the world worked and his place in that world. Among the photos were the framed historical documents that Winston had seen in his earlier meeting with Mr. Corbally and the painted portraits of ancestors. Unsmiling, they too radiated a confidence and self-possession that was certainly a Corbally trait. Or had been, thought Winston.

On the floor were the splayed hides of a zebra and a Kodiak bear, hunting trophies from another era. An assortment of antlers, some looking domestic, others African, sprouted from the walls in no discernable pattern. Somebody had adorned one burly rack with a string of colorful beads. To the left of the French doors, a glass-fronted gun cabinet exhibited its wares. Winston knew nothing about guns and had never been hunting, but he had to admit that the few times he'd actually held a revolver or a rifle he'd been intrigued by the weight and balance and by the power, real or imagined, that the weapon held over him.

The wall opposite the French doors was floor to ceiling in mahogany bookshelves with a large raised paneled cabinet set in the center. Opening the cabinet door, Winston discovered a well-stocked wet bar. Two rows of shelves held books about architectural history. Winston ran his finger along the titles. Mr. Corbally had been a man serious about his history. Venturi's *Learning from Las Vegas* and Christopher Alexander's *A Pattern Language* were not books read for amusement. On a long, low refectory table Winston was delighted to find a number of priceless old folios including the whole of Inigo Jones's Covent Garden elevations, Palladio's *Quattro libri dell-l'architettura* and a rare edition of Emmanuel Héré de Corny's *Plans et élévations de la Place Royale de Nancy*. He was carefully turning these pages when Lucille came through the patio doors.

"Good morning, Winston. I hope you slept well."

"Thank you, I did."

"How about some breakfast? It's Juanita's day off but I'm sure she's left something to heat up."

"Sounds good." Winston followed Lucille into the kitchen. The woman had been out jogging or exercising in some way. She wore a colorful combination of green Reeboks, purple sweatpants and an orange velour pullover. Her long hair, wrapped up in a paisley scarf, was wet from exertion.

"Out for a jog?" asked Winston.

"Heavens no. Walking. I've never been much for running, hurts my legs. A good brisk walk is always better from what I read. The countryside goes by at a much more pleasant rate.

Look, here're some scrambled eggs. Not to worry, Juanita uses Egg Beaters, and here's some juice, some English muffins."

"Let me help," offered Winston.

"No, no. I don't get to play cook very often. You sit. We don't want to contribute to the WASP Rot Syndrome now, do we?"

Winston sat in silence wondering what that meant. Lucille appeared cheery and she didn't appear to be forcing it. She finished preparing breakfast and sat down.

"Ready to research Longmeadow?" she asked.

"I'm ready to go." Winston helped himself to a portion of eggs. "I think today I'll begin with what I call the paper chase: deeds, old mortgages, surveys, maps, that sort of thing. Wills."

"Yes, wills." Lucille sighed.

"How *was* the reading?" asked Winston.

"The reading." Lucille said this as she might the title of a poem she was about to recite. "As for myself, the will held no surprises. Biff and I had gone over it in detail beforehand. The reading was really for the children so that if they had any questions Biff could answer them personally. Everything seemed fine until Biff got to the historic village trust. At that point, things took a turn for the worse, to put it mildly."

"I bet," said Winston. "Did Biff explain that it was only for ten years? Possibly fifteen?"

"He did all that. He also said that he was going to petition the courts to have one of them appointed as trustee to replace Clement. It was then that the reading fell apart. Biff asked if anyone was interested in being a trustee and Clemmy said he'd love the position. Sackett said something about kiddies and their rides and Clemmy stormed out through the French doors. Had it been another time, it all might have been quite humorous but . . . oh, well."

Winston remembered Inclement going by him last night. "Biff is going to try and get Miles, and possibly Dr. Harris, removed as trustees because of conflict of interest."

"He mentioned that," said Lucille. "They'll be up today, by

the way. They called to say they have a meeting with the local planning board. Perhaps . . ." Lucille gave Winston a look of supplication.

"An act of liaison?" asked Winston.

"If you wouldn't mind?"

The previous day, when Lucille had asked, or rather informed, Winston that he was to act as troubleshooter for the Corbally clan in their dealings with Miles and Sam, he had been doubtful. But the more he thought about it, the more it seemed that in many ways acting as liaison could help with his investigation. At least it gave him authority to ask certain questions without arousing too much suspicion.

"Should I advise them of my new position," said Winston, "or would you like to?"

Lucille smiled. "Thank you, Winston. Then I think it only fair that I give them notice. That should make them happy."

"No happier than when they realize the family is set against the project," replied Winston. "Once Biff makes known to them that he's petitioning to have them removed, it could get quite tense around here."

"I'm prepared for that," answered Lucille.

"What's the story on this Richie Baire fellow? Where does he fit into all this?"

"Richie's been here for almost eight months now. He was hired by Clement to be the head carpenter-restorer. From what I've heard, he's very good."

"Does he have a contract?" asked Winston.

"I don't know. I do know he's on salary and he gets to live in the trailer. He's spent the last eight months setting up the big shop down in the barn. I rarely see him, actually. He stays pretty much to himself. Seems to be a nice person."

"I should go talk with him later," said Winston. From what he had observed last night, Richie might be worried about his position now that his patron was gone.

Lucille nodded. She wasn't about to forget the real reason for Winston's residency at Longmeadow.

"This might sound silly," said Winston, "but where does Cybil live? I'll tell you why I ask. Last night I thought I saw a young boy, about Billy's age, moving around outside the house. I wondered if he might have come with Cybil or if he lived close enough to walk over on his own."

"A young boy?" Lucille shook her head. "Billy didn't come with Cybil last night. He could probably bicycle over if he wanted to. They only live a few miles down the road. When she and Gordon were together, that was her last . . . friend, Clement gave them some land down the road toward the lake. Ten acres or so. They built a barnlike thing. Too open for my taste."

"I was probably seeing things," said Winston reassuringly. "I wasn't all that sure." Lucille looked concerned and there was no need to worry her, although now that she was the new heir to the Corbally estate it might be a good idea to keep vigilant. Winston wondered briefly why Longmeadow had no dogs.

"The shadows can play tricks," said Lucille.

"It's true. Particularly for a city boy like myself." Winston finished his coffee. "Clement Jr. and George, have they been together long?"

"Yes, they have. Earlier, when Clemmy first came back to live at Longmeadow, he had quite a few friends. They would come and go. Of course, Clemmy didn't have the cottage then. He stayed here, in the apartment upstairs. Having his men friends in the house was difficult, to say the least. And then George showed up. That was almost two years ago now. George has been very good for Clemmy. Got him to renovate the old corncrib and start taking his art more seriously. I think I could say that George has made it his project to nudge my son in productive directions. It's something I applaud. Clemmy certainly wasn't going to do it on his own."

"Clement is lucky to have George."

"I think so." Lucille paused. "There are times, though, when I think he goes too far. By that I mean, I think his own life suffers because of it. I'm not sure it's a good idea to have all your eggs in someone else's basket."

Or to have someone else's eggs in your basket, thought Winston. "I better get to work." Rising, Winston went to pick up his plate.

"Please," said Lucille. "Let me do that."

"Thank you. Did Miles or Sam say when they'd be by?"

"Sometime late this afternoon," answered Lucille. "They said they had business with Richie."

"I see." Winston delayed his leaving. "One more question, if I may?"

"Certainly."

"I was wondering . . ." Winston hesitated as if searching for the correct words.

Lucille, who had been collecting plates, stopped and looked at Winston directly. "It's okay, Winston. You don't have to worry about inquiring about Clement's death. If you have a question, you can ask me."

"I appreciate that," said Winston. "Is there anything you can tell me about Clement's last hour at the house, before he went down to the barn? Sackett has mentioned that there was something important his father wanted to tell him. You wouldn't happen to know what that was?"

Lucille considered the question before speaking. "I'm sorry but I can't help you. Clement had said to me, just before he left, that he wanted to speak to Sackett and to send him down to the barn. That it was important. That was the word he had used. I'm sorry but I was busy with the caterers and not paying much attention. Clement hated these garden parties and I'd learned to ignore him and his quarrelsome remarks. It would have been like Clement to suggest such a thing in the middle of something else. He thought it gave him an advantage if the other person was upset or divided in some way."

"Sackett would never have said no?" asked Winston.

"No. Sackett, all the children, did what their father wanted. They might complain but in the end they would obey."

Winston wondered if Mr. Corbally ever used the threat of disinheritance to keep his kids in line.

"How long after Mr. Corbally left did Sackett follow?"

"I have no idea. It might have been a few minutes or half an hour."

Winston nodded.

"You might ask Juanita when she returns," said Lucille. "She usually has a better idea of what's going on than I do. I should pay more attention I guess."

Winston could see that Lucille's resolve to assist him was slipping quickly. "Thank you, Lucille. I know it's not easy to talk about."

Lucille forced a smile. Picking up the dishes, she hurried into the kitchen.

Standing in the study, Winston realized that he was too anxious to focus on historic matters. Maybe this would be a good time to go meet Mr. Richie Baire. They did, after all, share several important interests.

CHAPTER
18

Richie wasn't in his trailer and the shop was locked. Winston had brought his sketchpad and, after a survey of the architectural pieces in the barn, had decided to draw the Federal door unit. Concentrating was tough, though. Winston felt uncomfortable being in the barn. It had taken on a haunted feeling. Faces, too quick to see, peered down from the mow opening. Animal noises were the movements of things better left alone. From the corner of his eye, he kept seeing Mr. Corbally's body stretched out on the wood pile. He had just finished his sketch and risen to leave when Richie came through the door. Winston wasn't sure who was the more surprised. They had both visibly flinched.

In his early thirties, Richie was just under six feet in height with a long ponytail and a full drooping mustache. His face was long with high cheekbones. He wore black jeans, a black T-shirt and black motorcycle boots. A silver chain connected a belt loop in front to a wallet that stuck out of his rear pocket. It was the kind of oversized wallet that truckers used. The man reminded Winston of cowboys he'd seen in old photographs. He certainly didn't look like the type of person Mr. Corbally would have trusted.

"Sorry," said Winston. "I didn't mean to startle you."

Richie took a moment to assess the situation. His eyes ran over the lumber and then back to Winston.

"Likewise. I don't believe we've met."

It was difficult to tell if the man was welcoming or not.

Richie's eyes were gray and unsmiling and his mouth was hidden by his large mustache. Winston wondered which moniker he should assume first, Longmeadow historian or family troubleshooter.

"I'm Winston Wyc. The family has hired me to do a history of Longmeadow."

Richie considered that for a moment. "Richie Baire. I'm the carpenter around here."

"It's nice to meet you," answered Winston.

"You interested in the restoration of old buildings?" asked Richie with a nod in the direction of the door unit.

Winston said that he was. "I'm an architectural historian."

"I see," replied Richie.

"I was sketching that door. It's an unusual piece." Winston presented the drawing as if it were a peace token.

"Nice." Richie appeared to relax a little. "Did you check out those dormers over there? Came off the same house."

Next to a stack of clapboards were two dormers that had been removed from a roof all in one piece. The dormers echoed the oval pediment of the door.

"I saw those," answered Winston. "They're really beautiful. I don't think I've ever seen dormers with that oval piece and the paired colonnettes like those. And topped with rosettes. Very fancy."

"You probably noticed the outside casing on the door has the same banded colonnettes that extend over the arch. Looks almost like bamboo." Richie moved over to the unit. "Check this out." Richie pointed out that the half-oval hood of the recess was paneled, as were the sides. He pointed to the frosted glass. "This glass would have been leaded at one time," he said with authority.

"You're right," said Winston. "This leaf motif on the capitals looks Egyptian, though. If that is true, then these colonnettes might represent papyrus stalks. Instead of bamboo."

Richie eyed them closely. "Could be." He wasn't quite ready to concede.

Door Unit

"What's the date on this house?" asked Winston.

"Not sure. Early 1830s. Came from the east end of Connecticut just this side of the Rhode Island border."

"You take it down?"

"Nah. Some outfit from New Hampshire. Was trying to sell it to Old Sturbridge Village but they didn't need it. Mr. Corbally bought it instead."

"Is the rest of the house as interesting as these dormers and this door?" asked Winston.

"Not really. Just a mill owner's house common to that area at that time. Mr. Corbally wanted a very simple village with the usual buildings that might be found in an isolated community of the middle 1800s. Blacksmith shop, sawmill, tavern and store. And the houses the people would have lived in. What he looked for were simple structures with interesting details. And as close to original as possible. This house had the details."

"It sure did."

"We can't be sure of who the architect was here, but we think this doorway was copied out of Batty Langley's *Gothic Architecture*. There's one almost exactly like it on plate VII."

"You've done a lot of research here."

"You got that right. Me and Mr. Corbally. These buildings are like family at this point. On this particular house we have inventories of estates dating back to 1840. We could almost set it up the way it was originally, right down to the type of griddle pan."

Winston smiled to himself. Restorers were like old-car enthusiasts. Get them talking about what they loved and the rest of the world dropped away. But Winston was here for another reason.

"To be honest," said Winston, "I was down here before."

Richie raised an eyebrow. "Oh yeah. When was that?"

"I was with Cybil when she found her father." Winston let that sink in for a second. "We had actually come down to look for you. Cybil wanted to introduce us."

"She did?"

Winston could almost hear the doors slamming shut in Richie's brain. The man had paled slightly.

"You didn't see Mr. Corbally that afternoon, did you?" Winston tried to be offhand but it wasn't easy. Richie took a step back.

"I wasn't here. You said so yourself." Richie's tone was defensive.

"I meant before here. Up at the party. You didn't see him with anyone, did you?"

"I wasn't invited to any party. What are you? Some kind of architectural historian slash detective?"

Winston backed off. It was curious that Richie had become hostile so quickly but for now he would attribute it to the man's paranoia about his job—if indeed his job *was* in jeopardy. Briefly, Winston wondered if Richie had a stake in the Northingham business. He doubted it. Richie had been here before the television people, and from what Winston knew, which wasn't much, he had been Mr. Corbally's right-hand man.

"I was curious, that's all. I mean, finding someone like that you . . . well, it might sound a little weird but suddenly I've become focused on Mr. Corbally's last hours." Richie didn't seem to buy that.

"You find a lot of dead people?" Richie's eyes, which had become animated with talk of the door unit, had once again gone neutral.

"Well . . . no. Like I said, I'm the curious sort."

Richie gave the wood pile under the mow opening a quick glance. "He was a great old guy." Without looking at Winston, Richie headed for the barn doors and the outside. "I got work to do."

Winston followed him out. "Nice meeting you," he said to Richie's retreating back. Richie stopped and turned. He smiled, or at least Winston thought he did. The mustache certainly went in the appropriate directions.

"Likewise," drawled Richie.

Before he could turn back to leave, Winston asked one more question. "Did Mr. Corbally ever go up into the hay-mow by himself?"

Richie took a moment to answer. He glanced up at the second floor of the barn. "I couldn't tell you." With that said, the conversation was over.

Watching Richie's back, Winston wondered just where he might have been the Saturday afternoon that Mr. Corbally died. When the police did get involved, Richie Baire was going to need a good alibi.

After Richie went into his shop, Winston walked over behind the barn and peered up at the small rear door in the back. He eyed the path that disappeared off into the woods. I wonder where that might lead, he thought to himself. Only one way to find out. With some apprehension, Winston took off through the woods.

Miles Northingham had spread the Corbally Village renderings out across the wide folding table. Standing, staring at them, were Sam Harris and Sal Wantucci. The chairman of the Wistfield Planning Board was one of those short, pear-shaped men who cinch their belts six inches below the last chin. A retired plumber from Brooklyn, Sal took the position of chair very seriously. Looking properly pensive, he pulled at his left earlobe.

"Nice drawings," he offered. Sam looked up at the ceiling.

"No one would know it was there," said Miles, who had been explaining the project. Miles had worn his canary yellow sport coat for the occasion, combed his beard and was all smiles.

"The entrance would be here on Route 22, you can see there's plenty of sight distance, and the museum itself would be quite a long way in from the road."

"This all the buildings?" asked Sal.

"Well . . ." Drawing his mouth down, Miles gave it some thought. "There could be some expansion in the future but what that might be I couldn't tell you right now."

"More old buildings?" Sal looked at Sam.

"Sure," agreed Miles. "Although there might be some new ones later. You know, to house old things and such."

"I see."

"The board couldn't possibly find anything wrong with this, could they? I mean it's a sweet little project, nothing tall, no hazardous wastes." Miles ran his hand over the drawings. "Nothing here but American history. And hey, what can a person, a real American, say bad about that?"

"We're not talkin' history here, Mr. Northin'ham, we're talkin' the laws and rules of now. And by the way, I watch the show every Saturday. 'Tonia, my wife, she liked the ones about what the Indians lived in. She's into that shit, you know."

Sam looked away and chuckled. Miles gave him a look of annoyance.

"Always nice to meet a fan and please call me Miles. Sammy, do I have any of those signed pictures I carry with me? The ones with me standing in the doorway. Maybe you could get one from the car."

"Maybe." Sam didn't move.

"Like today." Miles raised his voice just enough.

Reluctantly, Sam headed for the door. Suddenly, he turned. "We've got company."

"What?"

Wantucci's office was separated from the reception area by a door and a large plate-glass window. Through the glass, Miles could see Clement Corbally Jr. talking to the receptionist.

"Well, what do you know," said Miles.

"Them Corballys," said Sal, pointing with his dead cigar, "they in agreement wit' all t'is? I mean, it's on their property, you know."

"It's all set up legally," assured Miles.

"That's good." Sal gave Clement a curious look. "This one I don't know. Maybe a little . . ." Pulling his mouth down, Sal wiggled his hand in a gesture of who-knows. At this point, Clement Jr. had his face up against the glass and was peering in. He waved. Sal motioned him in.

"Come in, Mr. Corbally. Join the party."

"I hope I'm not interfering in any way," said Clement Jr. "I was passing by and saw everyone come into the office. I

thought it might have something to do with the village project."
Clement noticed the plans on the table. "Ahhh, this must be it.
You know, I might have some ideas you could use."

Miles looked over at Sam. "What's that supposed to
mean?"

Clement smiled at each man in turn. "I was thinking the
village could use an amusement area."

"What?" Sam and Miles spoke in unison.

"I thought we might have a few rides." Clement spoke
quickly, his gaiety a little forced. "For the children?"

"What children?" Children weren't creatures Miles gave
much thought to.

"Ya might what?" Sal asked.

"For the kids, in case they get bored. Children can get bored
at these historical places," explained Clement. "It could be
useful in giving the parents a break. A place for the children."

"A carny?" Sal didn't seem to like that idea.

"Not a carnival. Just some rides," explained Clement.

"I don' know. Them carny people aren't very clean. They
been known to have drugs and stuff . . ."

"No carnival people, I can assure you. Now, we have to go
to the zoning board and ask for a waiver to have an accessory
provision attached to the historic project itself," said
Clement. "But if they approve the idea of the project then the
amusement part shouldn't be a problem. The regulations per-
mit 'specialty entertainment.' I went to the town hall and
looked it up."

Miles and Sam were speechless. Sal said, "That means like
a theatre or bowlin' alley, somethin's like that. Amusement I
don' know."

"Let's forget the rides," said Miles, smacking the prints
with some force. "You . . ." Miles put a finger into Clement's
chest, ". . . don't have a thing to say about it. Now, could you
please wait out on the sidewalk or someplace?"

Sam was the first to notice that Sackett had entered the
office and was staring through the glass at them. Sam tried to

get Miles's attention but he was too intent on selling the project to Sal.

"Now, can we continue? What do you think the board would feel about the village? This project could mean a few jobs in the area. People working, that's good." Miles turned back to Clement. "Are you leaving or what?"

"Jobs are nice," said Sal.

"Miles," said Sam.

"What?" shouted Miles. "Did you get that photo yet?"

"Sackett's here," explained Sam. Everyone turned to look at Sackett, who saw that as an opportunity to enter.

"What's going on here?" Sackett demanded.

"Jesus," said Miles under his breath. To Sal he said, "I apologize for these intrusions." He looked over at Sackett. "Would you get the hell out of here and take Six Flags with you." Reaching over, Miles grabbed Clement by the arm. Clement shook himself free.

"Don't you touch me," warned Clement. "George is out in the car."

"So what?" hissed Miles.

"Miles," asked Sam, "maybe we should do this another time?"

Sackett had gone over and was standing directly in front of his brother. "I might have known you were involved in this. No wonder you want to be a trustee."

"A trustee?" Miles appeared on the brink of apoplexy. He turned to Sam. "What in the hell is he talking about? What's with this trustee talk?"

"I don't know, Miles. Please, settle down."

"This village plan is going to turn into an albatross," yelled Sackett at Clement. He pointed at the plans. "Those should be burned."

"Just try it, pal." Miles placed himself between Sackett and the table.

"Whatta we talk'n here? Birds?" Although he was enjoying the situation, Sal was having a difficult time keeping up.

Sam raised his voice above the din. "If everyone could just be quiet for a minute, maybe I can explain." Everyone stopped to look at him. "Thank you." Sam turned and spoke to Sal. "The late Mr. Corbally set up a trust so that we," he indicated himself and Miles, "could go forward with this historic village should something happen to him. Unfortunately, Mr. Corbally has died, and now, Miles and I, being the trustees, are seeing that the plans go forward as Mr. Corbally wanted."

"Yeah," added Miles for emphasis.

"I'm sorry," continued Sam, "but I don't think the family has any input . . . legally. The matter is really out of their hands. That and the fact that the project won't be open to the public." Sam smiled at Clement. "Of course, Miles and I would be more than glad to listen to any ideas . . ." Sam looked back at Miles, "that someone might have in regard to the village. But I think we should do that at another time and place."

"And I think you might find that there's a space open for another trustee," said Clement.

"I don't think that's the way it works." Sam's voice was low but intense.

"Is this where the village is to be?" asked Sackett in a loud voice. He was peering over Miles's shoulder at the blueprints. "That can't be. I . . . That land . . ." Sackett's breathing became labored, his face red and mottled. He tried to say something but couldn't. Clenching his fists, he gave Miles and Sam a cold stare and then stormed from the room. He slammed each door as he passed on his way back outside. The receptionist stood and looked after him. Sal waved for her to sit.

"What a twit," said Miles.

"I think I should go, too," said Clement. "I think it would be a good idea if you two gentlemen talked to our lawyer. After that, we can talk about amusements." With a smile for everyone, Clement turned and followed his brother out.

"Ain't that the way wit' families?" said Sal to no one in particular.

"What was he talking about?" said Miles to Sam.

"Let's discuss it later." Sam looked at Miles in a way that indicated it was best to leave it a private matter.

Sal spoke and pointed at the blueprints. "Ya knows there's a whole process involved here. Particularly wit' somethin's this big."

Miles gave Sam a look of irritation. "We'll talk later." Turning back to Sal, he put on his television face. "Big?" Miles laughed.

"It's called the SEQR process."

"What's that stand for?" asked Miles.

Sal spoke as if reading from a page. "State Environmental Quality Review. In New York State any project that might affect the environment has to be reviewed. Ya have to fill out an assessment form which is then reviewed by the planning board. If the board thinks the plan could fuck with the environment, ya have to do an impact statement. Period."

"An impact statement. How long does that take?" asked Miles.

"Ya got a year from filing."

"It takes a year?"

"Ya can do it faster if ya want. Depends on you. But ya got to get a certified company to do the review. Understands." The two men stood staring at each other. Miles looked as if he wanted to smack someone.

"What's the next town?" With effort, Miles kept his voice cheery.

"Millbrook."

"Maybe Millbrook would like a museum."

"Could be," said Sal.

"Miles?" cautioned Sam.

Miles tried to smile. "We'll get back to you." He began to roll up the prints.

"I ain't going nowhere," stated Sal. "I'm retired."

CHAPTER
20

Winston had been back from his meeting with Richie for an hour and a half when the front door slammed. Looking up from Mr. Corbally's desk, he had watched Sackett storm by the door on his way to the kitchen. This had been followed by a loud and incoherent demand, a moment of silence and then his stomping back by the door. A minute later, Winston had heard muffled yelling coming from the second floor. Just as the tempest had seemed to subside, there had come another slamming of the front door. This time Clement had hurried by, not so much in anger, noted Winston, but in a determined way, as though he had something important to do and it couldn't wait. There was mumbling from the kitchen and then Clement had come back by the door on *his* way upstairs. Rising, Winston then went had gone into the kitchen and found Juanita peeling potatoes.

"Sure is noisy around here," he noted.

"Like *niños* those two," said Juanita.

"Do you mind if I ask what the problem seems to be?"

"Who knows, señor. Questions for Mamá."

Winston sat at the counter. "What are you making for tonight?"

"Tonight is salmon with a coriander sauce. Do you like spicy, señor?"

"I do, although I grew up eating things like bubble and squeak, bangers and mash and shepherd's pie. My mother's idea of spicy was Worcestershire sauce."

These dishes were obviously not part of Juanita's expertise. "We do not have shepherds here, señor. Like myself, your mother was from another country?"

"Ireland."

"Ahhhhh, yes."

Winston couldn't be sure of what but that seemed to answer a lot of questions for Juanita. Having rinsed the potatoes, she set them aside.

"Can I get you something, señor?" Her expression told Winston that he was in the way.

"No thank you. Do you mind if I ask you some questions?" asked Winston.

Juanita shrugged and turned back to the sink to wash some cilantro. She spoke over her shoulder. "Mrs. Corbally said that you would be asking Juanita some questions."

When Juanita didn't continue, Winston took that as a consent to help. "Do you remember if Mr. Corbally was with anyone the day he died? Before he went down to the barn?"

"You are a detective, señor? Like on the TV?"

Winston smiled. "No, I'm an historian but Mrs. Corbally has asked me to privately look into her husband's unfortunate death. I was wondering if you might have heard or seen something that day."

Juanita settled her slight frame against the base cabinets. She took a moment to remember that day. "Mr. Corbally was a very nice man."

"Yes, he was," answered Winston.

"On that day I remember he had a meeting with those two men in the study. I took them coffee."

"By 'those two men,' do you mean Dr. Northingham and Dr. Harris?"

Juanita nodded yes. "I think they are very upset."

"Upset? You mean angry about something?" asked Winston.

"I think so."

"What makes you think they were angry?"

"When Juanita is there they do not talk. But they are

upset. There is much . . . what is the word . . . tension in Mr. Corbally's room."

"Was Mr. Corbally upset?"

Bowing her head, Juanita thought back. "Maybe not so much as those two men."

Winston waited.

"That is all, señor," said Juanita. "I go in and come out." She gave him another shrug.

"Interesting. Were they at Mr. Corbally's desk?"

"Mr. Corbally was sitting at his desk, yes. And the skinny one. The man with the beard is walking around."

"I see. Did you notice anything on Mr. Corbally's desk? Were they looking at blueprints or papers of any kind?"

"I remember, I think, the skinny man was holding a paper that looked old," said Juanita.

"A big piece of paper?"

"No, no. Little, like this." Juanita held her hands up to indicate the size.

"Was it old, or did it just look old?"

"I . . ." Juanita paused. "Maybe it only look old. I do not know."

Winston realized that Juanita was uncomfortable. "Did Mr. Corbally see anyone else that morning?"

"I do not think so."

"What about after the meeting?" asked Winston. "Did the men leave?"

"The big man, he left. I saw him from the kitchen window going across Mr. Corbally's special court. I remember because no one is allowed to walk on there."

"And Dr. Harris?"

"I don't know."

"Thanks, Juanita. You've been a big help. Oh, one more question. Did Mr. Corbally have an appointment book?"

"Appointment book?" Juanita looked puzzled.

"A book that he wrote his daily schedule in. That sort of thing."

Earlier, when he had returned from the barns, Winston had looked for an appointment book. He had gone through the desk drawers, the shelves behind the desk and finally the liquor cabinet. Winston felt certain Mr. Corbally would have had an appointment book of some kind but he had not found it.

Finally, Juanita replied, "Maybe. I do not clean. Mrs. Walter does the cleaning."

Rising, Winston thanked Juanita again and went back into the study. He stood gazing out the French doors. So Miles and Sam had had an argument with Mr. Corbally that morning. And the piece of paper? Could that have been one of the threatening notes or something related to the project? Winston tried to recall his and Kiko's conversation with Miles and Sam that day in the front of the house. They hadn't mentioned seeing Mr. Corbally. And Miles, he remembered, had been curious as to whether or not Winston had spoken to Mr. Corbally before the accident. He wondered if Kiko would remember more. He had to call her anyway about this William Laird.

A door slammed on the second floor. Winston wandered out into the hall. He met Sackett at the bottom of the stairs. The man appeared less angry than before, although, Winston could tell, life wasn't perfect yet.

"Do you have any siblings?" asked Sackett.

"No," answered Winston.

"You are a very lucky man, Winston. I truly believe that the less family a man has, the more fortunate he is."

Was that a confession of sorts? "Is your mother up there?" asked Winston.

"She's in the trophy room with my brother. *Lupus est homo homini.*"

Winston had had it with the Latin. He tried not to sound too annoyed. "What does that mean? I stopped using Latin along with the Church."

Sackett looked genuinely surprised that Winston didn't understand. "I'm sorry. 'Man is a wolf to man.' It suggests

that pride and greed might be the cause for a certain predatory behavior in people."

"Families and wolves, heh? Someday we should sit down
over a good blood-red wine and talk religion. I bet there're a
few things you could tell me."

Sackett's expression indicated he wasn't quite sure what
Winston was getting at. "That might be fun. Flesh and spirit,
freedom and obedience, Bonhoeffer or Barth. Name your poison."

"I was thinking more along the lines of good and evil."

A wry smile from Sackett. "We must set aside some time
together. Now, if you'll excuse me, I need to get home. We'll talk."

Such a pleasant guy, thought Winston as he proceeded up
the stairs. Warm, selfless, at peace with those around him.
And a snappy dresser. That he should choose religion as a
career move was not surprising.

It took Winston a moment to find the trophy room. Lucille
was sitting in a Hepplewhite chair while Inclement stood by
the window. Lucille motioned for Winston to enter. She didn't
appear upset but the color was up in her face.

"Have a seat, Winston. We're having a lively discussion
about trusts and trustees."

Winston sat on a matching Hepplewhite across from
Lucille. The room was lined with shelves heavy with awards
and trophies. A few trophies were honored with their own
cases. Where there were no shelves there hung citations, letters of appreciation and many photographs. A battered old
mallet rested in the corner. As Winston surveyed the room,
Lucille explained to him that she and Clemmy and Sackett
had just been back over the whole trustee thing. That
Clemmy wanted to be a trustee and represent the family in
the project. Everyone already knew that, of course. And
Sackett was adamantly opposed. Everyone knew that, too. He
felt that if one Corbally showed an interest then the chances
of defeating the project would be all that more difficult.

"But it's not true," interrupted Inclement. He faced
Winston. "Let's say Biff can't get the trust dissolved, then

wouldn't it be better to have some representation? It would give the family some say in the matter." Inclement paused. "We tried to call Biff but he wasn't in."

"I think Clement has a point," replied Winston. He remembered that it was Inclement who wanted to introduce kiddy rides. "I'm sure Biff is working on both options."

"That's exactly what I said," answered Lucille. "Really. I'm getting to where I don't want to hear about it again." Lucille stood. "It's lunchtime. Would you two care to join me?"

"Not me, Mother," said Inclement. "George and I have to go back into town. I have a meeting with the caterers at two."

"Don't forget the bartender this time," chided Lucille.

"It's all under control. I'll talk to you later. Good-bye, Winston."

Lucille and Winston didn't speak until Inclement had left the room.

"There goes a happy man," said Winston.

"Life is odd, Winston. My husband tried to get Clemmy interested in the project and he could have cared less. Now . . ." Lucille sighed. "How's the history going?"

Winston followed Lucille out the door. "I've only just started. After looking through the files, I think most of the legwork has been done for me. It shouldn't take long. Is Clement having a party?" It seemed odd to Winston to be talking about caterers this soon after Mr. Corbally's death.

"Clemmy is hosting a croquet tournament this weekend. We had discussed putting it off but that, I guess, is out of the question. People are coming from far away. I think, too, it would be good for Clemmy. His father's death has depressed him so."

Could have fooled me, thought Winston. "I have a question."

"Yes?"

"Did your husband keep an appointment book?"

"Yes, he did. A rather large affair that he used as a sort of diary. Not a lot of detail but what he did, who he did it with, that sort of thing. It should be in the pencil drawer of his desk."

"I've looked but I couldn't find it," said Winston. "I was wondering if you could ask around. See if anyone took it. It would arouse less suspicion if you were looking for it."

"That's odd," said Lucille. "Why would anyone take it?"

"I don't know. A souvenir, maybe."

"Well, I'll certainly ask the children. Will *you* join me for lunch?"

"I'm afraid I'll have to bow out myself. I called Simon this morning and he invited me over. Will you be seeing Sam or Miles today?"

"Them." Lucille shook her head in dismay. "I told Sam when he called that I needed to talk to him. He said he'd come up after their meeting with Richie this afternoon." There was a teasing edge to Lucille's smile. "After that they're all yours."

"Gee, thanks," said Winston.

They had stopped at the bottom of the stairs.

"Where do they stay when they're up in Wistfield?" asked Winston.

"They used to stay here but . . . well, it's difficult now, obviously. I think they stay at one of the bed-and-breakfasts in town. I could ask."

"No, no, don't bother. If Sam wants to see me, I'll be back around two, two-thirty."

"I probably won't see him until after that anyway. Give Simon my best. He's been such a dear."

Winston watched as Lucille headed down the hall toward the kitchen. She must have been gardening or something earlier, for she wore baggy jeans and what must have been one of her husband's old work shirts. Her hair was tied up with a blue and white bandanna. Her bearing from behind reminded Winston of Cybil, a person he had been meaning to call. That was three phone calls he had to make, one to Kiko, one to Cybil and one to Biff. He hoped Simon wouldn't mind.

CHAPTER
21

"What? No dessert?" Winston's tone was mock serious.

"Dessert is to be a walk," answered Simon with a rueful expression. "Except for special occasions I've had to be prudent in my caloric intake." Simon patted his ample belly. "Doctor says I'm in some sort of danger zone. 'Low fat' is the new mantra. And after meals I'm supposed to take a short constitutional. Ridiculous, of course, but there you are. I've always thought of myself as looking like Joyce's Buck Mulligan: stately plump."

Winston laughed. "I thought lunch was a bit on the careful side. Although I did detect a hint of framboise in the fruit salad. And the sauternes beforehand?"

Simon called from the kitchen where he had disappeared to dump the dishes in the sink. "Think of yourself as a special occasion."

"I'm honored," Winston called back.

Simon reappeared. He had taken off his blue-and-white checked apron and put on a bright red sweatshirt. "I know," he said, "I look like a huge cardinal, but I'm supposed to work up some perspiration. Otherwise, I'm dawdling."

"Fruit salad and exercise. Who'da thunk it?" Winston laughed.

"Come on, city slicker. No pain, no gain."

Pain for Simon was a casual stroll to the end of the dirt road that connected the church to the main thoroughfare and back again, a total distance of half a mile. Winston told

Simon of his talk with Juanita and the incident in the study. The two spoke of suspects.

"So, in essence, there are two groups?" said Simon.

"That's right," answered Winston. "We have the project people and the immediate family, in which I include George. I think we can dispense with the idea of random violence."

"Or drive-by shooting," added Simon.

"You watch too much TV news, Simon. I believe Mr. Corbally was killed because of the project and I think it breaks down into two groups: the ones for and the ones against."

"Project people," mused Simon. "Miles, Sam Harris and the carpenter, Richie Baire."

Winston nodded. "Those were the ones present on that day, although Richie says he wasn't around. I'd have to check that."

"Why would anyone who is for the project kill Clement?" wondered Simon.

"I don't know yet. If indeed any of them did," said Winston. "But Sam and Miles were upset that day in Mr. Corbally's study. There may be a motive in what happened there."

"Sam or Miles." Simon was intrigued. "And the family." Simon bent to pick a blue coneflower, which he then used for emphasis. "Cybil was there with you the whole time. That would leave her out. Clemmy was in his studio, you say?"

"That's what Sackett said. By the way, what kind of art does Inclement do?" asked Winston.

"Sculpture of some kind. What kind I couldn't tell you. He puts things outside. Little scenes. Bits of automobiles hanging from trees, pathways strewn with mutilated plastic dolls, that sort of thing."

"Sounds like some kind of political constructivism."

"I know he once wrapped a piece of green string all the way around Walden Pond."

"Waltham Pond," corrected Winston.

"What?"

WITH MALLETS AFORETHOUGHT

"There's really no such thing as Walden Pond," said Winston. "It's actually called Waltham Pond."

"Really? Well, I call it Walden Pond like the rest of the world. If I said Waltham Pond to anyone other than an historian, they wouldn't know what I was talking about."

"That's true. I stand corrected."

Simon humphed. "Then there's Sackett," he said. "I'm afraid the more I think about him, the less sure I am. It makes me feel uneasy."

"I felt that way at first," said Winston, "but now I don't know. I was up in the hayloft and it was quite dusty. When I saw Sackett coming away from the barn, he wasn't at all dirty. No one could have dragged a body up there and not shown *some* evidence of the climb."

"We are still assuming that Clement didn't make the climb himself?" asked Simon.

"I feel it would have been impossible. As I said before, someone was up there and they went out the back. It would have been difficult for Mr. Corbally to have fallen and then scuffed his own tracks."

"True. What about George?" asked Simon.

"He was up at the party, remember? He was the one who dunked Uncle Carl into the pool."

"That's right. So of the family members we have Clemmy unaccounted for and a possible Sackett."

"It looks that way now," replied Winston.

"And the project people?"

"As I said, Richie claims that he wasn't around. I'd like to verify that. Kiko says she saw Sam in the study just before we met you, so I'd say that lets him off the hook."

"Maybe." Stopping, Simon thought back. "Between your meeting me and your going down to the barn, there's almost half an hour. There was the pool incident."

"That's true but I think Sackett had either already gone down to the barn or was about to. From what Lucille said, Mr. Corbally left about half an hour before that. That would be approximately one hour in which Mr. Corbally was unaccounted for. And less, if you include the twenty-five minutes that Sackett stood around waiting for him."

"And Miles?" asked Simon.

"Well, at the moment, the famous Dr. Northingham is my prime suspect."

"Well, well." Simon stopped. "We get to the prime suspect."

"Yes. What I didn't tell you earlier," said Winston, "is that after the meeting an unhappy Miles was seen taking off across the croquet court. According to Juanita, anyway."

"That would be away from the barn," said Simon, beginning to walk again.

"Correct. But the path that leads away from the back of the barn goes through the woods and around to the other side of the great lawn. I know because I took the path myself."

"So Miles could have doubled back?" Winston nodded that it was a possibility. "I wonder why he was upset," mused Simon.

"I thought I'd ask Sam when I see him later," said Winston. "Right now it could be the key."

"It would tell you how upset Miles really was, you mean?"

"Exactly."

The two men were back in front of the small church, a beautiful Carpenter Gothic built in the 1850s. The rectory had been built later and lacked the detail of the church building but it was still a graceful and well-proportioned structure. Both were in counterpoint to the little round man who inhabited them.

"It looks as if you might wrap this mystery up in record time, Detective Wyc."

"Maybe," said Winston. "Like I said, I need to know what upset Miles. I need a strong motive here. It'd be one thing if Miles was opposed to the project but he isn't. He and Mr. Corbally were in agreement there."

"Sam could provide some answers," stated Simon.

"If he's willing. Could I use your phone, Simon? I need to

make a few calls, two of which are long distance. I'll use my
credit card. I promise."

"Who are we calling locally?" asked Simon.

"Cybil," said Winston.

"I doubt if she'll be home," said Simon. "You should try
her at work."

"At work? Cybil has a job?" Winston was surprised.

"Not a job, really. She has her own business. Makes mustards
and sauces which she sells all over. Corbally's Condiments
they're called. And quite good, too. I believe she sells them
as far away as New York City."

"No kidding, a Corbally who works for a living."

"What a thought, hey? Come in. I'll get you the number."

Biff was not in his office but his secretary said Winston
should call back around five. Cybil was with a sales rep and
would call *him* back later that afternoon at Longmeadow.
Kiko was busy but said she'd give him some time if he made
it snappy.

"Gee, thanks a lot," answered Winston.

"We're shorthanded at the moment," replied Kiko. "*Some*
of us get to go on location."

"I'd gladly swap places, believe me. It's not all that much
fun up here."

"Actually," said Kiko with a chuckle, "it's not all that bad
here with the boss gone. Very quiet."

"I won't tell him. I promise. How're things?"

Quickly, Winston and Kiko caught up on business.

"Sounds like you don't need the boss down there. Listen,
there's something else I want you to do for me," said Winston.

"What's that?" asked Kiko.

"I want you to find a William Laird. I think he might have
something to do with restoration or museums or something.
I don't really know."

"That narrows it down."

"It's important. I'm pretty sure it has some connection
with Mr. Corbally's death, but what, I don't have a clue."

"Where should I look?" asked Kiko.

"Start with the *Landmark Yellow Pages* and go from there. Contact all of the historical organizations within a hundred miles of Longmeadow. Begin with the large ones and work down."

"That's a lot of calls."

"Keep a record, too. We'll bill for them. Well, that should keep you busy for a few days."

"More like a week. When do we get to see you again? I hate to say it but it gets lonely around here. No one to yell at me."

"I've never yelled at you and I'm planning to come back Friday afternoon. The way it looks now, I'll probably be up here part of next week."

"How's the investigation?" Kiko's tone turned serious.

"Too early to say." Winston looked over at Simon. "I've got the Reverend Mr. Tart on the case. Should be solved any day now."

Simon laughed from his seat across the room.

"Give Simon my best. And you, take care. There's a killer walking around up there. I worry about you."

"Thank you, but don't. I'm being very discreet."

"You?"

"That's right and don't sound so surprised. Take care of that convent stuff and don't forget the mysterious Mr. Laird. If you find him, call me immediately."

The two said good-bye.

Simon spoke. "You think this William Laird is connected in some way to Clement's death?"

"Not directly," replied Winston, "but his card was in with those notes for *some* reason. I would like to know what that reason was."

Simon chuckled. "I'm happy to hear that I'm now part of the investigative team. Do I get a badge?"

"You get to ponder the problem."

"That's okay as long as I don't have to go out in the field. Thinking I can do."

"Well, all thinking is greatly appreciated, as was the lunch, but I'm afraid there is going to be some fieldwork."

"What? Now wait a minute," objected Simon, "I—"

"It's okay," interrupted Winston. "There's no danger involved." He went and sat opposite Simon. "I want to do something, an experiment of sorts. It's a little silly but it would clear up a few things for me."

"I'll listen," said a skeptical Simon, "but it doesn't mean I'll participate."

"Oh, come on," said Winston. "Remember, no pain, no gain." He gave Simon a wide smile. Simon didn't smile back.

"Winston?" Sam Harris stood in the doorway.

"Come in, Sam." Winston was on his knees looking through a file drawer. Closing the drawer, he stood.

"How's the house history coming?" asked Sam.

"Not too bad. Mr. Corbally has a lot of the information I need right here."

Sam smiled. "Keeps the legwork down."

"It does that," answered Winston.

"I haven't done one of those in a while. What with the television work," said Sam.

It sounds like an apology, thought Winston.

Sam continued. "It used to be fun, though. Title searches in dark, dirty court basements. Tax records a hundred years old. Like a mystery in many ways."

Winston could see that Sam's good cheer and hesitant smile were being forced. "Just like a mystery," repeated Winston. No need to continue the small talk, he thought. "Did you talk with Lucille?"

"I did. It's why I'm here, really." The tentative smile disappeared. "I must say I was somewhat taken by surprise. I was hoping that you'd stay neutral in all this, Winston."

"I am neutral, Sam. I don't know what Lucille said to you, but one of the conditions under which I agreed to sign on was that I wouldn't take sides. That I would act as an impartial liaison between you and the family. With Mr. Corbally gone, the family wants someone who can interpret for them what's going on. Since I was here doing the house history, Lucille asked me if I'd do that for them, too. I said yes." This wasn't entirely true, but Winston needed information from Sam and he didn't want to alienate the man.

"That's not the impression I got from Lucille. She made it sound as if it was your battle now."

"Battle?" asked Winston. "I don't understand." Winston decided to play dumb.

"Well . . ." Sam hesitated. "You must know the family is opposed to the project."

"I knew Sackett was against it," said Winston. "He's made that plain to me on several occasions. But the others? I thought Clement Jr. wanted to be a trustee."

"I'm afraid he does." Shaking his head, Sam turned away and walked over to the French doors. He stood a moment staring out at the patio. "Lucille is also against the project." Sam turned back to Winston. "She made that quite clear just now. When she mentioned that you were speaking for the family . . . I naturally thought that . . . well, you understand." Sam offered a strained smile as a gesture of conciliation.

Winston uttered a noncommittal, "I see."

"I . . ." Sam started over. "Mr. Corbally's death has certainly complicated matters. Not with just the family, but the local authorities, too. Mr. Corbally had promised to take care of that end of things. Now . . ." Sam shrugged.

"If the family *is* against the project, Sam, why not move it? There must be other places that would welcome such a venture. Someplace closer to New York, maybe."

Sam gave Winston a look of suspicion. "I thought we were neutral here, Winston. That doesn't sound impartial to me."

"I'm only throwing out suggestions. You have the Corbally investment and you have the structures. All you really need is the land. I can't imagine the project's going to be much fun with the majority of the Corballys fighting you." Winston joined Sam by the doors. "There must be other people or organizations out there that could use a big tax break."

"There's more to it than that, Winston. The trust says specifically that the project has to be here at Longmeadow and has to be called Corbally Village. It even specifies a particular piece of land. I think that might be hard to sell elsewhere. Plus, we start speaking of moving the project, we automatically come in conflict with the trust. We can't do that."

"Sounds like it has to stay here," said Winston.

"Exactly." Winston's answer seemed to lift Sam's spirits, if only slightly. "Winston, listen to me. This project is important, not only to me, but to others. With the help of television, we have the chance of bringing the art of restoration and the need for preservation right to the American public. And once people get interested in something, it's amazing how they will support it. Believe me, I know firsthand."

Sam's colorless features flushed with the thought of Corbally Village being piped into every American home. Winston could see the attraction. For a man who had probably spent much of his time with the Historical Society trying to raise funds, the village project and its coupling with television must be a strong lure. Outside academia, much of a historian's energy is used up on the money issue.

"Can I ask you a question about this TV thing?" asked Winston.

"Sure," said Sam.

"How does the village project actually benefit financially from its partnership with television? I mean, does the network pay one lump sum to the trust, or does it pay individuals, like producers or someone? I'm curious as to how that all works."

Sam took a moment to answer. Winston had the feeling he was choosing his words carefully. "I'm not altogether sure of the details but the simplified version goes something like this: The network gets money from a sponsor who pays for commercial time. That money is divided, as to contract, between the network and the producer of the show. The producer uses his money to pay salaries, overhead, that sort of thing. In this case there are two producers, one from *From Mortises to Mullions* and the trust itself."

"Who is the producer of *From Mortises to Mullions*?" asked Winston.

"Actually, it's a group called Dovetail Associates. I've . . . eh, met some of the men but not all."

Sam had been with the show for three years and hadn't met all the producers. That seemed odd to Winston. His expression must have indicated such, for Sam added quickly, "The group has a few silent partners. Men who invest money but aren't directly involved."

"How is the money divided in terms of Miles's show and the project?" asked Winston. "Is it sixty–forty, fifty–fifty?"

Sam hesitated. Winston got the feeling Sam knew but wasn't going to say. "That hasn't been worked out yet. We need to get a sponsor . . . and, well, that sort of thing."

"Are the present sponsors for *From Mortises to Mullions* interested?"

"Possibly."

Winston could see Sam shutting down on the subject. The man had that distracted look about him, the one where magazine covers and furniture details are more important than the conversation. It was time to get his attention.

"The day Mr. Corbally died, Sam, you and Miles had a meeting with him in which you argued about something. What did you argue about?" Right to the heart of things, thought Winston. Usually, the use of shock investigation could go either way; either the person is so shocked he doesn't answer, or he says things he doesn't mean to. Sam, it turned out, was somewhere in the middle.

"Who told you that?" Sam's face became pale again.

"So you did have an argument?"

"I . . . we . . . we . . . didn't argue, exactly." Sam rallied somewhat. "Who said we argued?"

Winston bent the truth a little. "The cook delivered coffee

to you that morning and she told me that you and Miles were arguing with Mr. Corbally."

Sam became even whiter as he tried to recall that morning's sequence of events. "The cook saw us arguing?"

"Well, maybe not arguing but she said it was obvious that everyone was upset." Pretty lame, thought Winston. The professional bad guy would be in stitches at this point. Sam didn't actually laugh but he did appear to visibly relax. Some color returned to his cheeks.

"Ohhhh, yes, now I remember." Suddenly Sam was all smiles, and his head began to bob up and down as if the remembrance had somehow severed a few neck muscles. "There were these notes. Yes, that was it, these notes. Clement seemed to think they were threatening or something. He . . . eh, wanted us to see them. Wanted our advice. He was upset about them. I had forgotten that." Sam's head nodded to a stop.

Winston wondered how a person could forget something like that. "And that was it?" he asked.

"I believe so." Sam's cheerful countenance dropped into an expression of misgiving. "Why do you ask?"

"We found the notes," said Winston. "I showed them to the cook and she said she had seen you holding one of them in your meeting with Mr. Corbally."

"I guess I did hold one."

Winston was having a hard time keeping his emotions in check. "And what did you think, Sam? I mean, here were these notes saying Mr. Corbally better stop his project or else, and then the 'or else' happens. Didn't you put that together?"

Sam went white again. "But they didn't actually say that. I mean. they weren't that specific."

"I think they're pretty explicit in their message, Sam." Stopping for a second, Winston brought his voice back down to normal. "I'm sorry. I didn't mean to raise my voice. It's just that . . ." Winston took the plunge. "It's just that Mr. Corbally had a bad fall, Sam, and I find that fact a mite suspicious, particularly since he had received these threatening notes. I find it hard to believe that you and Miles didn't put that together, that you didn't talk about it."

Sam appeared wobbly. His eyes darted over to a chair and back.

"*Did* you and Miles talk about it?" Winston's tone was accusatory.

"No, we didn't," Miles proclaimed from the doorway. Both Sam's and Winston's heads jerked around at the sound of his voice. Slowly, Miles entered the study, his eyes boring into Sam's. "It never occurred to us," added Miles.

Winston collected himself quickly. His mind raced back over the last few minutes of his conversation with Sam. "And how long have we been standing outside the door, Mr. Northingham?" asked Winston.

With effort, Miles turned away from Sam to stare at Winston. "Oh, I think you were asking questions about television and its role in the world of historical preservation. Questions that Sam really knows nothing about." Miles turned back to Sam, who stood with his head bowed. "Do you, Sam?"

"No," answered Sam in a low voice.

Back to Winston. "And that's *Dr.* Northingham, thank you."

"I see," said Winston. "And where did you receive this doctorate, if I may ask?"

"I don't believe that's any of your business." Miles gave Winston a big smile to let him know he wasn't going to be rattled by any Mr. Wyc. Miles spoke to Sam over his shoulder. "We have a meeting in the village, Sam, or don't you remember? It's why I came looking for you, not, as Mr. Wyc here assumes, to eavesdrop."

"I had forgotten," intoned Sam.

As Sam moved toward the door, Miles continued to stare at Winston, his look assessing, his thoughts seemingly reconstructing the conversation he had overheard. "I'm not sure, Mr. Wyc, but I think I know what you're trying to get at—"

"What's that, Mr. Northingham?" Winston leaned back against the desk, his attitude relaxed and casual. He smiled at Miles.

"Please don't interrupt me." Miles smiled back at Winston. "Everything that has anything to do with the television deal and with the money is completely legal. We went out of our way to accommodate Mr. Corbally and to act in good faith where the trust was involved. The papers are there for anyone to go over. I suggest you take the time, Mr. Wyc. And as for Mr. Corbally's unfortunate accident, I don't think it serves his memory well to be going around suggesting that somehow his partners had something to do with that fall. That kind of talk could get you in a lot of trouble. Let's go, Sam."

Winston went to speak but decided not to. He watched silently as the two men exited the study, Miles with his canary yellow sport coat and confident stride and Sam with his head still down, his posture that of a beaten dog. After waiting a moment, Winston turned and walked over to the French doors. He opened them and stepped out into the warm day. He raised his face to the sunlight, letting it rejuvenate him. He thought back over what had been said. He had never accused Miles and Sam of any connection with Mr. Corbally's death. Winston had been careful about that. He had only asked why they hadn't wondered about the notes and the possible connection to the old man's fall. Miles had been quick in trying to shut down that possible train of thought. Did the man feel guilty about something? And that morning in the study. Winston was sure something else had gone on there. Why had they all been upset? Had Mr. Corbally accused Miles and Sam of writing the notes? But why would he do that? They certainly weren't, and aren't, opposed to the project. Winston remembered once again that Miles had asked him that day in the gravel drive if he had talked to Mr. Corbally. Damn, thought Winston. He had meant to ask Kiko about that conversation and he'd forgotten. What *had* Miles been worried about and what would Mr. Corbally have said to him?

174

"Mr Wyc?" Juanita's voice cut into Winston's thoughts. He looked up to see her standing in the breakfast room door.

"Yes, Juanita?"

"It's the phone, señor. Cybil is asking for you."

"Thanks," said Winston. "I'll be right in."

CHAPTER
23

From Lucille's description of Cybil's house, Winston had expected an open barnlike structure. The house was post and beam but it certainly wasn't open. For a relatively low price you can buy a post and beam kit from a company that will erect it on a foundation that you provide. Depending on what you buy, they give you a small or a large open space with four walls and a roof. It's up to you to fill it in. Cybil had bought the two-story version and put in a huge center chimney with two fireboxes. It could be used to warm either the kitchen or the living room. The kitchen was the largest room in the house, for it was also the family room and the dining area. The living room had that unused look and was carefully arranged with early American furniture, a collection of antique bed warmers by the fire surround and two old quilts which hung behind the sofa. Cybil had her bedroom downstairs and had given over the second floor to Billy and Gordon. A hand-printed sign at the bottom of the stairs read NO ADULTS ALLOWED.

Winston now stood in the kitchen sipping a beer and watching Cybil work. Against the fireplace wall rested a Garland stove, the huge, black industrial kind. One large pot and two smaller ones simmered quietly. On a butcher-block table next to the stove were a collection of herbs, a pot of honey and various unmarked containers.

"So Mom said you were looking for Father's appointment book," said Cybil. "Billy has it in his room."

"So he took it?" asked Winston.

"The day of the accident Billy went in and retrieved it. It was something he gave his grandfather every year on Christmas. They'd sit around on Christmas Day and make plans for the coming year. First day to go fishing, first day to go . . . that sort of—" Cybil stopped. Her eyes got watery and she bit at her upper lip. Grabbing a pan, she hurried over to the sink.

Winston watched as Cybil gave the pan the washing of its career. Setting the pan in the drainer, she rested against the cabinet.

"Sorry. Some things are difficult to remember." She took a deep breath. "I hope I didn't interrupt your house history or whatever it's called."

"Not at all," said Winston. "I've been stuck in the study all day," he lied. Cybil needed a change of subject. "What's in the pot?"

"My newest concoction," said Cybil. "I always experiment at home."

Leaning over the large pot, Winston took a whiff. "What is it? Smells good."

"It has hopes of being a new barbecue sauce. I wanted it done by this summer but I guess we're thinking autumn now."

Winston picked up a jar from the table. "Corbally's Condiments," he read. "Longmeadow Mustard. Hot."

"We have hot, we have honey, we have spicy, we have regular. Whatever your palette prefers." Cybil's refrain was sung like a commercial. She struck a pose and laughed. Winston laughed with her.

"It all looks great. How in the world did you get started in this field?"

"Oh, about four years ago, it was around the time Gordon was born, I started toying with the idea of concocting a mustard which I could sell at the local farmer's market. I needed something to do and I thought it would give me some time with Billy. He was upset about the new resident and I knew he liked being in the kitchen using the mixer, putting in the secret ingredients, that sort of thing. I bought some jelly jars and started experimenting with honey, herbs and mustard seed and voilà, there I was selling condiments on Saturday mornings. Father had a fit, of course. *His* daughter out there selling mustard as if she needed the money. I finally convinced him it wasn't the money. Still isn't, I'm afraid, but that could change soon. I've got a big grocery chain interested. Anyway, now there're six different mustards, two kinds of salsas and a new product called Gordon's Hot and Heavy. Well, almost a new product. That's it in the pot there."

"I'm impressed," said Winston.

"Don't be," answered Cybil. "I don't know if I could have made it on my own. Father helped me out and I didn't have to worry about support, really. Sometimes I wonder if I could have done it for real."

"I think it would have happened anyway," said Winston.

Cybil stopped her inspection of the sauce and looked over at Winston. "Well, thank you. It's sweet of you to say so."

The two looked at each other a little longer than necessary. Winston was surprised to find himself getting red.

"I . . . eh, came over to see Billy," he said quickly. Cybil had said Billy would be there.

"So you said on the phone." Suppressing a smile, Cybil turned away to look into the pot. "He's not here at the moment but he should be. I expect he'll be in any minute. Want another beer?"

"No thanks. Do you think he'd mind if I waited in his room?" asked Winston.

"I guess not."

"I can wait." Winston could tell Cybil wasn't happy with the idea.

"Well . . . go ahead. It's okay. You two share the love of a certain kind of music." Cybil's expression was teasing. "He won't care as long as you don't touch his comic book collection. He's got them all wrapped in plastic. He's going to sell them someday and make a killing." Shaking her head, Cybil smiled at the thought. "What have I wrought? But sure, go ahead. It's the second room on the left. It has a 'Death from Above' poster on the door."

Winston took a moment before entering forbidden territory. Billy's room looked like 'Death from Above' had come and gone, leaving no prisoners. If Winston, as a ten-year-old, had ever left his room looking this way, his mother would have grounded him until it was time for college. The only area remotely in order was that near the computer. Video games were stacked neatly and there was room to operate. It took Winston a few minutes to find the appointment book, although it was right on top of the bed. Sitting, Winston opened the book and turned to the day of Mr. Corbally's death. He wondered if Billy might have written something but the page only mentioned the garden party. Slowly, he turned the pages forward looking for a certain appointment. And there it was, July 11, nine days later. Monday at one o'clock in the afternoon. A meeting with William Laird. Winston stared at the entry. That afternoon had come and gone and no William Laird had shown. Not that Winston knew about, anyway.

"What's happening?" Billy stood in the doorway. He didn't appear upset but he didn't appear happy either.

"Hi, Billy. I'm sorry to invade your space but it was important. Maybe I should have waited." Cover all the bases, thought Winston. "I was looking for an appointment your grandfather made."

Glancing about the room, Billy appeared to be checking to see if anything was out of place. "That's cool." He came in and stood by the bed. "What appointment?"

"He was supposed to meet someone on the eleventh of July. A man named William Laird." Winston showed the page to Billy.

"Grandpa was dead." Billy's tone was suddenly sullen.

"I'm sorry about that, Billy."

179

"Yeah, sure."

"No, I am. I liked your grandfather. He could have taught me a lot."

"He knew about everything. He was great."

"I know," agreed Winston. "He would want you to help me right now." Billy nodded. "You don't know who this man is, do you?" asked Winston. Billy shook his head to indicate that he didn't. "Your grandfather never mentioned him?"

"Nope. Who is this guy?"

"I don't know. I'm trying to find out myself."

"You going to take the book?" asked Billy.

"I don't need to," answered Winston. "I just wanted to see if the guy was in here."

Winston had a feeling the appointment book was safer where it was. Lucille was sure someone had disturbed her husband's study. It was possible he had been looking for this very item. Winston stood. "Hope I didn't cause any grief?"

Billy took a moment to answer. Winston was going to have to pay some dues for trespassing. "As long as it was important."

"Believe me it was. Take care."

Back in the kitchen, Cybil was turning off the stove.

"Well, I think that's it. I'll have to wait until it cools to know, though. Billy get upset?"

"He was a real sport about it. I told him it was important."

"What was in that appointment book that was so important?" asked Cybil.

"I was looking for a man's name. I was hoping your father had written in the man's phone number, too, but he hadn't. I'll have to try elsewhere."

"That's too bad." Taking off her apron, Cybil straightened her shirt. She was wearing the same outfit she'd worn on the picnic only this time the tank top was dark green. Her hair was pulled back over her ears revealing the full oval of her face, the wide cheekbones. "It's getting late," she said. "I have to go pick up Gordon but you can stick around if you want. I'll be right back. How about staying for dinner?"

"I'm sorry but I can't," said Winston, who *was* truly sorry. "I have an appointment with Simon Tart. Another time?" he asked hopefully.

"Anytime."

"Well, I guess I'd better get back."

Cybil smiled. "Come again. You and Billy can listen to Dr. Didi together."

Winston laughed. "See you soon."

Out in his car, Winston thought about William Laird. The man obviously hadn't shown or someone in the family would have known about it. And he hadn't called. Juanita or Lucille would have taken the call. Or would they have? He would have to ask about that. Anyway, the man was still a mystery and Winston had a feeling that until he solved it, a major part of the puzzle was going to remain missing. He glanced at his watch. It was time to meet Simon at the barn.

CHAPTER
24

Already at the barn, Simon sat on a stump, his expression one of suffering patience. Winston backed his Volvo wagon up to the barn entrance. After getting out, he went to the back and opened the rear door.

"You're early," said Winston.

Simon huffed from his seat. "I just couldn't wait to get started." The sarcasm wasn't lost on Winston.

"Oh, come on, Simon. You don't really have to do anything. You only have to observe. Did you bring a watch?"

"I did."

"Good. Here, give me a hand with this."

"I thought I was only to observe."

"Don't turn sullen on me. I just left one gloomy face, I don't need another."

"What gloomy face was that?" asked Simon. Leaning in, he peered into the back of the Volvo.

"Cybil's Billy. Here, grab the other end of this," said Winston.

"That must weigh a ton." Simon backed away. "I'm not sure I'm supposed to lift anything that heavy."

"Come on, Simon. With the two of us it will be easy."

"What is it?"

"It's two fifty-pound sacks of potatoes joined at one end. I did it with twine."

"That's a hundred pounds!" Simon was horrified.

"Just pick it up, please. It will be dark soon."

Reaching in, Simon took hold of one end of a sack. "I should have brought gloves."

"Quit complaining. Now lift."

The two men were halfway to the back of the barn when Simon demanded that the burden be dropped.

"Set it on here," said Winston, indicating the stack of roof rafters where Mr. Corbally's body had been found. Winston waited until Simon's breathing appeared normal. "Haven't you been exercising, Simon?" His tone was one of mock concern.

"You are lucky I'm not a violent man, Mr. Wyc. Look at my hands." Simon thrust his arms forward as if they were bleeding stumps.

"I asked you to look for Richie," said Winston.

"He's not here." Simon massaged his fingers. "I don't think I can carry that one step farther. I'll be in pain for weeks. Why I let you . . ."

"Now here," interrupted Winston, "help me get this up on my back."

"I will not."

Winston could see that Simon was adamant. "Thanks."

"You're welcome." Simon stood firm.

With much heaving and grunting, Winston lifted the sacks by himself onto his right shoulder. One hung down his front, the other down his back. "Damn, these things are heavy," he moaned.

"Not as heavy as old Clement," stated Simon.

"Forty pounds lighter," grunted Winston, who was weaving under his load toward the ladder. "But good enough . . . ugh."

Slowly, Winston made his way up the ladder. After much grappling and groaning he disappeared into the second floor. Simon could hear the sacks as they were dropped. A fine mist of dust descended from above. There was the scraping of the sacks being dragged and then Winston's face peered down from the mow opening.

"Ready," puffed Winston. "I'm letting them go."

Backing away, Simon called up. "Ready!"

The two sacks fell end over end twice and crashed on the wood pile in a great explosion of dust and dry hay. A dark cloud chased Simon even farther back into the barn. He met Winston coming down the ladder.

"What a mess," exclaimed Simon. "Look at that dust. And my goodness, look at you."

Winston's clothes were smudged and streaked with dirt. Sweat dripped down his face in sooty little rivers. He leaned against the ladder.

"You're right. I'm a mess." Winston took a second to ease his breathing. "And that cloud of dust the sacks made. You don't even have to time it. That's going to take a while to settle."

"A good ten minutes, or more," agreed Simon.

The two men moved in a wide circle, avoiding the dust cloud. Standing in the barn doorway, Winston smacked at his clothes.

"Actually, it comes off fairly easy," noted Winston. "The pants, anyway."

"Not the shirt," said Simon. "That's filthy. You leaned against the ladder going up and rubbed the dirt in."

"You're right." Winston sat on a stump. "I'm glad that bundle didn't weigh any more than it did. I might not have made it."

Simon found an old chair to sit on and the two thought silently about what had just occurred.

"You know," said Simon after a minute, "this little exercise should eliminate a few suspects. At least, Sackett."

"He wasn't this dirty," agreed Winston. "Plus, I'm not sure he's strong enough, although he is tall and athletic looking."

"Miles is certainly big enough," observed Simon.

"That's what I was thinking. And he might have had time to clean up. He had several hours to do so. He might even have reached the house without anyone seeing him during the pool episode or after the ambulance came."

The two were silent for another minute.

"I wonder if Sackett ever actually went into the barn," said Winston. "If he did, and there was no dust, then Mr. Corbally's fall came early. If he didn't, then it might have happened later. I don't know what that means but it's something to think about."

"That's my job," said Simon. "Now . . . are we done? I need to go back to the rectory and take a long soak."

"What about the potatoes?" asked Winston.

"What about them?"

"Couldn't you use them in your soup kitchen or something?"

"St. Peter's doesn't have a soup kitchen. We're out in the middle of the woods, remember?"

"How about the Episcopal church in New Holland?"

Simon heaved a great sigh. "Couldn't we just leave them here?" He brightened. "You and Richie could get them later."

"Maybe Richie could use them," wondered Winston out loud.

"Excellent idea," said Simon, standing. "Now I'm off." He turned back to Winston. "And please, no more field trips. I'm positively inflexible on that point. We'll talk soon. Bye."

It was the first time Winston had ever seen Simon move faster than a stroll. He checked his watch. He'd better get moving himself, he had a dinner date with Lucille in forty-five minutes. Winston glanced over at the potatoes. The air had cleared but it was still hard to see them. It was possible that Sackett had come into the barn and never seen his father.

And those potatoes. They would have to wait. Standing, Winston looked off in the direction of the house. He would have to ask Lucille's permission but it might be time to ask certain people some pointed questions.

It was the next morning and Winston sat in the basement of the main house sketching an old chimney foundation. For such an elegant house the basement was low and dark and cobwebby. The section around the stairs had had a cement floor poured at one time but the remainder was dirt and dusty flakes of old coal. A single uncovered light bulb lit the bottom of the stairs. With a borrowed flashlight, Winston had first explored the dark recesses. The sills sitting on the foundation were ten inches square as were the joists that connected the sill to a larger center beam. The center beam ran the length of the house and the joists were mortised into it and held with trunnels. Trunnels, or treenails, are dowels of hardwood used as spikes and driven into drilled holes to fasten one piece to another. Three of the joists still resembled trees with one side flattened off to accommodate the subflooring. Without the aid of structural engineers, the early builders tended to over-build. It was safer.

From the written records Winston knew that the present house was built on top of the original. Winston could see where the original foundation stopped and the new foundation began. While the new foundation was block and mortar, the older was stones lain dry and later pointed up with mortar. In two old photographs that Winston had found of the first house there was a large center chimney which was typical of older Georgian houses. This had been removed for the new house so that Grandpa could have a nice center entrance hall. Winston had come down into the basement looking for the original chimney piers.

Winston had found two brick piers about five feet high, five feet wide, eight feet deep and set parallel with each other, partially hidden by the old coal bin. These piers rested on huge flat stones. Across the top of the piers and connecting them were eight hand-hewn timbers each over a foot thick. Placed on top of these timbers were more flat stones. There was only a space of several inches between the stones and the beams supporting the subflooring.

Kneeling, Winston had brushed cobwebs from a rusted metal piece attached to a strip of wood that ran down the inside of a pier. It was an old hinge bracket, its metal reddish brown and flaking. At one time there would have been a storage room between the two piers with a door.

Winston, with the flashlight dangling from a nail above him, was just finishing his sketch when the basement door opened and Lucille called down to him.

"Hello!" Lucille's feet appeared on the third step. "Are you still down here, Winston?"

Root Pile

"I am," shouted Winston. "Come on down."

Lucille carefully descended the wooden steps. "What a lovely place to spend the morning."

"Lovely and very interesting," answered Winston.

Lucille stopped at the bottom of the steps. "What a mess. Clement always talked about fixing it up but I think he liked it this way. When he came down here he'd say he was going spelunking."

Winston laughed. "It feels like a cave. I was just admiring this huge root pile."

"The what?"

"The old-timers called these chimney foundations root piles. Quite descriptive, don't you think?"

"Quite. There's an old well down here somewhere. Clement showed it to me once but I don't remember where it is."

"A well?"

Having finished his drawing, Winston unhooked the flashlight and came over to Lucille.

"That would suggest there was an even earlier house," said Winston. "A first dwelling with perhaps only a few rooms." He handed her his sketchpad. "Here. You can see what the pile looks like without getting dirty."

"Looks sturdy," observed Lucille.

"It had to be," answered Winston. "It supported one heck of a big chimney. I'll see if I can find that well." As Winston searched, he talked over his shoulder. "If there were still hostile Indians in the area, an early builder would put his house right over his well. Indians had a bad habit of poisoning those early water supplies."

"Now we do it ourselves."

"I guess in a way you're right. Here it is," said Winston.

In a far corner of the basement, Winston found a low cistern made of fieldstones. The opening was protected by a circular wooden cover. Lifting the cover, Winston shone his light down the hole. "It still has water in it. Doesn't look too tasty, though. I wouldn't want to use it."

"I wouldn't want any of the kids to find it, either," said Lucille. "Maybe I should have it filled in."

"Don't do that. These wells are really rare. You could have Richie provide it with a more secure cover. I bet he'd love to see this."

Winston passed his light over the foundation wall next to the well.

"This corner here could easily be from that original dwelling and added to when they built the Georgian structure. I can't tell but a good mason, maybe even Richie, would know where and if the old and new were bonded here someplace. I remember the land grant was issued in 1743, so that first house was built around that time."

"Two hundred and fifty-one years," stated Lucille. "That's a long time ago."

"A long time," agreed Winston. "There's a bricked-up passageway over here. Probably was a root cellar at one time or a way to the outside. When they rebuilt it would have been directly under the east wing. I would guess they just filled it in and bricked it over."

"Perhaps it was for runaway slaves?" Lucille's voice was hopeful.

"I doubt that. Everyone wants to think that their ancestors were abolitionists and hid slaves. The truth is, not many slaves, if any, were ferried through this part of Dutchess County."

"Oh. Well . . ."

Winston rejoined Lucille under the light bulb. The two stood in silence as he plucked cobwebs from his hair. Winston could see that Lucille had come down to discuss more than old wells. She had that expectant look she got when she was anxious about something.

"So," said Winston, "what's on the agenda for today? Spelunking?"

Lucille smiled. "No. I came down to apologize for my mood last night."

"No need," said Winston.

"Well, no, I think I should explain. I've been thinking about what you asked last night . . ." Lucille paused, "about being forthright with certain people as to why you're here. The investigation, and all."

Winston waited as Lucille thought about her next statement.

"I . . . I got upset because—and you didn't say *who* you were going to talk to, I appreciated that, but for some reason I . . . I suddenly realized that it might be one or two of . . . of my own." Lucille hesitated. "Last night was the first time I'd ever . . . even considered the possibility that—"

Lucille stopped. Winston waited.

"It upset me," continued Lucille. "I need reassurance right now, from you, that none of the children are suspected of . . . you know."

And what if they are? thought Winston. How do you tell someone you like that her children might have murdered their own father? You don't. You lie.

"I was thinking of Miles and Sam, Lucille. Of Richie Baire."

Lucille visibly deflated. Winston had realized that she was tense but he hadn't realized *how* tense. He had to restrain himself from hugging her.

"Even that prospect is unsettling," said Winston, his voice barely above a whisper.

The two stood once again in silence, each in their own thoughts, the cold and damp closing in around them. They could have been anywhere, a basement in East Harlem or in East Podunk. He'd been in many of these basements, realized Winston, and they all had that moist closeness, that dirt smell, the odor of the grave. Above: the skyscraper, the farmhouse, the elegant mansion; below: the dark, the decay, the unblinking worm. Winston shuddered.

Lucille broke the silence. "You should do whatever you think is necessary, Winston. Finding Clement's killer is the important thing. The only thing."

"Señora?"

Juanita spoke from the top of the stairs but her voice could have been miles away. It took a second for Winston and Lucille to come back to the reality of where they stood.

"Señora?" repeated Juanita.

"Yes?" answered Lucille.

"It's the phone, señora. Mr. Wiggins for Mr. Wyc."

"Ah yes," said Winston. "I left a message for him to call me." He touched Lucille on the arm. "Are you okay?"

"Yes, I'm fine."

"Excuse me."

It was with some relief that Winston ascended the basement steps. He took the call in the study.

"Mr. Wiggins? How are you?"

"Biff, please, and I'm fine, Winston. You called?"

"Yes. I wanted to ask you several things. Do you have a moment?"

"Fire away," said Biff.

"First. Before Mr. Corbally died, did he call you to relay anything important? Anything concerning the project?"

"Let me see. That was a Saturday . . . I'm looking in my appointment book, Winston. Yes, he called the day before but I was out. My secretary wrote it in. Whether it was important or not I couldn't say."

"I see." Winston was disappointed.

"I took off early that Friday to play golf. I would have called him Monday, but well . . . that was impossible, wasn't it? What was important?"

Winston explained.

"Goodness," said Biff. "No, I'm sorry to say, I didn't talk to him. You had something else?"

"When your office did its investigation of Miles Northingham, did it also do one on Sam Harris?"

"Why yes, we did."

"How was Sam's slate? Clean or dirty?"

191

"Let me remember." Biff was quiet for a moment. "Nothing that I can recall, really. He'd gotten a divorce recently. I remember that. I don't remember the particulars."

A divorce, thought Winston. Did Sam have money problems?

"Anything else?" asked Biff.

"No. That's it. Oh." Winston smiled into the phone. "How's *my* slate doing?"

"I beg your pardon." There was a pause and Biff chuckled. "From what I understand, it's quite presentable."

"Gosh," moaned Winston. "Nothing?"

"You realize it's not personal, Winston. An ounce of prevention, as they say. Call me anytime."

Click.

"So how are we doing?" Cybil stood in the doorway of the study, her hands held behind her. "Mind if I come in?"

"Not at all," said Winston. He stood to greet her. "How's the condiment business?"

"Gordon's Hot and Heavy appears to be a hit. With Gordon anyway. I was over to check on Mom and thought I'd peek in."

"How is Lucille?" Winston hadn't seen her since an hour before in the basement. She had gone to her room while he was on the phone with Biff.

"Okay, I think. She goes up and down."

"That's understandable. Have a seat."

"Thanks. Just for a minute. I know you're busy."

Winston was surprised at how glad he was to see her. "Stay as long as you like. I, eh, I like the company."

Cybil pulled a chair over next to him. "I keep wondering what it is you architectural historians do."

"Actually, this is a very small part of our job description." Winston smiled. "But it's the fun part."

Using both hands, Cybil swept her hair over and behind her ears. Leaning forward, with her elbows on her knees, she mugged an overly earnest expression.

"I said fun." Winston laughed. "You can relax."

"Okay." Cybil settled back in the chair. "I'm relaxed."

"Well, first of all, I've never seen such family records. Your ancestors saved everything." Winston lifted some papers off the desk. "At the moment I'm going over all the bills for the building of this house, the surveys, the bank stuff. Your grandfather even kept newspaper clippings from the local paper. That's over here." Winston pulled a file drawer open. He took out a folder. "Look at this headline. August 1927. TROTSKY BANISHED TO SIBERIA. And on the back a picture of your house being built."

"That's amazing. I never knew this stuff was here." Cybil began fingering the file. "Oh look. Here's a picture of Uncle Carl in the paper." Cybil laughed. "I don't believe it. He'd just won a turkey shoot." She showed the picture to Winston. "He looks no more than eighteen years old."

"Maybe he challenged the turkey to a duel," smiled Winston.

"I'll have to ask him about it," laughed Cybil.

"Now, usually the researching of a house is a game of hide-and-seek. Researchers do what they call a title chain, that is, they try to follow the house back through title. Who was the last to own the house and who they bought it from." Winston lifted a deed from a file. "Sometimes, like here, there's a 'same premises conveyed by' clause which is very helpful, for it tells you who sold the property to the sellers. This must've been the lake property. It describes the lake and several houses. Are they still there?"

Cybil looked at the deed. "One is. It's where Sackett lives."

"Oh yeah? Where's that?" asked Winston.

"We went right by the drive on the way to the picnic. It's on the right just as you leave the main road. It was an old tenant house." Cybil stared at the deed. "I wonder where the other was located."

"An old survey or tax map at the courthouse might have it indicated. Then you could look for the foundations."

"This *is* fun." Cybil rummaged through another file. "So how's the chain going?"

"I usually have to spend a couple of days searching through old deed indices but, like I said, most of it's here. Makes my job a lot easier."

"What's this mean, 'fee simple'?" Cybil held a paper up to Winston.

"That means the property is being transferred free of any and all conditions. That the title is clear. Now on this deed, dated 1838 . . ." Winston pulled out another document, "there is a condition stated. If Jedidiah Brooke let William Corbally's horses graze his land, then he had lifetime easement rights to some well or other. Here old Will was selling land to Jedidiah but he must have kept the water rights. I've seen old deeds that stated a certain person could keep using the property as a shortcut. The buyer had agreed to let that person continue crossing the land. You don't see that much anymore."

"I bet."

"Some things I'll have to follow up in the county clerk's office but not much. I've asked your mother to find me any old letters she might know of. And photographs."

"You get paid for this?"

Winston nodded happily.

"I mean, it's more fun than stuffing mason jars. Whatever got you started on architectural history?"

"My mother was a maid. She worked for many years on Fifth Avenue, in the seventies. Before I started school and later, on holidays, I would have to go with her to work. I'd sit in the kitchen and wait until she was done. Occasionally, the cook would let me help stir something but most of the time I'd just sit and read or color. But during my mother's lunch break, she would take me outside and we would walk up and down the side streets. That's where a famous doctor lives, she'd say, or some well-known lawyer. I'd get the work-hard-and-someday speech every time. She'd stop and gaze up at some ornate brownstone and imagine her little Winston living there. While she fantasized, I'd be fascinated by the architecture. I'd memorize every detail and when we were back in Brooklyn I'd draw them, imagining them on our simple row house. Little did Mom know that she was introducing me to the very things that would later capture my imagination and take me away from her dreams of my entering the professional life. It's an irony that has escaped her so far."

"Do you see your mother and father much?"

"Not as much as I should, probably. I used to see them more but . . ." Winston shrugged.

"I don't have *that* problem," said Cybil. "I've never ventured very far from the nest."

"I haven't either, actually. Manhattan is not all that far from Brooklyn."

"And how about your family? Are they all nuts, too?"

"I think every family has a member or two with a rung missing," said Winston.

"That's what they say."

Standing, Cybil moved over to the French doors.

"It is hard to imagine one nuttier than this," she said with a sigh. "Look at Inclement out there."

"I'm having lunch with Inclement today," said Winston. "I've been invited down to see the cottage."

Cybil didn't appear to hear him. "Croquet and art and George. And Sackett. The make-believe priest. Damn, Winston, there's more than one rung missing here. Myself included." Cybil laid her cheek against the glass. "There they all are, running around, not doing a thing . . . and Father. It's all so sad. So damn sad. Excuse me."

Suddenly, Cybil was out the door. By the time Winston got up from the desk and reached the outside she was gone. The patio and the croquet court were strangely empty, quiet. Mallets and balls were neatly stacked by the gazebo. Had Cybil actually seen her brother? At the far end of the lawn, Winston could see Lucille standing under the wisteria, looking out over the meadow, toward the barns. For an uncomfortable moment, he had the eerie feeling of being trapped in a Chekhov play.

CHAPTER
27

Clement Jr. and his friend George lived in the old corncrib. The two men could have lived in any of the old tenant houses still standing on the estate but Clement had liked the shape of the corncrib. The side walls slanted considerably so that the structure, from the front, looked like an upside-down, truncated pyramid or a funnel, depending on whom you asked. It was sixteen feet high and thirty-two feet long, twenty-four feet across at the eave line and sixteen feet, six inches at the foundation. Renovation had been costly, but in the end there had stood a charming board-and-batten cottage with a kitchen addition, two large picture windows and a cedar shakes roof. Lucille had upset Clement at the time by remarking that the house had an "elfin" quality. Clement Sr. had further exacerbated the situation by saying there was a reason for that: it housed fairies. Clement and his father didn't speak for nearly a month. It was with great effort and tact that Lucille had finally managed to mend feelings.

The first floor of the crib was an open space, one end having the kitchen addition and a small living room. The rest of the space was Clement's studio. Upstairs was a large bedroom with bath and a smaller guest room. Beneath the window facing the garden, George had placed his desk. From here he toiled over his book on Irish history. In all it was very comfortable and very private. Perfect for two people who preferred being alone.

Clement had dressed for lunch in a pair of tan linen slacks

197

(Clement preferred the word "slacks"), a white dress shirt and woven Italian loafers, no socks. He stood in the kitchen looking over the pâté and bread and timing a pot of steeping wild blackberry tea. A second past two and a half minutes and the tea was undrinkable, according to George. In the refrigerator, a curried chicken salad was cooling. Glancing out the window, Clement checked to see if George was cleaning the glass-top table. Once in the garden, George had a habit of finding a million things to do other than what he was asked. Sure enough, there he was pulling weeds from under the lavender. Hopefully, the table was clean. Nothing could ruin a pleasant lunch more than a gift or two from the resident blue jay.

Removing the tea bags, Clement wandered into his studio. Next to the north window hung strips of colored paper. He would use one of the colors in a future project. While appraising the strips, he noticed some movement in the bushes. A little head popped up and then disappeared. At that moment George came back into the house.

"Don't look now," said Clement, "but we're under surveillance." George joined him at the window.

"Merrill's little marauders?" he asked.

"Marauder," corrected Clement. "I saw only one. Billy, I think."

"I see him all the time," said George, "from my window upstairs. Sneaking through the bushes, spying."

Clement tsked. "I really should talk to Cybil."

"I can remember soldiering as a boy. Part of the male development."

"Oh, I couldn't agree more," said Clement, rapping on the window. "Father once yelled at me for stomping around in Mom's housecoat. Said I should play with soldiers like my brother. I told him I *was* soldiering. That *I* was a *WAC*."

George laughed. "That must've made his day." The two stared out the window. "And now your father's gone," added George.

"Yes."

"But you . . ." George added a slight edge to his voice, ". . . you follow along in his footsteps. I really can't believe you want to be a trustee. You were so against the whole thing. At least, I thought you were."

"I was against working with *him*. Good lord, that would have been deadly. I mean, I did the croquet thing for all those years hoping to get some attention. Look what good that did me."

"But what about the money, not to mention the time involved? You're doing too much: the croquet, the art and now a trustee for . . . for this project. It doesn't make sense."

"Oh, Georgie, relax. Get off your high horse."

"I am not on any horses." Smiling, George tried a different approach. "I'm worried about you. Aren't I allowed to do that anymore?"

"Wellll, to be quite honest, I'm getting a bit tired of the mother act. I *have* a mother, George." Turning his back on George, Clement stared back out the window.

George turned bright red. It was with great effort that he kept himself from exploding with anger. He knew the consequences. The tense, silent evening to come. The hurt looks. The stupid reconciliation.

Slowly, George spoke. "I thought you wanted to be financially independent again, Clemmy. If this village thing went away, it could happen, you know."

Clement turned. "That's not necessarily so, George. The money is already committed, I'm afraid. I think it's better to be in a position to make sure it doesn't go away."

George went to argue but decided not to. There was company coming. He turned and headed into the kitchen. Clement followed.

"Did you cut up the fruit?" asked George.

"It's in the frig. Blue bowl."

Opening the refrigerator, Clement took out the bowl and laid it on the counter. He also selected a bottle of sauvignon blanc.

"The fruit should sit out," stated George. "It's not good ice cold."

"You're the boss," said Clement.

George gave Clement a look of don't-start. "Please, let's not argue. We have a guest coming, Clemmy. It's not good if the host is colder than the fruit salad."

"Maybe you should brush off your knees then, George. You got them dirty yanking weeds." While taking down some wineglasses, Clement looked out the kitchen window for spies. "Maybe we should invest in some blinds. You don't think our little friend is out there at night, do you?"

George had moved out into the studio. "I can't hear you," he called.

"I said," Clement called back, "that we should . . ."

A knock on the door.

"There's our guest," said Clement, coming into the studio.

"Or maybe it's Billy," said George.

Clement spoke over his shoulder as he headed for the door. "Are we all smiles?"

"Sure. It's your world."

"Really, George, you're becoming a bore." Clement threw open the door. "Winston. Thanks for coming. You *are* a savior. George and I were just at each other's throats."

Winston smiled. "No blood, I hope."

"Heavens no. I hate blood. Come in."

Winston followed Clement into the cottage. He nodded at George. "Hi, George. You know, I think there's someone out behind the house."

"Cybil's Billy," said George.

"We use him to scare away the squirrels," added Clement. "Cheaper than a dog and we don't have to pet him. What do you think of the cottage?"

"Quite charming. They once stored corn here?" asked Winston.

"When Longmeadow was a cow farm," answered Clement.

"Jerseys," said George.

"I beg your pardon," said Winston.

"That's a type of cow," explained Clement. "My great-grandfather raised Jersey cows. How about a little tour?"

As Clement showed Winston around the cottage, George set the garden table.

"We added the kitchen, of course, and the upstairs bath. And the fireplace. Watch your head on that beam. They had to lift the whole thing up to pour a foundation. That took time."

The two men went upstairs.

"Master bedroom." Clement pointed to his left. "And the guest room on the right. It doubles as George's exercise room." Clement lowered his voice. "Being short, he's into lifting weights. It's an image thing."

"Very cozy," said Winston. "I envy you this privacy."

"Sometimes it can be too cozy. By the end of winter, it feels like a shoe box."

"Ready!" George called up from the foot of the stairs.

"Shall we eat?" asked Clement.

Set in the center of the luxuriant garden, in a small area of sunken bluestones, stood a wrought-iron table elaborately detailed with metal leaves and vines. In keeping with the floral surroundings, the bright colors of a Fiesta Ware set floated like large flowers on its glass top. The heart-shaped metal chairs had been made comfortable with cushions of green leather.

As the men sat, Billy could be heard sneaking away.

"The boy really must work on his skulking," said Clement.

"We should have invited him for lunch," added George as he rationed out portions of pâté and cheese onto small yellow plates.

"We'll leave him some food when we're done," said Clement. "I'm sure he'd rather sneak up and liberate it."

Everyone laughed. Clement swirled the wine around in its ice bucket and then filled each glass. He sliced the baguette.

"So," said Clement, "how's our history looking? Anything you can't write about?"

Winston could only think of the most recent scandal. "Not yet."

"What a boring book it must be," sighed Clement.

"I'm sure Winston will make it interesting." There was a bit of admonishment in George's remark.

"Oh, I didn't mean to imply that he wouldn't," added Clement quickly. "I was just hoping he'd dig up something to explain why we're all such nuts."

Cybil had used the same word, thought Winston. Nuts. "This garden is amazing," said Winston, admiring a spiked blue flower next to his chair.

"That's a *Veronica spicata,* or 'Blue Peter'," informed George. "I wanted to match it with dianthus, but no, we had to go with the spiderwort."

"It's much better." Clement smiled over at George. "That royal blue makes an excellent complement." Before George could offer a rebuttal, Clement turned to Winston. "How's it up there in the big house with Mother? Is she okay? She always seems to be putting on some sort of front when I see her. I worry."

"I think she's doing all right," answered Winston. "It's going to take a while for her to get over the death of your father."

"I know." For a second, Clement's face softened. But the smile returned quickly.

"Eh, more wine?" asked George.

"No thanks," said Winston. "This pâté is excellent."

"It's from the Buddha and the Boar in the village. Here, Clement seems to be skimping on the Brie."

It's time to add a little spice to the hors d'oeuvres, thought Winston. "I was wondering," he said to Clement. "Your father's death. I have some questions about it."

"Oh." Clement was surprised. "What questions?"

"This is between you and me, and George, of course, but I've been thinking about his death and the more I think about it—" Winston stopped. "No, it's silly. I apologize."

"What's silly?" asked Clement.

"Well, this accident business. I have a problem with that."
That certainly caught their attention, thought Winston.

George leaned toward Winston. "What in the world do you mean?"

Winston watched their faces. "Well . . . I don't think he fell." Winston let that sink in. "I don't think your father could have gotten up into the hayloft. Not by himself."

"But—" George went to speak but stopped. He shook his head.

"Then how did he—?" Clement's mouth formed a perfect little *o*. "You're not implying that he was—"

"Murdered?" George finished the sentence for Clement.

"I just think there're some unanswered questions, that's all," said Winston. Clement and George stared at their food.

George looked up at Winston. "You're kidding, aren't you? I mean, what unanswered questions? What do you think happened?"

Winston looked over at Clement.

"Please continue," said Clement, more intrigued than convinced.

"I think your father upset somebody and they followed him down to the barn. There was either a struggle or . . . or something was done intentionally. I don't know. And at the moment it's *just* a theory. I hope that's understood."

"But what a theory," marveled Clement.

"Who would be that upset?" asked George.

"I don't know that, either," said Winston.

George gave out a loud sigh of relief. "You *are* kidding."

"I don't think it's very funny," stated Clement.

"I'm not being funny." Winston sat back. "Neither of you happened to see him, your father, with anyone before he went down to the barn?"

"I wasn't at the party," said Clement, who was eyeing Winston with some apprehension. "I was mad at Sackett and wasn't up for his particular brand of agitation. I'm of no help. George was there. Until he got wet."

"You know," said George, deep in remembering. "I saw that man, Miles Northingham, wandering around in the woods down here. The man with the beard."

"When was that?" asked Winston.

"I . . ." George hesitated. "After I fell in the pool, I believe. I came back to the cottage to change."

"Did he see you?" asked Winston.

George nodded slowly. "I believe he did."

"Miles Northingham," said Clement. "He's a perfectly horrid man but you don't think—"

Winston realized he'd better stop the conjecture now. "I'm sorry. I've obviously opened a can of worms here without meaning to. It's just that . . . well, I can't seem to get the thought out of my head that something else happened in that barn." Shifting in his seat, Winston changed his tone from curious to self-reproaching. "But I'm being nuts myself. I've heard of people doing this before. Sometimes it's difficult to accept the fact that someone you like has gone. I really don't want people going around accusing others of murder. That might prove destructive for all concerned."

"Oh, I agree completely," said Clement. "This is strictly between us three."

I bet, thought Winston.

A phone rang in the cottage.

"I'll get it," said Clement. He stood up and then practically ran into the cottage.

Winston and George talked about flowers until Clement returned. Neither man bothered to pursue the question of murder. Sitting back down, Clement made a production of snapping his linen napkin and placing it on his knee.

"That was Mother," he said. "We've been invited up to the house tonight for cocktails and a cold buffet."

"How nice," said George.

"Guess who's coming?" Clement looked at each man. When they didn't guess, he said, "Miles Northingham and his sidekick."

"What?" said George.

"It's true. It seems they called and said they had changed their minds and were delighted that I wanted to be a trustee. That they welcomed the idea and wouldn't fight it." Clement's smile was one of triumph.

Winston's smile was more to himself. What could possibly have changed their minds? As if he didn't know.

Clement continued. "And so Mother invited them over. I think that's rather cavalier of her. Don't you?"

"But that man's involved," said George. "Northingham."

Everyone was suddenly pulled back to the earlier conversation, the earlier conjecture.

Before anyone could add comment, George stood. "I'll get the chicken and the salad. I take it everyone's still hungry?"

Everyone nodded silently that he was.

CHAPTER
28

Richie Baire held the chisel up to the light to check its edge. The angle looked good. Richie chuckled. A man could skin an ornery historian with that edge. Twenty years ago when Richie had apprenticed in Boston, the old guys would come into the shop early each morning *before* work and sharpen their saws and chisels. They'd do the saws with a set and a file. The chisels and planes with a medium block and a hard Arkansas stone. A little oil and a delicate touch. Those saws and chisels had been treated like old friends and the men had talked to them, held them as they might have dying birds.

Putting down the chisel, Richie moved over to the new post lathe. Leaning against the lathe, he peered back at the shop. It had taken eight months and one hell of a lot of work, but he had restored an old barn into a first-class shop equipped to reproduce anything the building project might need from cutting old molding profiles to forging hardware, from hand-splitting shingles to milling rough lumber. He had put the shop together with considerable intelligence, insight and affection. It sat silently waiting, gleaming and oiled, ready for work to start.

But that work was now in question. Richie had talked to the lawyer Wiggins about his future and the man seemed to think it was fairly secure but he could make no promises. Just like a lawyer not to commit. Richie also didn't like what he was hearing about expansion and amusements. The only person who seemed to care about the village was Sam Harris. Sam and Richie

206

had the same thoughts about the past, about the project and he knew *they* could work together. But Northingham needed to be watched. And that other guy, Wyc. Richie wasn't sure about him, either. Snooping around the barn. Where was he coming from?

Richie's thoughts were interrupted by a soft knock on the door.

"Come in," he called.

The lanky frame of Sam Harris entered the room. "Hi, Richie."

"Hi, Sam. What's up?"

"Not much. Just looking for some peace and quiet. You busy?"

"Nah. Pushing dust around. For quiet, you sure picked the right spot. Want some tea?"

"I'd love some."

As Richie went into his office to prepare the tea, Sam wandered among the machinery of the shop, touching this, inspecting that. He didn't know a thing about machines but he liked the way they looked and smelled and what they produced.

"Earl Grey okay?" Richie called from the other room.

"Perfect."

Richie came back into the room. "Like that planer? It's an old Walker Turner. Picked it up at Bass in New Jersey. Their used-machinery warehouse. If you know what you're looking for you can get some good deals there."

"It's a beauty. Looks like a big metal animal crouched to strike," observed Sam.

"Yeah, it has that look to it. I had an instructor once, up in Boston, who taught me to think of machines as wild animals. You didn't have to be afraid of them but you'd better have lots of respect or they might bite you."

Sam laughed. He picked up an axelike tool lying on a workbench. "What in the world is this?"

"Isn't that neat? That's an old gutter adze. Bought it at some antique place out on Route 7. You can tell it's old because it's poll-less and the haft doesn't have a curve."

207

"The what?"

"Poll-less means it has a flat back. Cows are called polled when they have their horns cut off. And the haft is the handle. The old-timers would use it like this."

Spreading his legs, Richie pretended to straddle a length of wood.

"See how the blade is cupped? They'd trim a log to a certain width and depth, and then they'd hollow it out with this to make a gutter that they could attach to the eave."

"I've seen gutters that were actually cut from the eave of the house," said Sam.

"That's right. Big mothers. Only problem was, once they started to rot you'd have to replace the whole eave. I'll get the tea."

When Richie returned, the two stood in silence for a minute, sipping their tea, enjoying the company.

Richie spoke. "Anything new on the project?"

"Clement Jr. is to be a trustee."

Richie looked surprised.

"It turns out," said Sam, "that the family lawyer, Wiggins, was going to petition the court. Our lawyers suggested we not fight it. It would only hold things up and accepting Clement could be a first step in placating the family. Sackett's not the only one unhappy with the project."

"But the project *is* going forward?" asked Richie.

"The village will be built." By the tone of Sam's voice, there was no doubt as to his resolve.

Richie's chuckle was mildly derisive. "I hear Clement wants to turn the village into an amusement park. What's that all about?"

"Clement wants a little amusement area for the kids."

"That's insane."

"It's a moot point," said Sam. "The village isn't open to the public. Depending on the number of employees, it's possible we could incorporate the idea into some sort of day-care facility."

Richie's brow furrowed. "Day care. That's a lot of employees."

Sam moved away. "I'm talking way down the line, of course."
Richie followed. "You're not buying into this big studio
idea of Miles's, are you? I thought you were against that."

"I . . . I don't think we can ignore the concept completely.
We start out with the summer shows and who knows, in a
few years we might expand. I say 'might.' " Sam could see
that Richie wasn't happy with the thought of expansion.

"Miles thinks he's going to be the next Ted Turner," scoffed
Richie. "THC he calls it. The History Channel. Miles's idea
of a show would be *Alf, the Alien Historian.*" Richie was quiet
for a moment. "I think he's jeopardizing the project. Correct
me if I'm wrong, but the trust says nothing about a history
channel. It might be the type of thing the Corballys could use
to trash the whole venture."

"I don't think so." Sam shook off the suggestion.

"How'd you ever get teamed up with that guy?" asked Richie.

"Some things seem like a good idea at the time," replied Sam.

"I hear that." Richie smacked the top of the table saw.
"Damn! You go to all this trouble and some ass like Miles
comes along. Famous Mr. Knows-Nothing."

"It will be okay, Richie."

"Yeah? Don't count on it."

There was a knock on the door.

"Come in," shouted Richie.

The door was opened by George. "Are you busy?"

"Not at all, George. Come in." Richie took a second to
calm himself. "How you been?"

"Okay." George nodded to Sam.

"I finished that piece for you," said Richie. He headed for
the back of the shop. He returned with what appeared to be a
four-foot walking stick that had a helix design running from
top to bottom, much like a screw thread. The foot had a brass
cap and the top had been carved to resemble a croquet ball.
He handed it to George.

Holding it in both hands, George admired the helix. "This
is beautiful, Richie. Clement's going to be so surprised."

Richie explained to Sam. "George had asked me to make a walking cane for Clement."

"It's a gift for this weekend," added George. "He's been in these moods since his father's death. I thought it might cheer him in time for the tournament."

"That's nice," said Sam.

"And it gives me something to do," said Richie. His expression darkened. "Hey, George, you don't happen to know about some things missing from the barn, do you?"

"No," answered George.

"Missing?" asked Sam.

"Yeah, some pieces have disappeared. And not small things, either. A window and quite a bit of molding. I noticed it on Monday."

"That's not good." Sam frowned. "Any idea who?"

"It might be someone coming in from the road. I was thinking of—"

Without knocking, Miles Northingham came bustling into the shop. He eyed the small gathering. "Well, well, boys having a little meeting."

"Not really," answered Sam. "We were talking machines."

"And since when did you start to like machines?" asked Miles. "You like machines, Georgie?"

George just stared back. Miles gave him a half smile.

"Not talking, hey? Why don't you beat it, shorty. I need to talk to the men." Miles put emphasis on the last word.

For a second, George's face reddened, the muscles taut. He didn't move.

Smiling, Miles moved away. He picked up the gutter adze. "What's this?"

"That's called a gutter adze." Sam's voice was a little too loud. He cleared his throat. "For making gutters," he added.

"And that's why it's called a gutter adze. Very clever." Miles's tone was only slightly sarcastic. "You like gutters?" Miles asked George. Miles grinned like a big bear.

"Miles, that's enough," said Sam. "If you—"

210

George interrupted. "That's okay. I consider the source."

"The source, hey?" Miles picked up the adze. "Maybe we'll carve a gutter right in your tiny, little melon head, heh pal." Miles's tone was playful, ironic. He smiled at everyone to show that he was just kidding.

Without another word, George turned and left the shop.

Sam was upset. "What in the hell was that all about? George is considered part of the family around here. It's stupid to antagonize him."

"He bugs me. And you want to know something, you bug me." Seeing Sam's expression, Miles changed his tone. "Hey, it's okay. Don't get that worried look. Nothing personal." Miles began to wander through the shop. He talked as he inspected machines, picked up a few tools. "I'll tell you what's wrong with me. I'm not real happy with the idea of cocktails at the big house." Miles put up his hand to stop Sam from interrupting. "I know, I know, it's all for the peace effort. But to tell you the truth, I'm not sure we need a peace effort. Legally, we're tight. We have nothing to worry about. I say we stay away from this family. The old lady, the preacher wannabe, the pervert, they're all weird. Inbreeding or something. It happened to the kings and queens of Europe. *They* got weird after a while. Who knows what this family is going to try and do? I wouldn't turn my back on any one of them." Back at the front of the shop, Miles stopped to address Sam and Richie directly. "Listen, you two. The Corballys don't have a leg to stand on. We do the trustee thing, fine. Sam and I can outvote him on anything that comes up. But we have to stick together. We have backers who don't want to hear or see dissension in the ranks. They have to think everything is cozy. Understand? A united front."

"Who are these backers?" asked Richie.

"Visionaries, like ourselves." Lowering his voice, Miles spoke in an earnest, almost reverent tone. "Men who want to commit money and energy to an idea they believe in. We're the seeds, us and this village. These men will provide the water, the fertilizer to make things grow. From little acorns . . . you know the saying."

Sam had to look away. Miles was unbelievable. The only fertilizer being provided around here was by him. If Miles had any brain at all, he wouldn't be mentioning any of this to Richie. Richie still thought in the same terms the old man had, small and educational. If Miles wanted a united front, he'd better be quiet.

"Mr. Corbally left plenty of money for this project," said Richie. "I don't like this talk about backers. And I'm not so sure about this TV stuff, either."

Miles's smile was generous, patronizing. "That's too bad. TV's the thing now, the power. You might want to reconsider. There're an awful lot of carpenters out there, cowboy."

"Don't call me cowboy." Richie was tense, his gray eyes hard.

Miles and Richie stared at each other.

"Please," said Sam. "Is this necessary?"

Miles forced a smile. "What? Is it something I said, something I did? I could be wrong but I feel some hostility here." He laughed.

"There's no hostility," said Sam quickly. He shook his head at Richie as if to say don't-push-it.

"Oh no?" Miles stopped smiling. "Well, that's good. So what were we talking about before I so rudely interrupted? Machines was it?" Miles ran his hand along the unisaw. "You've got some nice toys here, cowboy."

Richie glared. "You know about machines?"

"Nah. Cars. I know cars." Large machinery made Miles jumpy. The noise bothered him. That and the image of his sleeve or shirttail getting caught. Being dragged into one of these metal beasts horrified him. "I stay away from machines."

Reaching down, Richie threw the switch on the post lathe. The shop was instantly filled with a loud guttural rumble. Miles backed away. Richie ran his hand dangerously close to

212

the rotating head. The spinning metal threw flicks of light across his hand. He turned it off. "I like the way this feels. This is my idea of power."

"Yeah, that's great," said Miles. The whine of the lathe lingered in the air between them. "Sam, we gotta go."

Sam shrugged at Richie. "Sure."

Pausing at the door, Miles turned back to Richie. "I'd watch my hands if I was you. Woodworker wouldn't be much good without them."

The two men stared at each other. A united front seemed a long way off.

Winston sat in the study, the history of Longmeadow untouched before him on the desk. His thoughts were on lunch. Thank goodness Inclement had received his good news about the trusteeship. Lunch might have been rough going had that not happened. Bringing up his doubts about Mr. Corbally had proven vaguely successful in terms of information. George had seen Miles wandering about in the woods. Of course, Winston already knew that Miles had been down there, but it did place him, timewise, closer to Mr. Corbally's fatal fall.

Winston felt sleepy. Big lunches always did that to him. Two glasses of wine at noon and he spent the rest of the afternoon yawning. He didn't need to sit behind a desk right now. Maybe this would be a good time to visit Sackett and express his doubts to him, before the "secret" spread in his direction. It would be interesting to see what the would-be priest considered home.

As Cybil had said, Sackett's driveway was just off the main road. The dirt drive was long, rutted and ill-cared-for. Winston was beginning to worry about his old wagon when the house appeared around a tight bend. Sackett's BMW was not in evidence. Parking by the porch, Winston surveyed his surroundings. The house was a small saltbox, almost a house in miniature, but it was delightful in its simplicity and setting. Unlike the driveway, the house was obviously attended to quite carefully, with a new coat of red paint, a new shingled roof and a generous garden of perennials. In contrast to his brother's garden, Sackett's had the look of controlled anarchy. Plants pushed against one another, jostling for space and attention.

Upon reaching the front door, Winston knocked. He waited. Going to the back of the house, Winston checked to see if Sackett's car was parked in the rear. No car. He knocked on the back door. He didn't expect anyone but he wanted to make sure no one was there. An idea had formed in his mind and, since it could be considered illegal, he wanted no surprises.

Placing his hand on the doorknob, Winston counted to five and turned the knob. The back door was unlocked. Opening it, Winston called out Sackett's name. No answer. Standing in the kitchen, he called again. His voice in the empty house sounded odd to him. Was that the sound of anxiety? he wondered. Winston wandered through the rooms. He was looking for something and he thought he knew where to find it. Upstairs were two rooms. One was the bedroom, an austere little room with a narrow bed, a painted dresser and a low set of shelves. The other was the room Winston was seeking. It was Sackett's study. Over by the window was a simple desk made up of two wooden file cabinets with three pine boards laid across them. On the boards were an old typewriter, a telephone and some reference books. Along both walls were shelves heavy with books. A quick glance showed Winston that Sackett took his religious studies seriously. Or at least, he bought the books.

Winston inspected some papers on the desk. They appeared at a glance to be the beginnings of a novel. The first page was titled Chapter One and introduced a character who was in the middle of some life crisis. Winston put the papers down. Was this Sackett's secret ambition? To be a writer? Winston listened for noises. At this point, he felt really uncomfortable. His heart was pounding and all his senses seemed on some odd elevated level. It was as if he'd had too much coffee. Briefly, Winston wondered if burglars got the same rush. Was that part of the attraction? He heard a noise outside. Peering from the window, he could see nothing but the garden and his car.

Winston pulled open the desk drawers, one at a time. It was the bottom drawer on the right that held what Winston was looking for. A long minute passed as he gazed into the drawer. He picked up the phone and dialed.

"Simon, it's Winston."

"Hello, my friend. How are we?"

"Not so good. Look, Simon, I need some advice."

"What is it? You don't sound so great."

"Well . . . I've found the paper those notes were written on."

"What notes?" asked Simon.

"Those threatening notes that Mr. Corbally was receiving."

"My goodness, Winston. Where are you?"

CHAPTER
30

Winston watched Inclement and Miles from the edge of the patio. What an odd duo. Inclement in his white croquet outfit, Miles in his blue polyester pullover and tight designer jeans. Inclement's instructions to Miles on how to play the sport wove in and out of Winston's thoughts. Not that Winston wanted to hear them. His mind was full of what he had found at Sackett's and how he was going to deal with it. Simon had suggested he think about it overnight and agreed to come by in the morning to talk. They would have met this evening except for Lucille's little cocktail party. The timing wasn't right and obviously the problem could wait for one night.

"Place your feet parallel to each other just behind the ball," said Inclement. "Far enough apart so you can comfortably swing the mallet."

Bent at the waist, with legs spread, Miles could be seen taking a few tentative swings.

"Keep the swing even and straight," coached Clement.

"This mallet seems too short," complained Miles.

"It's not too short. Now, concentrate on the swing. Easy but firm. You need more control."

Winston turned to look at the others in attendance. Sackett stood alone over by the study doors watching them as if *they* intended on doing *him* harm. George and Lucille were conversing over the hors d'oeuvres and Sam stood near them, listening but not participating. For whatever reason, Miles and George had been giving each other hostile looks until Inclement had suggested, Winston had thought probably in desperation, teaching croquet to Miles. Strangely enough, Miles had accepted.

"Don't lift your head when you hit the ball. Never lift your head. I can't repeat that enough."

"So I've noticed," said Miles.

"And square the shoulders." Inclement took Miles by the shoulders and squared him.

"Maybe we could take a break. I could use another beer."

"In a minute," said Inclement. "I thought you wanted to learn croquet."

"I did. I do." Miles gave the ball a whack. It went through the wicket. "Hey, I did it. The damn ball behaved for once."

"It's not the ball, Miles."

"It's an odd sight, isn't it?" said Sam, who had come up next to Winston.

"I'm reminded of *Alice in Wonderland*," answered Winston.

Sam laughed. "I want to apologize about yesterday. Miles gets out of hand sometimes. I've learned it's easier to go with the flow."

"Forget it," said Winston. "Obviously, Miles had a change of heart concerning his croquet partner there."

"Miles isn't so bad. He's a big star and all, but he's one insecure guy. It makes him a control freak. If something gets explained more than once, he usually sees the light."

Sam the apologist, thought Winston. Was that part of the assistant's role? "Need another drink?" asked Winston.

"Sure. I'll come over with you."

The two joined Lucille at the food. Sackett and George were talking by the trellis. Something about the situation intrigued Winston. He couldn't think what, but something about the picture looked familiar.

"Line it up from both sides," instructed Inclement. "From here and on the other side of the wicket. Make a mental line on the grass. Actually, let's do this. Let's practice a Peel shot."

Miles was afraid to ask. "What's a Peel shot?"

"A Peel is when you use your ball to send a ball other than your own through a hoop. Here, try to strike my ball. Then for your croquet, do this."

Miles looked to see that no one on the patio was listening to them. Bending over his ball, he delivered his question in an offhand manner. "How much did your father tell you about the TV idea?"

"I remember something about it. It had to do with your show," said Inclement.

"That's right. What would you think about expanding that idea?" asked Miles.

"Expand?"

"Sure. Up to now Sammy and I have been thinking two, three shows a summer. Use the buildings as background, that sort of thing." Miles struck at the ball. It went wide. "Hmmmm. Lately, I've been thinking on a larger scale."

"You have?" Distracted, Inclement lined up the Peel.

"A television studio. Not a big one, a small one. Why do a couple of shows when we could do everything from right here?"

That got Inclement's attention. "Television studio?"

"I see it as broadcasting American history. The old buildings would be like a movie lot. Not only could we do restoration shows but historic movies. Get big stars involved. Right here at Longmeadow."

Inclement stopped playing. Miles continued.

"I know it sounds like a lot but not if it's done right, put in the right place. I see it as an opportunity that comes once in a lifetime."

"Movie stars?" That part of the idea intrigued Inclement. "I'll think about it."

"You do that," said Miles. "I think it's time for another beer." Without waiting for Inclement's objection, Miles dropped his mallet and headed back up to the patio.

Inclement watched him walk away. "That's okay," he said, frowning at Miles's retreating back, "you're dead on all the balls anyway."

"Sorry to hear that," said Miles over his shoulder.

Picking up Miles's mallet, Inclement placed both mallets upright against a wicket.

Inclement joined the others on the patio. Miles was describing his game to Sam.

"I did pretty well for my first time, didn't I, Clement?"

"Not bad, really," answered Inclement.

"I had to quit, though. What are you going to do when you're dead on all the balls?" Miles laughed at the thought.

"Rigor mortis," said Inclement.

"Yeah," said Miles, "the old rigor mortis."

"What did you say?" Winston, who had been avoiding the conversation by pretending to survey the food, turned at Inclement's statement.

"Rigor mortis," repeated Inclement. "It's a croquet term that *means* 'dead on all balls.' It's not a situation a croquet player wants to find himself in. It pretty much shuts you down, puts you out of the play."

Winston smiled back at Inclement. Those were the words written on William Laird's calling card. But why had Mr. Corbally written that on the card? Shut down. Dead on all balls.

"I hear there's a tournament here this weekend," said Sam. "Is that a big crowd?"

"Not that many," answered Inclement. "Fifteen players in all. As for spectators, I never know how many will show."

"I hope not many," said Lucille. "Last time it took a month to get the garden back in order. People we didn't even know were wandering about with my 'Perfume Delight' stuck in their lapel. It was horrid."

"That's a rose," explained Inclement. "And remember," he said laughing, "we ran out of food and some people got upset. As if we were *supposed* to feed them."

"Speaking of food," said Sam, "thank you for this delicious spread."

Lucille acknowledged his thank-you. She turned to

Winston. "I hope I'm not going to embarrass you, Winston, but I want you to clear something up for me. Juanita told me this morning that you ate mice as a child. Now where did she get that impression?"

"I don't know," said Winston. Thinking for a moment, he began to laugh. "I know. I told her my mother used to feed me bubble and squeak growing up."

Everyone laughed except Sackett and George, who were keeping their distance.

"What in the world is that?" asked Inclement.

"Cabbage and potatoes," explained Winston. "If mice were added, Mom never mentioned them."

Again, laughter.

"*What* in the *hell* is going on?!" Sackett shouted at them from the other side of the table. Everyone stopped and looked at him. "This does not make *any* sense. These people are the enemy!" He pointed at Sam and Miles. "How did they get in here? Where's the hollow horse?"

"Sackett." Lucille's voice was low and intense, her color high. "These people are *my* guests. If there's a problem, I strongly suggest we discuss it later."

Sackett gave his mother a belligerent look. "You don't get it. You just don't understand!" Sackett punched out each word.

"Maybe we should leave," suggested Sam.

"Why?" asked Miles. "We're here to mend fences. There is nothing going on that can't be . . ."

"SHUT UP!" yelled Sackett. "SHUT UP!"

Sackett's high voice bounced back and forth in the small enclosure of the patio. Everyone looked at Lucille and then quickly away.

Sackett threw his hands in the air. "This is insane," he said in a tense whisper. With that, he walked away, going over the barberry hedge and down onto the croquet court. He headed out across the lawn to the wisteria arbor.

Walking up to the barberry hedge, George turned to face

221

the others. "I agree with Sackett completely. I will not eat with these men."

"What are you doing, George?" asked Inclement.

"I'm going back to the cottage. You can stay if you *want* to." George's inflection implied that Inclement had better join him.

Inclement looked over at Lucille.

"I want you to stay, Clemmy," said Lucille. "This is important to me."

Inclement's tone was one of entreaty. "I'm sorry, George, but Mother wants . . ."

"I can hear perfectly well, thank you," said George. "I'll see you later." With a withering look of betrayal, he turned and raced after Sackett.

As if pulling a shade behind them, the sun set at that moment, sending long shadows over the house. Everyone watched in silence until the two had reached the end of the lawn, the dark shadow of the roof close at their heels.

Juanita appeared at the breakfast room door. "The buffet is ready, señora."

"Thank you, Juanita." Forcing a smile, Lucille turned to her guests. "Please, I hope you will stay and eat."

At that exact moment, Cybil came around the side of the house with her two sons. She stopped when she saw the small crowd on the patio.

"Sorry I'm late," she said. "Billy's game went longer than usual." She stared at the gathering. "What's going on? You all look like someone spiked the drinks with alum."

"Welcome to another episode of *The Days of Our Lives*," intoned Inclement. "I'm afraid, though, you've missed the best part."

The cocktail hour had been tense and unpleasant, but the buffet had started as a funeral. Thank goodness for Cybil, thought Winston. She refused to let the glum faces continue. Within half an hour, her high laugh and good spirits had cut through most of the gloom. At least people were pretending to enjoy themselves. Sam was being quite gracious, spending his time trying to make Lucille feel comfortable with the fact that he and Miles were there. Inclement tried to be humorous but he was obviously worried about George and kept glancing out the window. Once they had eaten, the kids had disappeared into the TV room. Miles ate.

"Sorry about yesterday." Cybil slipped her arm through Winston's. "I think I finally had my good cry about Father," she said. "It took me long enough."

That was the second apology Winston had received tonight. This one he cared about. "I came looking for you after you ran from the study but you had vanished. Poof."

"A witches' trick. Our way of getting out of a bad situation."

"Witches? Who could you be talking about?"

Smiling, Cybil lowered her voice. "This conciliatory dinner of Mom's isn't such a big hit, is it?"

"I'm afraid not," answered Winston. "Half of the guest list seems to have vanished."

"Did they go poof?" Cybil laughed.

Winston smiled. "There was a small popping sound."

"I know I shouldn't laugh," said Cybil, "but I've been through the alternative recently." Cybil looked over at Lucille. "Mom doesn't look so good."

"It's tough on her." But it's going to get a lot tougher, thought Winston.

Miles's voice rose above the others. ". . . that hard to believe," he was saying. "I'll get a wicket and a ball."

"I'll get it," said Inclement.

"No, no. I could use the fresh air." Stumbling to the French doors, Miles disappeared into the night.

"Where is he going?" asked Lucille.

"We were discussing the width of a wicket," answered Inclement. He sighed, obviously bored with the idea of pursuing the problem. "Miles thinks the ball and the opening are the same size. *I* think Miles has had too many beers."

"Anyone want coffee?" asked Lucille.

Everyone wanted coffee. Lucille went into the kitchen. The group made small talk until Juanita showed up with the silver service. Five minutes into coffee Sam went to the French doors.

"Where was this wicket?" he asked Inclement.

"Out on the court," was the answer. "Like I said," added Inclement, "Miles might have had one too many."

"Perhaps I should look for him," said Sam.

"Turn on the floods, Clemmy. Sam will need some light," advised Lucille. "Mr. Northingham is probably wandering around in the dark."

At the side of the door was a bank of light switches. Inclement flipped two. From the picture window the group watched as the great lawn was suddenly washed in pale light.

"My goodness," exclaimed Lucille. "What is Sackett doing?"

Out on the court Winston could see Sackett standing over the prone form of Miles Northingham. Hanging from his hand was a croquet mallet. He had turned to stare, blinking up at the sudden light.

"I *knew* Miles had had too much to drink," said Inclement. "He's passed out."

"I don't think so," said Winston, who was already heading out the door. "Something is terribly wrong."

CHAPTER
32

Lots of noise and colored lights are what you get when you call the police in the night. Winston stood staring out the French doors of the study at the commotion on the croquet court. Juanita and Lucille were bumping into each other in the kitchen, fixing everyone coffee. Cybil had taken the boys home. Inclement had disappeared into the darkness, apparently going back to the cottage to find George. He wasn't going to be happy when he saw his croquet court. Sam stood at the edge of the court looking shell-shocked. Winston could see Richie Baire haunting the far side of the excitement.

Captain Andrews, the area's homicide detective, had arrived half an hour earlier. Winston had watched him quiz his men at the scene and could now see him heading in the direction of the house. Noticing Winston as he stepped onto the patio, Andrews pointed a finger at him and then entered through the breakfast room door. A minute later he came into the study, a mug of coffee in his hand.

"I might have known you'd be involved," said Andrews gruffly. "How have you been?"

"I've been fine. At least this time I wasn't the one holding the mallet," said Winston. In a previous encounter with Andrews, Winston had had to convince the captain that he was not the prime suspect.

"That's a relief for all concerned." Andrews walked the room, taking it all in, talking to Winston in his gravelly monotone. The captain was of medium height and stocky. He had big hands and big facial features and moved as if he had nowhere to go and all the time to get there. He sipped at his coffee. "Unless, of course, you're that guy Sackett."

"I feel sorry for poor Sackett," said Winston.

"*Poor* Sackett?" echoed Andrews. "Not on any level from what I can see."

"He says he didn't do it," stated Winston.

Stopping, Andrews looked over at Winston, one eyebrow raised. "And you believe him? You know, it's strange. Thirty-two years in police work and never once has the killer said to me, 'Hey, I did it. It was me, officer, I slammed the guy with the mallet.' What do you *think* he's going to say?"

"I don't know. It's just that when I saw his face, when the light went on, he seemed so confused, so surprised."

"Oh yeah?" Andrews motioned for Winston to sit. "I thought our next meeting was to be for dinner or something."

"I thought you were going to retire."

"Who told you that?"

"You did."

Andrews looked at Winston as if Winston was crazy. "Enough chitchat. Tell me about what happened this evening."

Winston retraced the events of the cocktail party, the buffet and of Miles going out to find a wicket. As Winston talked, the captain took notes. Winston's own investigation kept nagging at him. What would be the right time to tell Andrews everything he knew and suspected? The captain wasn't going to be very happy when he found out what Winston had been up to.

". . . and Northingham was lying on the ground with his arm over his head like this . . ." Winston demonstrated. "And Sackett stood near him, maybe two feet from the man's feet."

"Holding a mallet?" prompted Andrews.

"He was holding the mallet," said Winston.

Andrews took a minute to pace and think about what Winston had told him. Stopping, he put his coffee mug down on the desk. "You're leaving something out."

"I am?" said Winston.

"You have that look on your face. I know that look. It says I'm not telling my friend, the police officer, everything."

Winston's laugh was one of release. "I do?"

Andrews stared at Winston for five seconds. "Okay, let's do this. It's late and I've got a lot to do. Lots of people to talk to. Why don't you think about what it is you're not leaving out and come see me in the morning. We've been through this before, Winston."

The last time Winston had taken on the cloak of amateur sleuth he had forgotten to mention a few important items to the captain.

"Late morning?" asked Winston.

Andrews's smile was not amused. "Eleven-thirty wouldn't be too early." With a disapproving shake of his head, Andrews went over and tapped lightly on the study door. Instantly, the door was opened by his aide, Sergeant Miller.

"Yeah?" asked Miller. He acknowledged Winston with a curt nod.

"Where's Corbally at?" asked Andrews.

"The front room. Officer Williams is with him."

"Bring him in here." Andrews turned to Winston. "Tomorrow. Now if you don't mind."

Outside the breakfast room door Winston bumped into Sam. For good reason, the man appeared dazed and distracted.

"You okay?" asked Winston.

"Not really. I'm still in the I-don't-believe-it stage. My mind refuses to focus on anything. The network is going to be very upset."

The network, thought Winston. Northingham has just been murdered and Sam is worried about the network?

"You want some tea or coffee?" asked Winston.

"Thanks, Lucille is fixing me some tea. I'd like to go back to the hotel but the police want to talk to me. This might easily be the worst night of my life."

Yeah, thought Winston, but not nearly as bad as it is for Miles Northingham.

CHAPTER 33

Winston had gone up to his room after talking to Sam. There had been too much noise and too many people running around. He had lain in bed listening to that noise slowly diminish to nothing. Sleep had been fretful and he had risen early. It was now seven-thirty the next morning and Winston was in the living room drawing a picture of the fireplace surround. He had no idea what had happened to the others or what they were doing this morning. If Lucille was up and about, he hadn't heard her. As for Sackett, Winston had no idea. He might have gone home or gone to jail.

As he drew, Winston thought about Miles. Why had Miles been killed? The man had been his prime suspect in the Corbally incident, and now that he was dead Winston was having to rethink the situation. Of course, it was possible there had been two separate murders, two separate killers. But Winston doubted that scenario. It was becoming more and more difficult for Winston to dismiss Sackett as the killer in both instances. In both cases, he had motive and access. And right now, he appeared to have been the author of those threatening notes.

"Señor?"

Winston jumped at the sound of Juanita's voice. He turned to see the cook standing in the doorway. "Yes, Juanita."

"There is coffee if you want."

"I'd love some, thanks." Rising from his chair, Winston joined Juanita at the door. He showed her the picture he'd drawn. "What do you think? A good likeness?"

Juanita took a moment to compare. "It is very good." The cook went back to the kitchen. The tone of her assessment suggested that the drawing might be okay but it certainly wouldn't stand up to a well-managed flan. Winston followed. He sat at the counter and Juanita handed him a cup of coffee.

"Thanks. What time did you finally get to bed last night?" asked Winston.

"Two o'clock. After Mrs. Corbally goes to bed. The police are here very late."

Winston watched as Juanita began kneading dough for biscuits. "Do you know what happened to Sackett?"

"Mr. Corbally left with the police, señor."

"Oh." That wasn't good. Lucille must have gone to bed extremely upset. "How is Mrs. Corbally?" asked Winston.

"I do not think she is well this morning."

Winston could see that the conversation was upsetting for

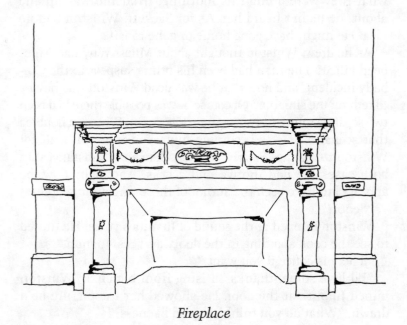

Fireplace

Juanita. She wouldn't look at him and kept her head slightly bowed. Finishing his coffee, he went into the study.

From the French doors Winston looked out on the croquet court. The police had driven four metal rods into the ground and joined them with a yellow ribbon. The grass on the court was so short and hard that within this defined square had been drawn a chalked outline of where Miles Northingham had lain. Other than a few obvious divots the court appeared to be in good shape. Would Inclement still have his tournament the following day? Winston couldn't begin to guess. The Corballys seemed to follow their own rules on things like that. Maybe croquet players could incorporate the police line in their game.

Winston could hear the doorbell ring and Juanita hurrying down the hall. The voice in the entrance foyer was unmistakable. Winston caught Simon as he was about to go up the stairs.

"Winston, Winston, when will it end?"

"Then you've heard," said Winston.

"Lucille called me this morning at seven. Is there a place we can talk?"

Simon followed Winston down the hall and into the study.

"Now . . ." Simon took a deep breath, "what do the police know? Did you mention the paper you found in Sackett's drawer?"

"No I didn't. In fact, I didn't say anything about what I've been doing. Is Sackett in jail?"

"For another hour or two probably. Lucille said that Biff was arranging for an attorney up here to post bail this morning first thing. What are you going to do? What will you tell the police?"

"I haven't decided yet." Winston sat in a chair by the French doors. "I'm exhausted thinking about it. I know I should tell all I know and suspect but I find myself fighting the idea. Even now I have a hard time believing Sackett did it."

"But the paper in his desk and Lucille said Sackett was holding the mallet."

"I know, I know. But here's what I'd like to do." Winston leaned forward. "I want to wait and talk to Sackett's lawyer before I do anything. I'm supposed to meet with Captain Andrews late this morning and I'm going to have to tell him what I know, I guess. It would be nice to have some legal advice first. Does Lucille know who this lawyer is?"

"I'll ask her." Simon sat opposite Winston. "You've lost your prime suspect, Winston. I think you're going to have to face the facts. There's really not anybody else."

"Well, that's not entirely true. Not everyone was in the breakfast room last night when the light went on outside."

"Oh?" Simon lowered his voice. "Is there something you're not confiding?"

"Something keeps nagging at me but it won't focus. It feels like . . . if someone said the right word or two words, or even did the right action, I'd suddenly know. It would all fall into place. And it has nothing to do with Sackett."

The two men stared out through the glass doors at the patio. Slowly, Simon huffed to his feet. "I must go see Lucille. I hope for her sake that you're correct. I'll be back down in a while. Will you be here?"

Winston said that he would. Simon had just left when the phone rang. Juanita leaned into the study.

"It is for you, señor. From New York."

"Hi," said Kiko on the other end. "How's paradise?"

"I think we've just eaten the forbidden fruit," answered Winston, "and we're about to get the big boot."

"What?"

Winston took five minutes to explain about Miles and Sackett. When he had finished, Kiko remained silent. "Are you still there?" he asked.

"I'm digesting," replied Kiko. "So television loses one of its big stars. I think it might be a good idea if you came back to New York."

"I can't. I'm a witness."

"There's a killer up there."

"I'm okay. Really." Winston was surprised at the anxiety in his voice.

Kiko was quiet for a moment. "Miles Northingham. The newspapers will have fun with this one."

"It's true," answered Winston. "TV star victim of mallets. Scion of wealthy family to blame. They'll have a field day."

"That does leave an opening on the show, though," said Kiko. "Maybe the network would like a real historian?"

"*What?*"

"Forget I said that. Listen, I called for a reason. I have good news, I hope."

"What's that?" asked Winston.

"I found William Laird."

"You found him? I don't believe it. Who is he? What is he? Where is he?" Winston felt like laughing.

"He's a buyer-seller for old homes and he lives in Hartford, Connecticut."

"How many phone calls?" asked Winston.

"Don't ask but I reached his home this morning and he'll be there until noon. He's expecting you to call."

"Kiko Hamaguchi, you are beautiful. This is really good news. I think."

"You don't sound too convinced. Do you think he can solve this thing for you?"

"I have no idea but it's been so long since I've heard a positive note that anything sounds good."

Kiko gave Winston the number.

"I'll call him right away," said Winston.

"Could you do me a favor," said Kiko. "Please be careful."

"I'm a study in vigilance," replied Winston.

As soon as Kiko hung up, Winston dialed William Laird's number. The call was answered on the first ring.

"Laird," said the voice on the other end.

"Mr. Laird, this is Winston Wyc. I believe my assistant called you this morning."

"She did. Had quite a nice voice, too." Mr. Laird must have

been using a portable phone, for his voice sounded as if it was at the end of a long tunnel.

"I'll tell her you said so."

"I already told her." Laird laughed. "Can you hear me?"

"Yes," answered Winston. Sort of, he thought.

"I'm out in my garden on this portable phone. Sometimes it doesn't work so well. Do you have a garden, Mr. Wyc?"

"No I don't, Mr. Laird. I live in New York City."

"That's too bad."

About which statement? wondered Winston. "I have a question for you, Mr. Laird." Winston realized he was shouting and brought his voice back to normal.

"Shoot," yelled back Laird.

"You had an appointment with a Mr. Clement Corbally back in July. On the eleventh, I believe. Could I ask what that meeting was about?"

The line was silent for a moment. "Yup, I remember."

"I don't know if you were aware, Mr. Laird, but Mr. Corbally died."

"My goodness," said the voice at the other end. "That must be why he canceled our appointment."

Winston had to think about that for a second. "Must have been. I, eh, understand you buy and sell old houses?"

"That's true. Move them, too. You want to move something?"

"No I don't. I'm here at Mr. Corbally's trying to settle up his estate, Mr. Laird. Now, could you tell me if Mr. Corbally was buying or selling?"

"He was selling. He said he had a bunch of old structures he wanted to move and wondered if I would broker the deal for him. I said sure but then he called me back and said he'd changed his mind."

"When did he call back?" asked Winston.

"Let me see."

Winston heard a muffled "damn" and then a loud noise that almost took out his eardrum. Laird came back on the line.

"Sorry about that. I hit a mosquito with the phone. You still there?"

"I think so."

"Well . . . he called me back on the . . . on the Monday following the second of July. I remember because we were supposed to meet one week later on Monday the eleventh."

Winston thought about what Laird was telling him.

"You okay?" asked Laird.

"Yeah, I'm fine. You're sure he called you on the fourth?"

"Positive. Said he had a change of heart. Too bad, I thought at the time. Sounded like a big job."

"Thank you, Mr. Laird. You've been a big help."

"Think nothing of it. I'm still available if you want to move anything."

"Thanks. I know where to call."

Winston hung up. He got up and went to open the French doors. Somebody had called Laird and canceled that meeting and it sure wasn't Mr. Corbally. Once outside, Winston sat in one of the patio chairs. His mind began to sort out what he knew, trying to place things in order. Mr. Corbally had said something was important and it certainly had been. He had decided, obviously, to end the project. He had wanted to meet Sackett at the barn, away from the crowd of the party, and tell him of the decision. Why he had decided to abandon the project was of no consequence now. Health, family, money . . . threats? Mr. Corbally had shown Sam and Miles the notes. It could have been a combination of them all.

Winston stood and walked out onto the lawn. Slowly, he made his way to the croquet court. Mr. Corbally had told Miles and Sam. They must have been very upset. No wonder Miles had taken a walk. But later, when Winston had seen them . . . Winston smiled. No wonder Miles had asked if he'd talked to Mr. Corbally. He and Sam must have agreed between themselves not to tell anyone of Mr. Corbally's determination to end the project. But *when* had they made that agreement? In reaction to Clement Sr.'s death or in preparation for it?

Winston stood looking at the court. Rigor mortis. Dead on all the balls. Mr. Corbally had probably written that on the day he'd made his decision and called Laird. For Old Wicket the game had been over. Little had he known.

"Winston!"

Winston turned to see Sam standing by the patio waving at him. He hurried back across the lawn.

"Sam. What are you doing here?" asked Winston.

"I left my sport coat here last night and I came by to pick it up. I'm going back to New York this morning. I have some arrangements to make."

"I bet. Look, Sam, do you mind if I ask you a few questions? I know it's probably not the right time but I may not see you again. Not for a while, anyway."

"What questions?" Sam looked as if he'd been asked enough questions for any twenty-four-hour period.

"They have to do with the day Mr. Corbally died."

"Winston, I think we've —"

Winston interrupted. "I talked to a Mr. Laird this morning, Sam. He had some interesting things to say."

Sam swallowed hard. He suddenly looked as if the last bad thing that could happen had. "Can we sit?" he asked.

Sam took a moment to gather his thoughts. With his elbows on the patio table, he placed his head in his hands. He spoke to the tabletop.

"Clement had asked us to come see him. Miles and I had a good idea what it was about. The old man had been hinting at it for several weeks. Miles thought he could talk him out of it. Clement had several reasons for stopping. It seems his health was deteriorating fast. And then he had these notes. Someone was threatening him." Sam looked up. "You know, for a while there I thought that his death might *not* have been an accident, but . . ." Sam shrugged. "Never mind. Anyway, after we heard the news we decided not to say anything. We'd wait and see if anyone else mentioned it. Of course, no one did."

"Did you call Laird and cancel the meeting?" asked Winston.

Sam sighed. "Yes. Clement's appointment book was right there. I went through it and found the meeting. I made the call."

Sam was silent for a minute.

"It doesn't matter now but the project meant so much. I needed the money. I needed to get my self-respect back. I wanted to work on something that was vital." Sam sat back in his chair. He shook his head. "Sackett put an end to all that."

"It would seem so." Winston's voice sounded far away to him.

Sam continued. "Miles went through everything looking for any mention of Laird. All the drawers, the files, anyplace that Clement might have put his number or name. Clement had these brochures of Laird's on his desk so Miles thought there might be more."

"When did Miles do that?"

"Just before we saw you, actually. Miles had taken a walk he was so mad, but he had come right back. He had decided to have another go at Clement, but Clement had already left to go down to the barn."

"I see."

"We sat in the study and tried to figure out what to do. Then we heard the news about Clement's death and, well, I told you what we decided. You probably think I'm terrible, but at the time it seemed the right thing to do. I was desperate."

"I'm not sure I wouldn't have done the same thing."

"There's probably a law against what we did." Sam's statement was more a question of Winston.

"I don't think it matters now," said Winston. "The village project is over."

Sam looked up. If the thought had occurred to him, it hadn't actually been said aloud. The fantasy was over. Water welled in the corner of Sam's eyes. He stood.

"I'd appreciate it if . . . you wouldn't . . ." Sam shook off the thought. "Maybe we'll talk someday. I . . . I'll get my coat."

Without another word, Sam hurried by Winston and into the house. Winston heard some mumbled words by Juanita and then nothing. At the front of the house, Winston could hear a car start. Sam must have gone through the house and out the front door.

Stretching his legs out before him, Winston stared off at the wisteria arbor. He frowned at all the beauty. Was it possible that Miles had beaned himself? It sure would simplify things. It sure would simplify his meeting with Captain Andrews.

It was late afternoon on the same day and Winston was standing in the front room of the main house with Lucille and Sackett and the lawyer known as Joseph Conrad, of all names. It would have seemed, according to Captain Andrews, that half the lawyers in Dutchess County had shown up to represent Sackett and bail him out. Even Andrews had been impressed.

Winston's meeting that morning with Andrews hadn't been *that* bad. Andrews had been relatively understanding. The raking over the coals had been short, only about forty-five minutes. Winston had claimed he felt there wasn't enough information to support cries of murder and then revealed all he knew. Well, almost everything. He had taken the notes but he did forget to mention the paper he had found in Sackett's desk. He had mentioned it to Mr. Conrad, though, and that had motivated the present meeting. Sackett sat next to Lucille with his head bowed. The lawyer sat opposite them and Winston stood over by the fireplace wishing he was anyplace but in that room. He had said nothing about the fact that Mr. Corbally had decided to can the operation. That would have been too painful for all involved.

"I thought it would scare him," said Sackett, his voice low and uncertain. "And that is all. What I could have been thinking . . ." Sackett shook his head. "You must understand, I was at my wit's end with this project. If I had only had the courage to confront him directly. He knew it was me, I'm almost sure of that. Who else would have left notes with a religious tone?

Father even asked me several times if I knew anything about some mysterious notes. I, of course, denied it. I felt it was a game. But the notes got nastier and at one point I realized I'd turned a corner of sorts. I had honestly thought that if I persisted, Father would consider dropping the project. And when he had his accident . . ." Sackett massaged his forehead with the fingers of his right hand. "I have never felt so guilty."

Lucille looked across the room at Winston. She touched her son on the arm. "That was not your fault."

Sackett looked at his mother. He appeared on the verge of tears, his expression one of self-loathing. "But that's beside the point. I realize now that it would have been just as easy to have worked with him on the project. Gotten to understand it on some level and then made an intelligent argument against it. Or who knows, maybe I would have been won over. But no, I was like some child denied his way, petty and self-serving." Sackett was silent for a full minute. He raised his head. "I was afraid of him."

Standing, Mr. Conrad came over to Winston. "And you say you didn't mention these papers you found to the police?"

"That's right," said Winston.

"Why?"

Winston looked at Sackett. "I forgot."

Mr. Conrad didn't believe that for a minute but he'd let it pass. He spoke to Lucille. "I'd like to talk to Mr. Wyc alone if I could. Is there a place we could do that?"

"In the study," said Lucille.

"Would you mind, Mr. Wyc?" asked Conrad.

"Not at all."

Mr. Conrad closed the study door behind him. He stood for a second taking in the room and watching Winston. Finally he came forward.

"Mr. Wyc, there's a lot more going on here than some young man threatening his father. I've listened to what you have to say and I'm receiving a subtext that doesn't sound all that healthy for my client. Threatening notes, a dead father;

hatred of some project, a dead trustee. Can or would you enlighten me on this situation? Is there something I should know? I can promise you it will remain confidential."

Winston hit the highlights. An improbable fall by Mr. Corbally and Sackett's being at the scene. Of course, Conrad knew of Sackett's being discovered near Miles with a mallet in his hand. With a search of Sackett's house, the police would figure out quickly that Sackett had written the notes. From there it was a short leap to realizing that Mr. Corbally may not have fallen by himself. If they didn't have a search warrant at this point, they would soon. Mr. Conrad looked glum.

"I see," was all he said. Then he went to collect his client.

Winston stayed in the study. Soon after, he heard Sackett and Mr. Conrad leaving. Winston figured they were going to Sackett's house to rearrange evidence. Who could blame them? Winston felt like rearranging himself.

Once again he found himself staring out those French doors. How many times in the last three days had he done that? How many times had Mr. Corbally done that? Thousands of times, probably. Unlike Winston, though, he would have looked out and realized that it was all his. What did that mean to a person? Winston didn't know. Possessions were the least of his worries. Winston thought of Sam and Sackett. The needs that both men had. The sadness of their lives. The dependency.

Winston stared at the croquet court and the men working on it. He had learned from Lucille that the croquet tournament was to go forward. She could have canceled it, but that would have been an admission of something. Besides, the people involved were already on their way. Some were to arrive that evening. Everything was to proceed as if nothing had happened. After the tournament, the Corballys could hunker down. The walls could go up.

Winston thought of Cybil. Maybe he could hide at her house for a day. Listen to music with Billy. He couldn't face Lucille and he didn't want to see Inclement or George. He picked up the phone.

CHAPTER
35

Cybil had responded to Winston's phone call by insisting that he come right over. He had shown up with two large pizzas, two pounds of coleslaw and two liters of Yahoo. Winston and Cybil, Billy and Gordon, had eaten themselves silly, played Monopoly, listened to ten minutes of Dr. Didi and called it a night. Winston had been offered his choice of sofas.

Briefly, during the evening, Cybil had worried about her brother, but that had been it. At one point she had talked privately to her mother on the phone for twenty minutes. If she had any questions to ask Winston, she had seemed to understand that that evening was not the time. Winston had been grateful. For the first time in three nights, he had slept soundly.

It was now twelve-thirty the next day and Winston, Cybil and the kids had just arrived at Longmeadow. It was the day of the croquet tournament and Cybil had promised Inclement she would attend. Winston noticed two vans parked in front of the house, the media kind with antennae and twirling dishes attached.

Together they walked around to the back of the house. A yellow striped canopy had been erected near the gazebo, its interior filled with food and large coolers of drinks. The weather seemed good for a croquet tournament, bright blue skies, full sun and no discernable breeze to blow those balls about. A number of what appeared to be visiting white-clad club members stood at center court inspecting Miles's chalked outline. Inclement, or somebody, had removed the metal stakes.

Men were arranging a gallery of folding chairs near the court. As quickly as a chairs went up, someone sat down. The lawn was already a hotbed of spectators standing in little groups watching the workmen, staring at the house. They all turned to gape at Winston and Cybil. Their curious expressions made Winston uneasy. Winston gave them a big smile and a bow. Now *they* looked uneasy.

Juanita stood next to the breakfast room door tending a table that held a coffeemaker, a steeping pot of tea and several kinds of Danish. There was also a pitcher of what appeared to be Bloody Marys and a pitcher of what must have been mimosas.

"*Hola,*" said Juanita. "Coffee?"

"Thanks," said Winston, taking the offered cup. Cybil declined. The boys made off with several Danish. "Is that pitcher with or without alcohol?" he asked.

"With. You would like?"

"A little early for me. I need to eat something before I have a drink, otherwise I tend to do silly things."

"This crowd could probably use a silly thing or two," said Cybil.

"Me standing naked at center court belting 'Take me out to the ole Croquet Game' would probably try their patience," said Winston. "Certainly their ideas on how to act in public."

Cybil laughed. "Don't count on it. And you'd better not call croquet a game around this crowd. They'll get all red and sputtery. It's a sport. Ranks up there with tennis and trapshooting."

"So I've heard," said Winston. "Does it help your play if you dress like an attendant from a home for the bewildered?"

"You don't need a drink to be silly," chided Cybil with a smile. "Whites are traditional, like pinks for foxhunting or greens for beagling. Tradition is important to us old families. We like to think we invented tradition. Somewhere back in our remote robber baron past we came up with certain rules of conduct, and as the generations went by the reasons for those rules became more obscure and therefore more admirable. It's what separates us from the common folk." Cybil poked Winston in the stomach.

"God help me," groaned Winston. "So what's with all these people, and the news vans?" asked Winston.

"I don't know," answered Cybil.

"Excuse me," said Juanita. "This thing that happen here is in the newspapers. Mrs. Corbally is very upset."

"Boy," said Winston. "It doesn't take long for good news to get around."

"Where is Mother, Juanita?" asked Cybil.

"Your mother is in her room."

Gordon bounced up. "Hey, Mom, can I go for a swim?"

"Not right now, sweetie. I think the pool's off limits today."

"I don't care."

"Yes, but Grandma does."

"Oh, come on," chuckled Winston. "Dripping male youth *au naturel*, chasing through the crowd. Has a bucolic drift to it, don't you think?"

Cybil wasn't amused. "You'd make an interesting father."

"No I wouldn't," said Winston.

Cybil smiled up at him. "You say the things I like to hear. Look, I need to find Mother. Can you watch the boys?"

"Sure," said Winston, if he could find them. Already they had vanished.

As he looked for the boys, Winston watched the crowd gather. Within a half hour, all the chairs had been taken and Inclement was calling for more. The media had also arrived in number. At the back of the seating gallery were three teams with battery packs and shoulder-mounted cameras. Aggressive types holding microphones, accosted spectators as they walked by. The croquet players sat in the gazebo waiting, eyeing the newspeople and looking nervous. Inclement hadn't mentioned national coverage. At center court, Winston imagined he saw the hovering, grinning ghost of Miles Northingham.

"Ladies and gentlemen . . ."

At the front of the seating section, Inclement stood nervously calling to the crowd. He held some kind of walking stick with a croquet ball carved at the top. The crowd was getting so large that Inclement's voice was just audible to Winston, who stood in the back.

"Ladies and gentlemen, if you please . . ." Inclement waited for the crowd to quiet.

"HEY!" he shouted, smacking a metal chair with his stick. That got everyone's attention. "Thank you. Let me welcome you all here and say thank you for coming. It's a beautiful day for some top-notch croquet and we expect it to remain so. Before we begin, I'd like to extend a special thanks to Bippy Cunningham and Regina St. Tookums for all they've done . . ."

A polite round of applause.

". . . and to my mother, Lucille Corbally, the grande dame of the deadness board."

Polite laughter.

"The Wistfield Wickets are honored to have the visiting club from Cape Cod, the Hyannis Wicket Whackers, and from Long Island, the Center Moriches Mallets . . ."

Winston eyed the spectators. How many were here to see croquet and how many to see the spot where *it* happened? Over to his left, he could see George being interviewed by a thin blond woman. George seemed to enjoy the attention. Richie Baire stood down by the canopy talking with someone. Winston noticed he'd put on a clean black T-shirt. He wondered if Sackett was here somewhere.

The crowd became quiet as the first players were introduced. There was a short conference between competitors and what looked to be a referee. Everyone involved moved off to the sidelines as the first person set up for the game. There was some walking around and checking of imaginary boulders and aligning of the ball and then, with a faint pop, the blue ball flew through the first hoop. A murmur of approval went through the crowd. Winston watched as the game progressed. Eventually all the competitors were in play and balls darted back and forth. Some strikes sent balls down to the other end, while others traveled hardly any distance at all. Balls were picked up and set next to other balls before being hit. Through it all very little was said except an occasional low remark to the referee or short, hurried whispers between teammates.

Coming up behind Winston, Cybil took his arm. She handed him a newspaper. "Check this out."

Winston read the headline. "TV STAR FOUND MURDERED." It went on to say where and how. "No wonder your mother is upset," he said.

"No wonder croquet has suddenly become so popular," added Cybil. "How's it going?"

"I wouldn't know," said Winston. "I've noticed, though, that no one wants to cross over the white outline of Miles. Must add another dimension to the game."

"Croquet people are a very superstitious lot."

"Maybe Clement has introduced a whole new wrinkle to croquet. Cross over the victim and lose points. Land in the victim circle and the others get to club you with their mallets. You *become* a victim. Might bolster the TV ratings."

Cybil shook her head. "You're incorrigible."

"How's your mother?" asked Winston.

"Not good. She might have made it had it not been for the media attention. She says she's going to watch from the second floor."

One of the camera crews had ventured dangerously close to the action and Inclement had hurried over to object. Most of the curiosity seekers, those not here specifically for the match, were getting bored, their voices loud, their movements distracting. The media were shoving microphones in faces everywhere, asking questions. Winston could see that some players were getting annoyed. One of the media had been threatened by a raised mallet, and at the front of the gallery a reporter was being removed forcibly from people's sight lines. A woman in spandex pants stood near Winston grumbling that she'd been refused a second helping of salmon mousse.

"How much more of this game is left?" asked Winston.

"This match is ninety minutes," said Cybil. "I'd say there were twenty minutes left. The thing is, there're probably four or five more games scheduled."

"Not today," said Winston. "I'd say within the next hour the croquet players are going to start swinging mallets at things other than balls."

"I'm afraid you're right. Oh, what a beautiful tice," exclaimed Cybil.

"A what?"

"A tice is when a player places his ball in a position where his opponent is tempted to shoot at it but will probably miss."

"Uncle Carl know about this?"

Cybil laughed. "Uncle Carl should be here."

"He'd be good on crowd control," said Winston. "I think this media thing is about to get out of hand."

Billy came running from the house. "Hey, Mom. It's great, we're on TV. Want to watch?"

"On TV?"

"Yeah. Gordon was looking for cartoons and found it. Come on, Mom. Uncle Clement looks really silly."

"Want to come?" asked Cybil.

"No thanks," answered Winston. "I'll stay and watch the cartoon from here."

As he watched Cybil walk toward the house, Winston noticed for the first time the uniformed police officers. Two were standing out past the pool and one was quietly leaning at the corner of the house. Were they looking for Sackett? Were they waiting for Andrews or was he already here?

Winston turned to find himself staring right into the face of a tall razor-thin woman with stiff blond hair, a predatory expression and a microphone. Over her left shoulder poked the lens of a TV camera.

"Hi there, I'm Carol Ruskin of NBC News. Could I ask you a few questions?" The woman didn't wait for an answer. "Is it true that Dr. Miles Northingham was struck down in a highstakes croquet game by an angry loser?"

Winston could only stare.

"And is it also true that his body lay undisturbed for one whole day before anyone notified the authorities?"

Winston cleared his throat. "Well . . . I'm afraid Miles did behave rather badly during a 'Peel' and well, yes, someone objected. But as to his lying there for twenty-four hours, that's untrue. Tradition, which is a wonderful thing, don't you think? Tradition dictates that the offensive person lie for no more than half an hour. A reminder, of sorts, to others to behave."

"That would explain the chalk marks." Carol Ruskin's face had taken on a euphoric glow. "What is your name, sir?"

Winston lapsed into a mid-Atlantic accent. "Corbally, Winston Corbally, and yes, Miles and I go back a long way. Let's see . . ."

Over the woman's shoulder, Winston could see a laughing Cybil suddenly appear at the study door. She waved at him to stop. It was obvious she had seen him on television. Winston looked down his nose at the camera and continued.

". . . it was around 1951 and the North Koreans had just . . ."

The cameraman reached over and touched Carol Ruskin on the shoulder. "This man's putting you on," he whispered.

"It doesn't matter," hissed Carol. "Go on, Winston. You, Dr. Miles Northingham and the yellow horde."

Winston went to speak but stopped. From the direction of the house, out of view, could be heard what sounded like an approaching tornado.

"What is that noise?" asked Winston.

Others in the crowd had heard it, too. A number of spectators had turned to stare at the roof of the house, their eyes and mouths little circles of apprehension. Ms. Ruskin seemed to know what it was, her expression suddenly comprehending and angry.

And then, rising over the west wing could be seen the spinning rotors of a helicopter, and then the beast itself, hovering there, a noisy black metal dragonfly from hell. Everything and everyone stopped to look at it. Winston could hear Carol Ruskin behind him, her voice shrill and maniacal.

"It's those CNN bastards! Quick, Harry, follow me!"

As the helicopter began to move toward the spectators, pandemonium broke. All of a sudden, three hundred people had to be somewhere else. Forty maddened media personnel spilled out onto the croquet court, trying to capture for their viewing audience close-ups of the tidy white outline of Miles Northingham. Colored balls were kicked this way and that. A reporter tripped on a wicket and went down. Inclement swung his walking stick and bits and pieces of a camera took to their own airways. Striped wooden balls became missiles. Winston was impressed with the fighting spirit of these croquet players. People caromed here and there, chairs were overturned, the noise was unbearable. The helicopter had reached the court area and was flattening people with its brutal downdraft.

Keeping to the fringes of the action, Winston worked his way toward the house. People were stampeding through the rose garden. Four or five spectators had been pushed into the pool and the police were trying to pull them out. Winston stood and stared at the splashing bodies. Something in his mind clicked. Nodding, he smiled to himself. That's it, he thought. That was the last part of the puzzle.

Running over, Winston grabbed one of the policemen.

"Have you got a radio or something here that you could call Captain Andrews on?" yelled Winston.

The officer shouted back that he did.

"I need to talk to him. It's an emergency."

The man looked at Winston as if he could see that much, but he nodded and motioned for Winston to follow him. Off in the distance could be heard the wail of approaching sirens.

It had taken Winston twenty minutes to get all the family into the study. He had even asked Richie to attend the little meeting. Lucille had come down from her bedroom on Sackett's arm. Outside the French doors the bedlam had diminished considerably, the now occasional shout or bang acting as counterpoint to the pin-drop quiet in the study. A stranger's face peered through the window, then was gone. Winston started his little lecture with an explanation of why he was really at Longmeadow. Lucille nodded in affirmation.

"You mean," said Inclement, "that we were the research material instead of my father's files?"

"In a way," answered Winston. "Lucille had asked me to do some quiet investigating. As I've already mentioned to a few of you, there was some question as to how Mr. Corbally actually died. Lucille and I both felt that it was not an accident." Short gasps from several of the group. Winston paused for a moment.

Cybil spoke. "If it wasn't an accident, then . . . then he was killed."

"That's right," replied Winston. Everyone looked at one another. Winston watched one particular face. He explained about how the fall couldn't have happened.

"I think all of you were used to the *idea* of Mr. Corbally going up and down that ladder, but I wasn't. It didn't seem to me a possibility."

Shaking her head in dismay, Cybil said, "It's true. I

remember seeing him up there so many times. It never dawned on me . . ." Her voice trailed off.

"He didn't fall," muttered Sackett.

"It took me a while," continued Winston, "but now I know who the killer is."

Everyone went tense. Eyes darted from one face to another.

"Originally, I had suspected Miles Northingham. I hope, if he's out there somewhere, that he'll forgive me. I must also ask forgiveness of Sackett. He was on the list at one time but, with a little experimentation, I realized it couldn't be him. Whoever killed Mr. Corbally must have gotten very dirty. Cybil and I saw Sackett right before we found the body and he was clean. He didn't have the time to carry his father up to the hayloft and then clean himself off before we saw him. Plus, I would realize later, that the killer must have gone out the back of the barn."

Everybody shuffled in his seat.

"Where did he go?" asked Inclement.

"Well," answered Winston, "unless it was some stranger passing by in the woods, that person had to get clean before they reappeared. There was a party and people were everywhere. They might have gone back to *their* house but someone was there and might later put two and two together. Plus, they'd been seen, hadn't they, George?"

George stood. "What are you saying?"

"Miles was in the way, wasn't he?" continued Winston. "You didn't see him after the pool incident, like you said at lunch. You saw him before and he saw you."

Reddening, George looked at those present. "He's nuts."

"You had to cut up to the wisteria arbor where you noticed that everyone was focused on Uncle Carl and his duel. All you had to do was dash up to the pool and dive in. Suddenly, you were all clean."

George spoke to Inclement. "It's not true. I was at the party the whole time."

"You're a weight lifter," said Winston. "You had the strength to carry Mr. Corbally up that ladder."

Everyone was staring at George. Inclement appeared on the point of tears.

"You realized after our lunch together," added Winston, "that you had to eliminate Miles. That he had seen you on the path *before* the pool incident and that you weren't wet, you were dusty. Once the rumor began circulating that Mr. Corbally's death might *not* be an accident, Miles could very easily have put two and two together because he would have remembered seeing you coming *from* the barn and not the pool. The other night you saw an opportunity to kill him, too, and you acted. Poor Sackett happened along and picked up that mallet at the wrong time."

George was trying his best to remain in control but his breathing was getting labored. The veins on his neck stood out. He kept eyeing the exits. Richie Baire moved over in front of the French doors.

"You're crazy," yelled George. "Why would I do that? Tell me that?

Inclement's quiet voice broke the ensuing silence. Tears had come to his eyes. "George? You said that morning that you were going to speak to Father about us but I said no. You told me later that you hadn't seen him. But you did talk to him, didn't you?"

George could only shake his head in denial. Lucille had stood. Unlike Inclement's voice, hers was ice. "Why, George?"

George tried to speak but words wouldn't come. Tears had welled up in *his* eyes and he suddenly looked collapsed, as if the weight of his crimes was too large a burden for the internal pressures that keep us round and firm and human. No one moved. Haltingly, he found his voice.

"I followed him down to the barn. He'd been so horrible to me and Clement. I wanted to set him right about us. To explain. He laughed and said he wasn't interested in my explanations. He said to go away and he called me names. I flew into a rage and pushed him. All this time of having to listen to him, to suffer his insults. I didn't mean to . . ." His voice stronger, his words coming in a rush, George spoke to Inclement. "He fell and hit his head. I wasn't sure at first. I tried to revive him with mouth to mouth. I pumped his chest. You must believe, Clemmy, I did everything in my power." Unable to look at Inclement's expression, George turned to Winston. "It was an accident. But who would believe that? I had to make it *look* like an accident. I . . ." George's voice trailed off.

Winston thought that George looked like the loneliest person he'd ever seen. Small and sad and isolated. Suddenly, Winston realized it must have been George he'd seen that night on the patio, eavesdropping on Biff's visit. Not being an actual member of the family, he'd had to sneak up and listen through the door. His life with the Corballys must have been a series of listening through doors, of being the outsider. Lucille had said that George would do anything for Inclement. And he had.

The door behind Winston opened quietly. He turned to see Captain Andrews and Sergeant Miller. The captain nodded that he'd been listening. Outside, the noise of the helicopter could be heard fading in the distance.

The small party had gathered in a clearing down in the woods. Inclement was unveiling the memorial to his father and had invited only family and some family friends. A table had been set up to the side with a nice Chardonnay and a few canapés. Winston stood between Cybil and Kiko. Lucille was on the arm of the Reverend Mr. Simon Tart and Sackett moved about taking photographs. Gordon and Billy had disappeared into the underbrush.

It would seem that Inclement had been the one taking items from the barn. With the architectural details, he had built a small room in the clearing, or rather, the suggestion of a room, and in the center of this room stood Mr. Corbally's old club chair. Moldings hung from the trees, a door unit stood staked to the ground and a window, leaning against a post, had been opened. The History of Longmeadow, a gift from the small firm of Wyc and Associates, had been placed next to the club chair on an upturned oak stump. Various personal articles, including the mallet Mr. Corbally had given his son, the one with which he'd won the Nationals, had been laid on the ground. A photo of Mr. Corbally had been pinned to the chair. The Old Wicket looked out at the gathering with a casual smile and a slightly embarrassed tilt of the head.

Inclement raised his wineglass. "I would like to drink a toast to my father. I won't say much. I'll let my piece do the talking. But I would like to say something without boring everyone about relationships and their inherent mysteries.

My father taught me many things, whether I wanted to learn them or not, and I wish he were here today. I miss him." Inclement bit at his lower lip. His voice quickened. "He'd be delighted, though, to know that his death has forced me to concentrate on living. I have never seen the world so vividly or wanted so much to be a part of it. And for that, and I know he has to be listening somewhere, I would like to thank him with all my heart."

Sackett raised *his* glass to the photograph pinned to the chair. *"Ad perpetuam rei memoriam,"* he added to his brother's toast.

And everyone drank. Something the late Mr. Corbally would have approved of, thought Winston. Amen.